About the author

Julian D. Parrott was born and raised in Wrexham, Wales. He attended Manchester University and the University of Illinois. He lives in Urbana, Illinois with his wife and, on occasion, can be found travelling the canals of England and Wales.

FIT FOR PURPOSE

Julian D. Parrott

FIT FOR PURPOSE

Vanguard Press

A CIP catalogue record for this title is
available from the British Library.

ISBN 978-1-80016-030-9

*Vanguard Press is an imprint of
Pegasus Elliot MacKenzie Publishers Ltd.*
www.pegasuspublishers.com

First Published in 2021

**Vanguard Press
Sheraton House Castle Park
Cambridge England**

Printed & Bound in Great Britain

Dedication

For Beth

Prologue
Tel Aviv, November 1st

Viktor Rabinovich was nervous. The Russian journalist was always nervous these days. A car backfiring on the Tel Aviv street below his apartment would send him into a paroxysm of anxiety while an unexpected knock on his door would ice him with fear. A quiet, gentle man who had always modestly viewed himself as a mediocre local journalist, he never intended to become an international cause célèbre.

He had been sent to eastern Ukraine by his pro-Kremlin newspaper to write a warm, human interest piece on the camaraderie of the pro-Russian separatists, but he'd ended up reporting on what he observed: secret Russian military intervention and human rights abuses. The drive to be a good and honest reporter overcame his natural timidity. His editor, of course, censored the story but it leaked out and was picked up by western news agencies. To many in the west, Rabinovich was a free press hero, but to the Kremlin he was nothing but a traitor. The Kremlin issued an arrest warrant for him. Warned not to return to his Russian home, he fled to Israel.

Rabinovich had adjusted to life in exile. He lived a low-profile life in Tel Aviv working as an occasional consultant to press agencies while writing features about the Russian state's suppression of speech or more personal pieces about his life in exile, and his fear of Kremlin retribution. His fear was justified but he hoped his high media profile would give the SVR and FSB, the Kremlin's external and internal intelligence agencies, pause before they attempted any action to silence him. Rabinovich was very aware of the Kremlin's campaign to quash its critics. He knew that at least fourteen opponents of Putin and the Kremlin had already died in mysterious circumstances while living in exile in the UK. He also knew there had also been brazen attacks on émigrés in the US, France, and even in his newly adopted home of Israel. He justifiably feared the SVR and FSB and their long reaches.

He looked at himself in the mirror that hung in the small alcove by his flat's front door. He was short, plump and getting plumper. He wore large plastic framed glasses, was heavily bearded, and his bald pate was covered by a plain yarmulke. Dressed in plain blue slacks and a short sleeved white shirt, he thought he looked like a regular Israeli citizen. Rabinovich rarely went out of his flat and almost never met journalists in face-to-face meetings but the recent request came from a legitimate source, a respected Irish daily. Rabinovich had personally checked the journalist's credentials and read some of her features online, and the meeting had even been approved by the Shin Bet, Israel's domestic intelligence agency. He had arranged to meet in a popular and very public cafe.

The cafe was refreshingly cool with a nice view of the Mediterranean and the fine beaches that lined the opposite side of the street. Rabinovich would have preferred to meet at one of the open-air beachside cafes, as it would have been more public, safer, but he would have been bothered by the heat. He was breathing heavily as he entered the cafe after the short but hot walk from his flat.

"I really need to do more exercise," Rabinovich thought and then smiled. "Who am I kidding, I need to start some exercise first."

He wiped his forehead and back of his neck with his handkerchief. He was early for the appointment, just as he planned, and ordered a sealed glass bottle of water and removed the bottle's cap himself as he sat down at a small window-front table. Recalling how Alexander Litvinenko had been poisoned, Rabinovich was taking no chances with the possibility of anyone adulterating his beverage. After a third gulp of water, he noticed a small, red-headed woman, dressed as a tourist, enter the cafe. Rabinovich recognised the journalist from her online profile picture. The journalist smiled at Rabinovich, ordered coffee and then took the seat opposite the Russian. After quick and perfunctory introductions, Rabinovich settled in to answer the journalist's questions.

Outside, across the street at a beachfront cafe, comfortably relaxing at a table, Feodor Kamenev,

Russian temporary cultural attaché visiting Israel along with the Kirov Ballet, pretended to read his newspaper. As he moved his coffee cup up to his lips, he surreptitiously glanced across the road at Rabinovich in the cafe's window. Colonel Kamenev of the FSB listened to his team's chatter coming through his hidden earpiece. He listened as the team talked through the logistics of their plan, he watched as the team's motorcycle, taxi, and minibus took up their prearranged positions. Pleased with the professionalism of his team's preparation, Kamenev carefully turned his full attention back to Rabinovich. He checked his watch and mentally confirmed the set time for the journalist, who was a member of Kamenev's team, to conclude the interview.

"Any minute now," he whispered. He watched the cafe across the road as Rabinovich stood, smiled, and shook hands with the Irish journalist. Kamenev spoke quietly as if to no one, "OK, he's on his way out... any second now."

Rabinovich stepped out on to the beachfront street's pavement; he squinted in the sunlight. As his eyes adjusted to the glare, he looked up and down the road and across to the beach suspiciously but, seeing nothing out of the ordinary, started on his walk home. The minibus approached from the north, a taxi from the south. Rabinovich looked across to the road when he heard the loud, noisy acceleration of a motorcycle; he watched as the bike dodged in and out of the light traffic before cutting in front of the taxi and slowed. Multiple car horns blared. Rabinovich slowed his pace to watch the traffic shenanigans with slight amusement. The motorcycle veered in front of the taxi, purposefully forcing it to lurch as if out of control. The taxi fishtailed across the centre line into the path of the oncoming minibus. The taxi clipped the side of the minibus which appeared to simultaneously speed up and slide. Rabinovich saw what was happening, but too late. He opened his mouth as if to scream as the minibus jumped the curb swerved onto the pavement, and ran Rabinovich down. He was dead before the minibus' wheels had stopped rotating.

To the casual observers, who now crowded around the scene of the crash, it looked like a horrible, tragic accident. They would report it as such to the police collecting witness statements. Across the street, Kamenev neatly folded his paper and placed it under his arm as he stood and left the beachfront table and slowly walked away. The motorcycle had disappeared. Police sirens wailed while the taxi and minibus drivers disappeared into the gathering crowd that stood around the dead Russian journalist. The redhead walked down the beachfront without looking back.

Chapter One
Montreal Trudeau Airport, November 20th

Sarah Jones had already finished her shift when she volunteered to help staff the ticket counters teeming with storm-displaced and angry passengers. She was a tall, striking Canadian of Jamaican heritage with eyes so deep and green that men, particularly, sometimes got lost in them. As a psychology graduate, she was always interested in how people responded to her professionally and she often played a game with herself where she observed travellers in line and determine whether they'd be pleasant, demanding, entitled, angry, or passive. During this shift, so far, she had hit the target more often than not: delayed passengers were almost universally angry, demanding, and entitled. She finished with yet another disgruntled passenger when she scanned the line in front of her. There, about two people back, she saw a good-looking man in maybe his late thirties, touch of grey at his temples, so probably early forties, who exuded a sense of tranquillity. She liked him immediately.

Sarah surreptitiously kept glancing up at the man while she dealt with the customer in front of her. She noticed how his fine features set off his pale blue eyes and she surmised that he wore his good looks with ease, as if he didn't realise how handsome he was. She thought that he wouldn't be one of those guys who used his looks or substituted handsomeness for a genuine, natural charm. She noticed his sports jacket, quality, not American, she thought, probably Italian or British. The jacket had a classic looking check, British, she thought. He was one person back now. Sarah looked up and held his gaze over the counter passenger's shoulder. He smiled, shyly and sweetly she thought. He's genuine. He's a nice guy and I like him, Sarah thought, it's a shame he's flying out.

The passenger's mind was somewhere else when the tall, beautiful ticket agent waved him to her counter. He smiled feeling somewhat embarrassingly self-aware.

"Sorry," he explained. "I was miles away."

Sarah noticed his accent as he handed over his passport and e-ticket. He was a Brit. Sarah scanned his passport: Thomas Price, place of birth, Manchester.

"Sorry, Mr Price, but as you probably know the flight is delayed. The storm," Sarah said almost regretting she was stating the obvious,

"Yes," Tom Price replied. "It's not a problem." He looked around and lowered his voice. "At least not for me. I'm in no rush. But it's probably made your job more difficult."

Sarah smiled sweetly and held Tom's gaze, "Going home, sir?" She noticed his eyes, grey blue with a hint of sadness. She scanned his left hand, third finger unadorned.

"Yup, on my way home."

Sarah detected an underlying melancholy in the passenger's response. Her fingers zipped across the keyboard in search of Tom's flight and seat. She leant forward over the counter conspiratorially, "I can offer you an upgrade if you'd like, sir."

"Brilliant," Tom grinned with genuine excitement. "I've never flown business class."

"Then how about first class?" Sarah whispered with a smile.

"Seriously? Even better. Wow. Thanks."

Sarah's fingers flew across the keyboard and her printer rattled as it produced a new ticket.

"Any luggage to check?" She asked.

"Just this," Tom held up his hand grip. "Cabin baggage."

"Ah, a light traveller," Sarah said wondering where he had been in Canada, what he had done, and how long he'd been in the country. "Quick business trip was it, sir?" she enquired.

"Quick trip for fun," Tom responded genuinely. "Visiting an old friend."

"Well, I hope we can have the pleasure of another visit in the near future," Sarah said and handed Tom his passport and his new ticket. "Enjoy your trip, sir and thanks for flying with us."

"Cheers. Thank you," Tom said. "I will."

Tom collected his documents and smiled with a nod to Sarah. He was a bit confused as to what had just happened. He left the counter with a little more of a lighter step than he had approached it with. He slowed momentarily almost turning back to the ticket agent to ask her, ask her what, he pondered, for her phone number? Idiot, he told himself, he wouldn't know what to say, wouldn't know how.

Sarah, watched Tom's first few steps in the direction of security, noticed his limp, sighed a little with the desire of a missed opportunity, then turned to the line in front of her, smiled again and said with a hint of wistfulness, "Next."

***

Montreal Trudeau Airport Departure Gates

The airport gate was crowded, and the passengers' frustration was palpable. Outside a cold wind whipped and hail pelted the floor-to-ceiling windows. Inside, the terminal's air was warm and dry and doing nothing to calm the weary passengers who continued to crowd the overwhelmed gate agents for information on their delayed flights. All the gate's chairs were occupied, people and bags appeared to spill out into the aisles like clothes from overstuffed drawers. Slightly back from the melee, the actress stood leaning on one of the many pillars that held up the wing shaped ceiling, observing.

Although she was slightly hungover from the previous night's wrap party and dying to sit down, she people-watched almost out of professional curiosity.

She observed the nervous flyer read and reread a page in a novel, the businesswoman in the expensive suit constantly checking her phone, the elderly couple, clearly still in love after goodness knows how many years, sit patiently deep in conversation. What were they talking about? She watched the harried mother with a toddler in a pushchair and a baby on her hip trying to soothe both children while animatedly talking to a gate agent. The actress saw the toddler throw a stuffed toy from her pushchair; the mother missed it deep in conversation with the agent. The actress noticed a guy, early forties, fit, kind face, air pods, leave his seat and retrieve what looked like a blue bunny. The man squatted down next to the toddler looking as if he was making funny voices as he made the bunny dance for the child who was now laughing. The harried mum, blonde, pretty but understandably tired looking, gazed down. Concern changed to a gentle smile as the man straightened, with a little difficulty, from his squat, the mum nodded a thanks and the man smiled. Nice teeth. The actress noticed that the man's seat had been taken by a teen with greasy hair, giant wireless headphones, and an air of surliness. The man noticed too and gave an 'Ah well' motion and wandered off to find some floor space. He had a noticeable limp.

All these personal, small human interactions and dramas continued to be training for her. It was real-life acting school. She never tired of these moments; locking away a small facial expression, a pause in a conversation, a shift of body weight, a smile, the change of gaze, a touch. She saved them for her own usage to bring depth to a character she may play. She was good at it. She was a jobbing actor, always working and always grateful for work. She was heading home to London from the shoot in Montreal.

Her role had been a good one. It was one of those secondary characters that had, since her late thirties, become her métier. Still, she reflected, it had been a role that she brought a rewarding depth to. The actress noticed a seat become vacant and she stepped quickly towards it. The kind faced toddler whisperer also made a play for the empty seat but pulled away when he saw her move to sit. The actress nodded her thanks and moved her gaze down into her cabin bag as she rummaged around for one of the two novels she carried, the Iain Banks or the cheap thriller. She grabbed the thriller with a rather lurid cover. She missed the toddler whisperer's return nod.

**

Tom Price didn't mind being gazumped for the seat. He moved to the pillar the elegant woman with the nicely fitted sweater and tight jeans had just vacated. There was a vague scent of something floral, herby, ephemeral. He inhaled the aroma deeply without drawing attention to himself. Tom liked the fragrance. Was it hers, the woman who grabbed the seat? The scent reminded him of something, there was a hint of spice and he immediately felt the dry heat of desert, but then there was a softer, floral nose. This scent evoked the cottage garden that had been attached to a country pub close to his childhood home.

Home. His flight was taking him home but Tom was in no rush. Jack would be happy with Rachel, so the delay didn't bother him. He sniffed again, the scent was evocative of times and places now distant and he remembered L.P. Hartley's statement that the past is a foreign country. In his case, he felt it to be literally true. At least his trip home would be different, at least it would be more comfortable than he had expected, and it would certainly be more comfortable than his past.

Chapter Two
Montreal Trudeau Airport

Home was but a fleeting construct for Tom. After twenty years on active duty, very active duty, home had become a rucksack and kitbag and whatever base he had been sent to. After leaving the army he felt unmoored, unable settle back into the small house that he had never lived in and had never felt like a home. He had only bought it because that's what people did at a certain time of life and with a certain salary.

Tom had retired from the army exhausted and restless. He felt the need to keep moving, to keep to himself, to be surrounded by quiet and peace. Especially peace. He'd temporarily moved into a narrowboat and, four years later, was still there. Now he was looking forward to collecting his dog from his sister's farm and getting back to his boat and, if the weather allowed, moving slowly up and down the UK's labyrinthian canal system.

Tom looked at the sleet that was now streaming against the terminal's broad windows. He moved his gaze down to his phone, touched the screen, went to his music, found ELO's 'Mr Blue Sky' notched up the volume, and took a surreptitious look at the woman who had taken 'his' seat. Lovely, he mused, I wonder who she is and where she's going?

There was an announcement from the gate agents and the flight was called. There was a collective movement, and, as one, the mass of people retrieved bags, corralled kids, and searched pockets for tickets and passports. A crowd formed at the gate while the uncomfortable sorting by class began. First class was summoned and somewhat embarrassed, the actress moved to the gate with ticket and passport in hand. She disliked the term 'first class' as she had bridled against class and privilege and entitlement all through her life. Many of her roles reflected her own politics and sense of class — pink and working. Her politics had remained steadfast even as her roles and lifestyle evolved. She was cleared by the ticket agent, hoisted her cabin bags and moved off down the jet bridge without a look back.

The big Boeing was almost full by the time Tom made his way quickly down the cold jet bridge. He had completely ignored the call for first-class passengers as he was still stuck in the economy class mode. He was greeted at the plane's door with an obvious additional level of service courtesy and shown to his seat, which was more like a self-contained pod. He smiled at the flight attendant who returned it with something more than the usual fake plastic smiles found on most cabin crew. The first-class cabin was relatively sedate. Most passengers had already stowed their luggage and were all in various stages of settling in: some reading business newspapers, he recognised the pink of the

Financial Times; some were sitting back, eyes closed lost in the reveries of whatever music or podcasts they were listening to through complimentary Bose headphones; most, however, were furiously typing on their phones, tablets, or laptops. There was one empty seat, front row, second seat, slightly angled next to the third pod to his right in which sat the woman who had gazumped him for the terminal seat. He quickly glanced at his ticket for his seat assignment. Yup, this was him.

The actress had just finished arranging her space, champagne flute next to her book on the pod's small table, magazines piled up next to the microfibre pillow in its hygienic case, when she noticed the flight attendant showing a passenger to the adjacent pod. It was the toddler whisperer. She again gave him a quick, professional appraisal. He was indeed a nice-looking guy, she thought. In her younger days she would have enjoyed the frisson of having a handsome man sitting next to her on a long flight and the possibilities that such a situation conjured. There had been that knee trembler in the toilet on a flight to LA with a Hollywood A-lister, some fifteen years ago. She remembered it, somewhat fondly. He was a terrible actor, but he had been beautiful. But that was then. Time and the bottle, she thought, had not been kind to him. Given her profession she was aware how opportunities changed with age. Her roles had already changed, as they did for all actors.

She had been the ingénue as a late teen while still in drama school. Casting agents viewed her as lovely, but not beautiful, strong yet vulnerable, and she was often cast as the rebellious daughter, the runaway, or the bad boy's girlfriend. Through her twenties she was seen as sexy, thoughtful, and deep but lead roles were infrequent. She played anger and indignation and insouciance so well that it made casting directors nervous. Perhaps, too, it was the dark eyes that often looked black on screen, the raven hair, the Welsh accent, the full lips over slightly wonky teeth. She was always the consummate professional and recognised and accepted casting directors' limitations for she was never short of roles. She weathered a personal and professional wobble and was still enjoying a solid career working on stage, frequently on TV, and occasionally in Brit cinema. There had been a couple of Anglo-American movies in her younger days, but Hollywood had never really come calling. Her disappointment had been short-lived.

As the actress returned to her novel, Tom settled into the oversized and extraordinarily comfortable chair pod next to hers. The plane's safety video played to a distracted audience. Almost no one watched; all, Tom presumed, knew how to fasten their seat belts, find the exits, and how to place the dangling oxygen mask over their own faces before helping anyone else with theirs. The first-class steward who introduced herself as the purser, made a quick check of seats belts and electronic items being turned off and then Tom felt the short shunt of the Boeing being pushed back from the gate. He looked to his right to the window. He had travelled extensively, enough to know that there was a ubiquity to airports, but he wondered whether the weather would break enough to allow a view of the city to emerge during take-off and ascent.

The actress noticed Tom's stare but then realised he was trying to look out of the window. As she caught his eye, he looked at the first-class pod and mouthed "Wow." Tom noticed the book she had laid out to read.

"How's the book?" he asked with a gentle smile.

"Not good. Pretty crappy really, one of those trashy beach thrillers with gratuitous violence and bad sex. Not my cup of tea really, but a friend gave it to me as a plane read," the actress replied diffidently.

"Aha. I see. What do you normally read?" Tom continued.

"Well, I'm also actually reading an Iain Banks. It's a bit heavy, so was taking a little break from it. Thinking of picking it up again, oh, around Iceland."

"Ah, good," he said. Then, after a pause, "I like Iain Banks too, *The Bridge* is one of my favourite books, brilliant."

"I prefer the *Wasp Factory*," the actress said somewhat disdainfully.

Tom was aware of the difficult attitude the woman exuded but he found her intriguing. In a situation like this he would normally smile, put in his air pods, get lost in a book or magazine, and retreat further into himself.

"I'm Tom, Tom Price," Tom said, with a 'damn the

torpedoes' attitude which was unusual for him and he held out his hand.

"Hi, Tom, I'm Nia," the actress said a little coolly and just brushed his hand in a facsimile of a shake. She stared up at Tom as he stood to take off his sports jacket and then settled back into the pod. She was anticipating a look of recognition followed by a statement like, "Are you the actress Nia Williams?" or "I loved you in that episode," or "Has anyone told you that you look like Nia Williams," or, a little less these days, "Hey Nia, give us a kiss then." None of these happened. Did he really not recognise her? Shit, she thought, had she aged that much?

***

The Boeing taxied onto Montreal's main north-south runway. It had been de-iced, but the pilots were still anxious to get the wide-bodied jet into the air as quickly as possible. They knew the troublesome sleet that lashed their windscreens would be no match for the jet's speed and climb rate. The big Boeing would soon rise above the clipper system that had dropped the temperature along with a nasty stew of hale and sleet. The pilots received the okay from the traffic controller. The captain nodded to the co-pilot and applied pressure to the throttles and the two huge General Electric turbofan engines responded sweetly. The two-hundred-and-fifty-tonne aircraft accelerated down the runway as smoothly as a Ferrari from a traffic light. Its nose wheel appeared to almost levitate off the runway's surface before the jet leapt into the air.

Inside the warm cabin Tom felt the plane become airborne and he pushed himself further back into the seat willing the jet to continue its climb. He missed sitting next to a window and attempted to look across the seat pod to his left, but the passenger had closed the window blind and appeared to be settled in for a nap. He looked to his right, across Nia, who was staring straight ahead with a blank determined look, to her window. He couldn't see much through the window; different shades of grey and precipitation streaming across the window giving him a sense that they were under water. Then his gaze fell on Nia. Blimey, he thought, she really is lovely. He should travel first class more often. He found her looks and air of insouciance attractive. He continued to steal quick glances in her direction taking in the thick black hair with red highlights that fell past her shoulders, her generous mouth, and as she turned and captured his stare, her slate-dark eyes. Tom smiled reflexively and Nia half smiled back and pushed herself deeper into her seat to afford him a better look through the cabin window. She's thoughtful as well, Tom recognised, nice.

It's going to be a long flight, he thought, may as well try to make some conversation. "Flying home Nia?" he asked.

"Yup." She exaggerated her novel reading body

language for a moment but then felt rude. She put down her book. "I've been working in Montreal and Toronto for a few weeks, what about you?"

"Over here just for a long weekend really. An old friend was defending his doctorate and having a bit of a bash afterwards."

Nia was now intrigued. "Sounds fun. What was the doctorate in?"

"Strategic studies, something to do with international terrorism," Tom answered with a bit of feigned ignorance.

"And what is it that you do?" Nia asked looking into Tom's face. It was a good face. She noticed his eyes, calm and blue grey, close cut dark hair with some pepper and salt at the temples, a face that was slightly weather burnt, he must work outside she thought. Close up she reconfirmed he had a warm, genuine smile. Yes, she thought, a nice face.

Tom hesitated, partly because he felt himself being sucked into Nia's big dark eyes. He tried to think of a colour to describe them and felt 'brown' didn't do them justice.

"Oh, I do a bit of writing now and then."

He noticed Nia's eyes immediately register suspicion. Why?

"Oh God," she began with an obvious eye roll. "You don't write for newspapers and magazines, do you?"

"No, not for newspapers but, errrr, I do write the

occasional pieces for magazines." He let the sentence trail off interested in how she'd respond.

"What magazines?"

"Um," he smiled. "Well, would you believe magazines devoted to narrow-boating on British canals and some related touristy things?"

She stared at him for a moment, he watched light return to her eyes and her eyes crinkle as her full mouth broke into a smile.

"You're joking," she asked, and he noticed more of a Welsh accent creep into her speech. Was she relaxing, getting a bit more comfortable?

The jet emerged through the pregnant clouds to find its ceiling and cruising speed. The captain turned out the seat belt lights and gave the passengers permission to move about the cabin albeit in a rather discouraging tone. As if by magic, a flight attendant appeared with another tray of champagne and hot, moist towels for the passengers to freshen up with. Tom and Nia both took a towel and a glass. He wiped his forehead and his neck and felt immediately refreshed, more so when he took a long draw on the champagne. He raised his glass in Nia's direction and was happy to receive a slightly raised glass and a smile in return.

Nia took a gulp of her champagne. She leant towards him in her pod.

"Seriously, you write about barges?" she enquired.

"Yup, I write travelogue pieces about British canals and living aboard rather small boats." Tom answered with a smile. Then, in an exaggerated pompous plumy voice,

"Narrowboats to the cognoscente rather than barges."

Nia laughed again until she realised, he was serious. Tom noticed how she tipped her head back while she produced a deep throaty laugh. He liked it. He liked her.

"I'm sorry," she said. "I didn't know, obviously, and anyway I didn't mean to sound condescending."

"That's okay. It's not really my career, actually more of a lifestyle thing and helps pay the bills. Well, more like offsets the bills. And, what do you do Nia?" he asked.

She looked at him quizzically, "I'm an actor." Then she moved on quickly.

"Well, you must be doing well," Nia made a gesture summing up the first-class cabin.

"I was upgraded," he said.

He saw her embarrassment. He had already guessed that class was something she was very aware of. You don't keep that accent as an actor if it wasn't a point of pride. He kind of liked that.

"Have you always been a writer?" she asked quickly.

Tom paused for a moment before replying, "Errr, no. I don't actually really think of myself as a writer. It's still relatively new for me so I'm not really sure what I am. I noodle around a bit enjoying the kind of writing that I do but, now I think I'd like to write a novel… one of those trashy beach thrillers with gratuitous violence and bad sex."

They both laughed again, and Nia moved closer to Tom.

"What did you do before the writing then?" Nia asked.

"I was in the army," Tom sighed internally. He was proud of his service, but he'd had these conversations before. Some people responded excitedly, some thanked him, whereas some others withdrew. In the pod next to his, he felt Nia withdraw ever so slightly.

"How long did you serve?" she asked.

"Oh, a little under twenty years," he said.

"Wow, a lifetime."

"Felt like quite a few lifetimes actually," he said and immediately regretted it. He was trying to be flippant but had opened the door to a room full of uncomfortable histories. He anticipated the follow up, oft-asked question that accompanied the knowledge that someone had served in the armed forces in the past two decades: whether he had killed anyone? He hated the question because he didn't like the answer. Neither, usually, did the questioner.

Nia didn't ask it. She moved a little closer to him in her pod and stared deep into his eyes. She had long ago realised that there was a psychology in understanding a role, embodying a character. You took on that character's feelings, their joy, their pain, their hopes and fears. In many ways she was a trained empath and she recognised that there was some real pain here. This Tom was a genuinely warm and funny guy, but there was something deeper to his personality. She was intrigued and she didn't want the conversation to end.

"Look," he began hesitatingly, wanting to keep the connection going, "Would you like another drink?"

"Yes," she said. "Let's split a bottle of red."

Nia was going to ring for a flight attendant, but Tom unbuckled his seat belt and went in search of the wine.

Nia smiled. Fuck, she thought. She had vigorously protested the wars, had attended some mass demonstrations, and had marched in protest into Trafalgar Square. She couldn't understand why anyone wanted to join the army.

Tom returned with six small, plastic bottles of red wine. He opened the first bottle and poured the wine into their empty flutes. With the first glass the conversation returned to the light banter they had both previously enjoyed. He asked her about her career. She was now comfortable with the genuineness of his not knowing. Seldom did she encounter people who didn't recognise her, at least vaguely. She wasn't a marquee name, but she was still well known. For a few years, earlier in her career she, had been more recognisable, famous sometimes for her work, but almost as frequently for her personal life.

They continued talking as flight attendants passed out menus and then took orders for dinner. Through dinner, Nia talked, and Tom listened intently. At first, she didn't notice his attention, but as the conversation continued, she reflexively kept checking to see if he was still listening, still connected. He was, and she realised that most of the people she talked to couldn't wait to interject and move the conversation to focus on themselves. It was refreshing to feel such a connection and it inspired her to add greater depth to her anecdotes. She watched Tom's eyes, felt increasingly more comfortable and less guarded. She told personal stories and regaled him with some of her favourite tales from her theatre days as they shared the wine, some laughter, and the occasional close head lean-in conspiratorial conversation. Tom liked her sense of humour and her infectious giggle as it grew into a full laugh. Two Canadian flight attendants who slyly observed them thought them a well-established pairing still deep in the throes of love.

Nia became aware of the cabin crew and leant closer to Tom, she was tired and a little tipsy now.

"You're used to uniforms so what do you think of the cabin crews' uniform then?"

Tom glanced up and noticed the two flight attendants. They were both wearing tight purple pencil skirts, white blouses under purple bolero jackets, with small, elegant gold wings over the left breast. Blue scarves rounded off the ensemble.

"Quite nice really," he said. Then, with effete pomposity, "Smart, with a hint of a timeless classic style, but the manufactured material, although unquestionably durable, leaves a lot to be desired."

Nia looked at him and laughed.

"I've worn lots of uniforms in my time. For some reason I've played a helluva lot of coppers," Nia said. "Some good roles really, but I always feel their uniform makes me look a little… dowdy, matronly even."

"Nonsense," interjected Tom. "I bet you look really lovely. Look at you, you're so beautiful, you'd rock any uniform." What the fuck, you blithering idiot, he thought immediately.

Nia smiled but warily this time, took a gulp of wine and politely excused herself to go to the toilet. It had been a long time since anyone had called her beautiful. It was an odd remark given the context and she wasn't sure how to take it. She instinctively felt it had been genuine, but she wondered if it was loaded somehow. And, what was with the "you'd rock" remark? She giggled as she looked at the reflection in the mirror. She reached up to her hair and pushed it off her forehead. She took in the fine lines emanating from the corners of her eyes and around her lips, age and all that damn smoking in her youth she thought. Her cheekbones were still fine, and she had always liked how her dark eyes glistened when she was happy or tipsy. Too many of her acting friends had panicked when age began to show, or when scripts were suggested with character parts and not leads. Many resorted to needles and knives, or worse, pills or the bottle. She'd had her moments with pills and bottles and powders but only recreationally.

Still, she couldn't help comparing her face to her twenty-year-old self and the face that landed her first roles. She had definitely been pretty as numerous casting directors and cast members had remarked. But she had worn the prettiness lightly, she never let it define her, and she knew she hadn't possessed the looks that would have been mainstream romantic lead. As she matured, she was cast as the love interest's best friend or rival. She was the mistress not the wife, but she had her fair share of romantic and sexy characters. Life reflected art, for she had had her fair share of real-life romance and drama as well. She stepped back from the mirror and smoothed her sweater down and over her hips. She had moved on to character driven supporting parts, accepting the arc of the actor's life with good grace. She was still in good shape but, she thought, there would be no more underwear or nude scenes. At least on film. She refreshed her lipstick, dabbed a smidge of her scent, Floris No 89, behind her ears and smiled to herself in the mirror.

Back in the cabin, Tom was mortified. Idiot. Lovely, pretty. It sounded like he was either trying to pick her up or damning with faint praise. Either way, he sounded like he was thirteen. And where the hell had the "you'd rock" phrase come from? He'd never used it before and probably never would again. He looked towards the closed toilet door. Was he trying to pick her up? He didn't really know. He felt something. He couldn't tell whether his pupils had dilated or whether his heart rate and respiration were elevated or whether he had had too much wine. But the strange look she had given him when excusing herself to go to the toilet had involuntarily worried him. His stomach had hollowed.

Nia returned and quietly sat down and buckled her seat belt. Tom watched her in silence, aware of the ambient engine noise for the first time in hours. She leaned over their seat dividers, she found his hand and held it tightly. She had decided to move this, whatever it was, forward.

"I like it that you think I'd... rock a uniform," she said. "You flatter this girl from the valleys, for you, sir, have a fine line in sophisticated patter."

"Well, yes. I am, after all, nothing if not considered urbane," Tom said and added a shy smile. "Sorry, it's been some time."

Nia laughed, "That's hard to believe."

Tom had experienced a few relationships with women since leaving the army, but most had been one- or two-night stands. Intense, sweaty tumbles where both parties didn't confuse momentarily passion or lust for any deep emotional coupling. There had been a longer relationship with the woman his sister now called Marina Girl, but that had been a disaster. It wasn't that he couldn't have a deep relationship, it was that he'd just convinced himself that he wasn't ready for one.

They talked quietly; simply sitting next to each other, holding hands, they were both surprised how natural and how comfortable this connection felt. Nia squeezed Tom's hand as the jet wobbled through some turbulence. He liked the physical connection to this amazing woman. Tom tried to ignore the change in the pitch of the Boeing's engine noise, but it morphed into an all too vivid a memory.

Chapter Three
Afghanistan, Five Years Earlier

The big RAF Chinook's engines screamed loudly as it swooped into the valley, flying low and fast. It was a dangerous night to be out. Intelligence had reported an uptick in Taliban activity and the night was cloudless and a half-moon provided enough light to read by. The helicopter's veteran crew were nervously scanning the valley sides stretching above them for the tell-tale flashes of assault rifle fire or worse, the fiery streak of an RPG. The Chinook's passengers were a mixed bunch; wiry, tanned men sporting large, grizzled beards that usually meant special forces, most of whom slept, a group of wide-eyed female nurses, looking small under their helmets, and a platoon of regular army guys rotating out from a Forward Operating Base. Major Tom Price MC couldn't help catching the eye of the nurse who sat opposite. He had already been captivated by her large brown eyes, the wisps of red hair that snuck out from under her helmet, and her shy smile when they had chatted briefly at the FOB. She had been apprehensive about the helicopter flight; he had tried to assuage her fear even though he, too, hated helicopters. He had made sure he sat opposite her. They nodded to each other across the Chinook's cabin as it was too loud to talk, and they exchanged smiles. He quickly took in her uniform again; fresh and reasonably clean, her name on her chest, Roberts, the single pip of a second lieutenant. He knew that she was at the fresh-faced start of her career while he was in the tired twilight of his.

The Chinook reached the head of the valley and swung hard to port. Suddenly, there was a change in the pitch of the helicopter's engines. All the special forces guys were now awake and alert. Through the cabin noise, they all heard a shearing sound followed by a deafening crack and then the Chinook began to rotate at sickening speed. Price shut his eyes. The helicopter spiralled violently until it crashed into the valley side.

Price came to and vomited, then he felt someone grabbing his webbing and pulling. His body screamed in pain. He screamed in pain. His vision cleared and he could see one of the special forces troopers was pulling him away from part of what had been the Chinook.

"No worries mate," the trooper said. "You're good. You're going to get through this."

Price wasn't convinced. His tunic was covered in vomit and blood and something that looked like Chinook bulkhead was sticking out of his right thigh. Every movement was agony. He moved gingerly against the valley side forcing himself into a sitting position, grimacing and sweating with the pain. Sitting up, he observed the scene around him. A couple of the special forces' lads had taken up defensive positions constantly scanning the valley sides above and around them. The Chinook had broken in two on impact. The front of the chopper lay out its side and was ablaze. The rear, containing the passenger and cargo compartment, had apparently burst on impact. The trooper who had freed Price from the wreckage had been joined by one of Price's own men and a nurse as they sorted through the human wreckage. There were several broken bodies. Another soldier was carried and laid next to Price. He recognised the brown eyes. They were impossibly large with fear. Roberts was in a bad way. Silent and pale in shock. She had been placed on her left side and faced him.

One of the nurses knelt in front of Price and began to apply a field dressing around his thigh wound.

"Work on her," Price ordered through gritted teeth and nodded towards Roberts.

The nurse almost imperceptibly shook her head. Price noticed the tears running down her dirty, blood smeared cheeks.

To his right, Roberts reached out a bloody hand and Price held it while the other nurse continued to work on him. Waves of nausea and darkness began to break over him like surf. He turned to face Roberts through the descending haze. Price watched a single tear leave her eye, follow the contour of her cheekbone and down her face before falling onto the rough sand. He stared deeply at her and squeezed her hand as the light appeared to fade from her eyes.

"Roberts," he shouted. "Fight it. Stay with me

kiddo."

He felt her grip on his hand loosen, he tried to hold on, but her hand slipped out of his and she slipped away. Her eyes remained open, but he knew that she was gone. Then, a wave of nausea spread over him, his vision clouded and then he felt or saw nothing more.

***

Present. Mid-Atlantic. November 21st

Tom held Nia's hand as she drifted off into a shallow airplane sleep. He watched as she snoozed. He wondered just who this exciting woman lying next to him was? He felt he had connected more with her in four hours than he had with his wife across their four years together. To be fair, he recalled, he had spent most of their relationship bouncing from trouble spot to war zone to army base and back again. But, also to be fair, she did sleep with his best friend and his best friend's best friend. She had really wanted to marry an officer, any officer. He had heard she was now on her third. He felt that he never did really know her.

Tom released Nia's hand gently. He carefully manouvered out of his seat pod and made his way to the toilet. There, he washed his face in the tiny sink. He was tired, he recognised it in the corners of the blue grey eyes that looked back from the mirror. He still wore some of the familiar fatigue from the years of taking and giving orders, of mentoring young men with hopes and fears he no longer shared, of dealing with civilians who barely concealed their contempt for his uniform, of making life and death decisions. It was the tiredness that had come with being around so much death and killing. He had done quite a bit of it in his time but now he was done with it. Tom had retreated to his narrowboat still burdened by emotional hurt, not to punish himself, but to ensure that he remained constantly aware of those that were lost. He brushed his teeth with his finger and smiled in the mirror to check his teeth. It was a strong and surprisingly gentle face that smiled back.

He returned to the seat pod. Nia stirred in hers as he sat. She opened her eyes and smiled. Tom smiled back. It felt both odd yet natural. Nia shut her eyes again. Tom watched her for a moment, knowing he was smitten and thinking how truly lovely she was, then, with his free hand he pulled out his phone, popped in his air pods, opened the screen, found Kate Bush's *Babooshka* and hit play. Nia stirred again next to him and opened her eyes.

"What are you listening to?" she asked.

He gave her one of his air pods and she put it in her left ear.

"Oh, I like this," she said and closed her eyes again.

After the song was over, she opened her eyes and asked him about his music. She remembered that he was wearing air pods when she first saw him at the gate. They talked about their favourite music, favourite bands. Although they were of similar ages, they had different tastes. Tom had eclectic tastes but was anchored by eighties' music. "Inherited from my sister," he explained.

Nia's tastes were 1990s' Britpop: Oasis, Blur, and Pulp. She didn't feel the time was right to mention she had partied with most of the bands. She quickly mentioned that she had also grown fond of musical theatre and had had roles in several productions. Tom had only seen one musical, *Evita*, and that was only because a college girlfriend had dragged him to the theatre to see it.

"Next time I'm in one, I'll send you a ticket," Nia joked, and Tom quite liked the idea of them remaining in some kind of touch after the flight's end. They continued to talk, occasionally awkwardly, but mostly engagingly for the remainder of the flight.

It was a still and dark dawn as the big jet crossed the English coastline. Nia pointed to the twinkling lights of little villages, the orange glow of streetlamps, tiny traffic alive with the shining of miniature head and taillights, she wondered aloud where they were all going so early in the morning. The enveloping soft glow of dawn spread across the patchwork landscape exposing towns and roads that Nia recognised from her numerous approaches to Heathrow. She was happy to be approaching home but, as she turned to Tom, she was struck by the sudden reality that whatever they had shared over the last seven hours was about to end. Tom felt it too and he wanted to say something to her, but he struggled to find the words. They were suddenly quiet. Nia, who made her living with and through words, found herself suddenly at a loss for them.

**

Heathrow. That Morning

The landing was smooth. The bump and jolt of the heavy jet's landing gear touching the runway at one hundred and sixty miles per hour was barely perceptible.

"Good pilot," Tom exclaimed really to himself and Nia nodded in agreement.

"Nice to be on the ground," she said.

Tom nodded, "I don't mind flying in these big jets, but I bloody hate helicopters. I'd be happy if I never set foot in another helicopter again. It's always nice to be back on the ground."

"Yes, always nice to be home," Nia said again with just a hint of wistfulness.

Both were wondering how they could transition into something that would serve as a bridge to an ongoing connection, something more than what could so easily become the transient connection of two passengers thrown together for the duration of a flight. The seat belt light was extinguished with a ding and the big jet filled with the sounds of hundreds of passengers standing, opening baggage bins, and removing bags and sundry items. Both Nia and Tom stood and retrieved their various personal items. They both looked at each other willing the other to say something. Neither did.

Tom wrestled for the right words to say and the right way to say them. Nia struggled with the desire to connect and her imperative to remain detached. They were shepherded out of the aircraft by still smiling flight attendants. Tom shouldered one of Nia's bags. They talked about the London weather. Through the terminal's glass sides, a cold London winter waited. Passport control was mercifully smooth and quick. Nia waited for Tom to emerge from the border force booth and together they proceeded to move to the next stage of airport experience. Tom hesitated as they approached the signs for baggage claim.

"Don't you have any bags to pick up?" Nia asked looking at the small cabin bag he carried with a sense of incredulity.

"No, I travel light," Tom answered patting the bag. The phrase, 'travel light, travel alone', came to mind. "Occupational hazard of army life and then from living on a narrowboat," he smiled.

"Will you wait for me to get my bags?" Nia asked.

"Of course," Tom replied gallantly. "I'll help if you'd like."

Tom retrieved Nia's bags noting that she did not travel light and loaded them onto a trolley. Together, they emerged through the frosted glass doors that formed the barrier between passport control, baggage collection, and the rest of the airport. The overhead lights appeared to diffuse the area in an unnatural harsh yellow light. Nia quickly wrapped her scarf up and over her chin and slipped a bobble hat on her head, tucking a lot of her hair up and under it. She also appeared to shrink as she changed her gait. She was a different character.

There was a small crowd as the glass doors hissed open and out on to the concourse. Family members and loved ones were waiting for the return of their dear ones, business associates mingled, and there was a handful of drivers, some liveried, some in jeans and heavy coats.

"Is anyone meeting you?" Nia asked, hoping Tom's answer would be in the negative. She had suddenly realised that neither she nor Tom had asked whether there were significant others in the picture. She got a strong sense that Tom didn't have one. She hadn't had a significant relationship for a long time.

"No, not here," Tom replied. "I'm catching a train up north, to Chester, my sister is picking me up there."

Good, single, she thought.

"Look," she said directly. "I have a car service. I can get the driver to drop you off at a Tube station if you'd like."

"Yes," Tom said. "I would like that."

He appreciated the offer as it would mean more time with Nia. Tom noticed a driver was holding a home-made sign that simply stated 'Nia.' Tom pointed to the sign.

"I know it's a relatively rare name," Tom said. "But

the one name thing. It's a bit Cher isn't it?"

Nia laughed. "It's more like a habit now, but I still need to be a little protective of some privacy, of some personal space."

"Are you really paparazzi famous?" asked Tom.

"No, not really any more," she answered without any hint of regret. "I never really was, consistently, but I did have my moments."

He was intrigued, "Moments?"

She stopped walking and turned to him, "So you don't know who I am at all? And I don't mean that in a pompous arseholey kind of way."

"Err, no. I'm sorry," he responded, and she felt his honesty and a little of a shared embarrassment. "I got out of the habit of theatre and TV when I was in the army. Should I know who you are?"

"No, but I still occasionally bounce into people who still see me as some kind of public property or think I'm actually one of the characters I've played. The press were, at one time, brutal. It has made me a little wary, a little defensive."

They paused in front of the already tired looking driver. They both wanted to say something, the same thing.

"Look, do you have time for a coffee?" Tom asked.

"Yes. I'm sure the driver could find a cafe close to a Tube station for you." She didn't want to break the connection. She turned to the driver, "An extra fifty do it?"

The driver nodded. Tom felt his heart beat a little faster with genuine excitement.

***

London

The cafe was one of those nondescript, shopfront, neighbourhood affairs loved by retired locals and hipsters alike. Nia and Tom both ordered flat whites and took a small table by the steamed-up windows. It was raining outside. The heavy tiredness of the long travel night came over them both.

Nia smiled at Tom over the rim of her mug. He felt a part of him melt. He knew that he had lived so deeply inside his head for the last five years that the feelings he was now experiencing were both rare and liberating. Everything seemed to have a new resonance; the coffee tasted richer, the steam hiss from the latte machine sounded fuller, the winter light appeared softer. He felt as if he was breaking a swimming pool's surface after a deep, lung bursting dive. Nia looked lovelier in what natural light was available than she had under the airport's harsh fluorescents or in the jet's semi dark cabin.

They talked, and laughed, and talked some more. Go for it, thought Tom.

"I would very much like to see you again," he said.

She smiled; her dark eyes shone like wet lead.

"I'd like that."

Nia asked for his phone and swapped phone numbers.

"I'll text you soon," she said. "I have a busy, few days, but I'll get in touch."

She saw his face register disappointment. Nia held out her hand across the table and he took it gently.

"No, I promise. I will. This has been nice, Tom. Unexpected, but really nice."

She was distracted by the driver's entrance. The driver theatrically tapped his watch.

"Look, I have to go," she said. "Don't worry. I mean it. I'll text you, okay." She squeezed his hand encouragingly but Tom was already feeling the sensation of loss.

Tom watched her leave the cafe. He liked the way she moved, the bounce of her hair, and the quick, over the shoulder gaze towards him as she opened the cafe's door excited him. He turned his chair to watch her through the heavy condensation on the windows as she moved through the haze of the late morning drizzle and into the waiting car. He continued to watch as the car pulled away from the curb and disappeared into traffic.

He replaced his air pods and took out his phone. Something cinematic he thought and chose Jon and Vangelis 'Friends of Mr Cairo'. He hit play then switched screens to his web browser and typed her name into the search box. His eyes scanned the results. "Holy fuck," he said loudly enough for the people at the next table to turn around with displeasure.

Outside, rain drizzled down the car's windows and Nia pushed herself deeply into the warm, pliant leather of the rear seats. She was tired. She had been excited to return home and get back into the regular routine of her life but the last hours had been something completely surprising. She wasn't a stranger to desire; indeed, it was something of another occupational hazard. She had drifted in and out of relationships, but they were usually fun, short, and shallow. Love wasn't a reality any more, she had thought. It wasn't that she couldn't love. There had been several lovers, but very few loves. Fewer loves than her marriages. There was at least the big one, but she had convinced herself that that relationship was the ONE true love of her life. It was partly why she had never attempted to build a lasting relationship since. Oh God, she thought, Tom would find it on Google. She was interested in seeing Tom, again but she grimaced and remembered another airport scene over seventeen years past.

Chapter Four
London, 2002

Nia's career was on a high. A regular role as a femme fatale on a beloved weekly drama series had made her a household name. There were rumours that Hollywood would come knocking. Nia had been thrilled by the role and the accompanying public profile, but the lens of fame quickly lost its glitter. Her anonymity had been replaced with requests for selfies and gossip columnists couldn't separate her role from her reality. Her first husband, married and divorced in her early twenties, sold salacious stories to the press along with some racy, intimate photos. Paparazzi caught her tired and emotional at parties or after award shows. There was talk of voracious appetites for wine, coke, and men. Little of it was true. She liked a glass or two of wine, she believed she had her cocaine problem under control, and there weren't men, there was a man.

He was a fellow actor, of course, leading man material, recently discovered by Hollywood. He was a Goldenboy. Nia found him beautiful and tender, clever and witty. He wore a background of Harrow and Cambridge with a faux lightness. He charmed her, as he did everyone, and she found herself in love with him. He loved her, too, but conditionally. He was voraciously ambitious. The press presented them as the golden couple when they were dating. There were wedding photos in *Hello* but then the failings of their two-year-long marriage was played out in the full glare of the public. There were the rumours of affairs, his; accusations of crockery being thrown, hers. There were private stories leaked by so-called friends, and there were the public fights in restaurants, at parties, and then, finally, Heathrow. Goldenboy left her standing broken and crying on a concourse, while he flew off for a movie shoot. The marriage was over. He never returned to her or to the home they had shared. Goldenboy sent his agent to collect his possessions, all but one.

Nia's heartbreak, but not her secret, played out in a very public forum. Goldenboy's charm offensive worked wonders with the British press and the Hollywood glitterati. Her working class, fuck you attitude didn't sit well with newspaper editors and gossip column hacks and so she was viewed as the villain of the piece. While Goldenboy, all cool and collected, was seen as a potential future James Bond, she was the fiery, mouthy Celt. Nia discovered that most of her friends were actually Goldenboy's friends. Doors closed. For the first time since she was a young teen, she felt alone and, worse, abandoned. But, not completely alone, there was the little life she carried and her agent, Jane, provided some support and comfort.

Against Jane's advice, Nia decided to take a break. Discussions with her TV show runner didn't go well, they wouldn't give her the time away that she needed. She had tough decisions to make and she made them. Her character was written out of the weekly TV gig. It was a professional and financial blow, but Nia felt it was freeing. She hoped that she would have something good from the whole personal debacle. She travelled alone seeking some anonymity, solace, and healing. Then, her hopes for a new kind of future came to a distressing and bloody end in a small Scottish hospital where Nia lost her baby and was left utterly bereft.

Nia let her life spin out of control. She drank too much, had too many one-night stands, and let herself slip into the arms of a deep depression. She knew that she was punishing herself but felt that she deserved it. It was Jane, her agent, who saved Nia from herself. Jane used job options as a kind of therapy for Nia. There was some regional theatre, TV guest roles, the West End, and then back as TV recurring characters. Nia threw herself into the parts with determination and effort. She was a good actor and parts continued to come. She reforged a professional life while, outside of the public eye, she continued to nurse her personal wounds. Her upbringing had made her resilient but the experience with Goldenboy and her baby hardened her heart. She moved on determined to guard her emotions closely and to never let anyone get close enough to hurt her again.

It didn't help that her personal reputation remained damaged. With every career success the Goldenboy enjoyed, the press would regurgitate a Nia rumour just on the safe side of slander. The press always seemed to like to juxtapose a photo of Goldenboy, usually staged, all tan and teeth and expensive suit, with a gotcha photo of Nia with no make-up, gym-wet hair, leaving a supermarket clutching a frozen meal and a bag of toilet paper.

***

London and the Marches. Present. November 21st
Nia and Tom separately made their ways home. Tom walked to the nearby Tube station then on to Euston and then on to points north. Nia headed east across the city. She arrived at her home long before Tom arrived at his. The driver helped her with her bags. She opened her front door and stepped inside, putting her bags down in the hall. A dog came running up to her signalling joy with its wagging tail. Nia squatted down to rub the dog's head. She stood up and said loudly to the interior of the house, "Darling, it's me. I'm home."

***

Chester train station was grey with rain. Tom's sister, Rachel, was waiting for him inside the station. She caught sight of him and waved as he walked across the station's small concourse. He'd snoozed only lightly on the train but felt more refreshed than he had in years. They hugged.

"How was Canada?" Rachel asked.

"It was good. It was great to see Jacques. He sends his love," Tom replied.

"Flight okay?"

"It was… fine." Tom paused and then added, "It was quite interesting, actually."

Rachel cocked her head quizzically.

"What?" he said.

"What?" she said.

"What nothing," Tom said emphatically.

They stepped outside. He looked over to the vehicle she had driven.

"Oh, Rachel, you had to bring the bloody Land Rover? I hate those things."

"You know the more you get used to these kinds of things the better it will be. Look at it, it's blue not army green," she replied.

Rachel drove and they talked of his trip to Canada, Jacques Gagnon's PhD defence and subsequent party, the food, hotel rooms, the flights again. Tom looked out of the Land Rover's windows at the increasingly familiar countryside. Icy frost still clinging to hedgerows and trees sparkled in the afternoon sun. It felt magical, it felt different, more vivid somehow. He shut his eyes momentarily wanting to enjoy the memory of the recent flight.

Rachel had looked after Tom's Jack Russell terrier while he had been on his Canadian trip and she talked about the terrier's enjoyment of farm life. She talked of the farm, how hard her husband Owain still worked, pushing sixty. But Rachel sensed there was something. She had been concerned that Gagnon's post-army accomplishments, a career position with Canadian military intelligence and now the doctorate, would send Tom deeper into his shell. Tom's reticence worried her and she began to fear that the trip had not gone well.

"It's going to snow," she said.

"Looking likely," Tom answered. Ah, the comforting feeling of the classic British conversational topic of the weather, he thought.

Almost as soon as they entered Rachel's farmhouse the kettle was put on. "Tea?" she asked more of a statement than a question. Jack, the Jack Russell, bounded up to Tom, Tom knelt, with some difficulty keeping his right leg outstretched, and rubbed his dog's powerful chest. Jack licked Tom's hand repeatedly.

"She does look good," Tom said.

A few minutes later Rachel passed him a big mug of tea; steam twirling from the mug.

His tiredness was mixed with a fresh excitement.

"Okay, little brother," Rachel began emphatically. "Tell me what's up."

Tom stared into his tea.

"It's crazy but I think I've met someone," he said. He surprised himself with the remark as he and Rachel, although close, increasingly so over the past five years, did not regularly share personal intimacies. But Tom felt the need to say something. He felt lighter for saying

57

it as if sharing the information made it more real somehow.

"You think? Well, you either met someone or you didn't." Rachel then twigged. "Oh, I see, you think you MET someone." She was stunned.

She knew her brother had the occasional fling with women he would meet in a canal-side pub or a single female boater who made herself available; two narrowboaters that pass in the night. He was a good-looking chap, but Rachel knew that he had avoided any real connection since leaving the army. She didn't think it was because of the residual feelings for the ex-wife, those wounds had long healed. She looked up towards the sideboard to the framed picture of Tom in dress uniform. Other wounds were taking a lot longer.

"Yes," Tom smiled. "Met in that way, but I'm not sure."

They both sat down at the kitchen table, cups of tea in hand.

"Well, you can't just say something like that and go all quiet on me," Rachel said. "Come on, who is she, what's she like?"

Tom felt embarrassed by candour, but in for a penny in for a pound.

"She's smart and funny and lovely. She's an actress," he said. "Quite well known, apparently."

"Oh yeah," Rachel responded. "Would I know her?"

"Maybe. Nia Williams."

Rachel's face registered shock.

"Oh my God, the Welsh Spitfire?"

***

Rachel dropped Tom and Jack off at the narrowboat basin at the small, pretty Welsh village of Llangollen. Light flakes of snow seemed to drift in a mild breeze. Tom unlocked the rear door of his narrowboat. Home. He had had no idea what he was going to do after he left the army, but remembering an enjoyable family holiday from his youth, he impetuously sold his house, his Mini, and bought a forty-eight-foot narrowboat.

The boat, Periwinkle, was in good shape when he purchased it. He asked the boatyard about changing the name but was advised not to as changing boat names brought only bad luck. The boatyard gave him a thorough training on the boat operations and maintenance and even accompanied him on a thirty-minute test sail. After about another thirty minutes of solo boating, he was hooked. He had since spent five years living on the Periwinkle and had travelled a few thousand miles on the canals of England and Wales. It had become his lifestyle, his profession, his therapy. Tom loved the Llangollen canal and the region around it, its proximity to Rachel, and had decided to winter up at one of the canal's marinas.

He stepped down into the boat, dropped off his small flight bag. Everything was familiar but everything felt different. The boat was cold and Jack immediately curled up on her bed in the front cabin. Periwinkle was plugged into an external electrical outlet, so Tom switched on a small electric heater, while he started a fire in the boat's little pot-bellied Danish Morso stove. He fired up the kettle and emptied the contents of a supermarket plastic bag he'd carried under his arm. It contained a few essential groceries and a selection of DVDs which spilt out onto the small galley table. They were the fruit of his and Rachel's labours of visiting several video shops and supermarkets. Rachel had curated a small collection of Nia Williams' work. As the boat's cabin warmed nicely, he took a seat in one of his two comfy chairs, Jack jumped up into his lap, then, tea in hand, he pressed play on his small TV/DVD combo. The first DVD was of a two-decade-old TV drama; within ten minutes of watching, a young Nia emerged on screen. She was playing a pugnacious teen runaway. She turned to face the camera and Tom thought she was stunning, her dark eyes sparkled through the screen and through the years. He ached to be with her again. He took a sip of his tea and wondered what she was doing at that moment.

***

In her London town home, Nia was remembering how nicely Tom had smiled. Ben, the handsome young man who had greeted her, was shouldering a rucksack and was about to push his bike through the open front door. Nia held the door for him and passed him an envelope containing an overly generous amount of cash. She knew the young actor struggling for parts would need it.

"Thanks again for house-sitting," she said.

"No problem darling. Anytime. You have such a lovely house. It was fun to stay and eat all your food and drink all your booze." Ben leaned down and patted his Lab on its head. The dog licked his hand. "We love it here. Do let me know if you need me again." Ben looked at her. "You are positively glowing darling. Jet lag must be good for the skin."

"I'm just happy to be home," Nia said recognising it was only a half truth.

Nia held the door open to watch Ben cycle off into the city followed by his trotting Lab. She closed the door and leant against it as if catching her breath. She was tired, almost overcome with fatigue. She would unpack her bags later.

"Time for a cup of tea," she said out loud, her voice echoing in the empty house.

Tea made, Nia sat down in her study surrounded by the books she loved so much. She wondered whether she should get a dog. She sipped her tea thinking back on her last few weeks. The job had been fulfilling, fun, and well paid. Bills would be paid; savings account would be topped up. Nia wouldn't have to worry about her finances, but she was anxious for the next role, the next job. There were some scripts to read, auditions to prepare for, and call backs were already on her calendar. She didn't care for auditions but was rarely just given roles these days, and she had accepted that as another part of the actor's life. But now, there was this Tom guy and, for the first time in a long time, her thoughts weren't just about work. As she went through the rest of the day, her imaginings filled her house, making it feel less empty.

Over the next day, Nia and Tom went on with their separate and regular routines. As they moved through what was so familiar; boat duties, making cups of tea, talking with agents, sitting down with a book, listening to the news, they both, unknown to the other, felt attached by a gossamer-thin thread of connection.

Chapter Five
Llangollen, November 22nd

Tom woke to a cold cabin. He exhaled breath clouds as he slipped out of bed with an audible 'brrrr' and, put on slippers. Jack moved from the foot of the bed to the warm spot Tom had just vacated. Jack watched Tom throw on sweatpants, T-shirt, and a sweatshirt before Tom made his way down the narrowboat. His limp was more obvious on cold mornings. Tom went to light the little Morso stove in the forward cabin. He was always good with fires and the kindling took immediately. He placed a few coal bricks on top of the kindling and waited for the first wafts of warm air. He closed the stove's grill and held out his hands to absorb the heat. Sufficiently convinced that the fire would now hold, he made his way back down the cabin to the small kitchen. His phone was plugged in, charging. He held his breath involuntarily while checking his texts. Nothing. It's still early, he told himself. He put the kettle on. The window, above the small cooktop and sink, was almost at water level. Tom watched a few hardy ducks and coots navigate the semi-frozen canal, drawn to the narrowboat's window in the hope of some crumbs. Tom opened the window and supplied some as he always did. The canal bank opposite opened on to a meadow, tinged with heavy frost. Tom, now with tea in hand, watched a dog fox scuttle home, like an anxious husband who had stayed out too late. Perhaps there was a vixen waiting, perhaps kits, in a nearby den. Or, perhaps, like Tom, the reynard was alone. A loner, Tom considered, but not necessarily alone. There was Jack and Rachel and her family. His thoughts then turned to Nia.

Tea done and cup placed in the sink, Tom moved down the cabin to the tiny bathroom — a child-size toilet, a half-size sink, and a small shower stall that required Tom to duck his six-foot-one body into to get his hair wet. He knocked on the thin wooden wall that separated the bathroom from the bed's cabin, "Hey, don't go back to sleep," he said to Jack. He quickly washed his face, saving water had become second nature on the narrowboat. He checked his face in the mirror above the small sink. To shave or not to shave. He rasped his hands over his two-day stubble. He'd go without a shave again. He was still tired of shaving. Twenty years in the army with its over emphasis on personal turnout, freshly shaved faces, spit polished boots, blancoed webbing, and cleaned and oiled rifles had led now to a bit more carefree an attitude to such things.

"Okay Jack, morning piddle."

Tom picked up the terrier off the bed and put her down on the cabin's rough carpet. Tom slipped on running shoes, threw two bolts and opened the stern doors off the bedroom cabin and immediately felt a rush of cold air. He kept the roof hatch closed and ducked up the three steps on to the narrowboat's stern, Jack at his side. The boat was rock still. There was a sheen of ice on the canal, frost dusted the mooring ropes, and the towpath was frozen hard. Tom grabbed the short boat pole off its roof housing and tested the ice. Thin. Thin enough for another day's journeying. Jack had already jumped off the barge onto the towpath where she was leaving a steaming puddle. Tom grabbed gloves and scarf, padlocked the stern door, and took off down the towpath with his dog.

It was their routine. Although free of the strictures of army life, Tom still liked the cadences of certain routines. He enjoyed the brisk morning jogs, checking what lay immediately ahead on the canal while enjoying the company of the young, inquisitive terrier. Today, however, felt entirely different. He looked down at his watch, it was now seven a.m. He wondered whether she, miles away, was up. He took a huge breath in, the cold air stinging his lungs. There was an incredible stillness across the basin. Tom opened his phone's music app, decided on Kraftwerk's 'Computer Love' as accompanying music, he liked its ambient, trance-like quality, and he and Jack began to run down the towpath at a decent pace. Tom never really knew how far or how long he'd run. He let the soreness in his right leg be his guide.

Later, he showered, dressed in warm clothes, and quickly finished a breakfast of tea and toast. He listened to the radio news and weather. Freezing temps and snow predicted for the day ahead. Freezing drizzle for London. Her home. Out on the small rear deck he opened the engine compartment. He checked the engine oil and water levels and eyeballed the compartment for any water ingress that needed to be pumped out. He checked the engine was in neutral and then pushed the start button to fire it up. While the engine warmed up, he went back into the cabin, boiling the kettle for a thermos of coffee, double checking his canal guides, he quickly jotted some notes for his own guide. He then cast-off bow and stern, put the engine in gear and pulled out into the canal moving slowly past a couple of lonely looking moored narrowboats. As a distant church bell tolled eight o'clock, Tom swung the tiller and pushed the Periwinkle through the onion skin of ice, out into the main body of water and set off south-easterly down the Llangollen canal. The Dee valley below to his right was shrouded in whisps of morning mist and a low winter sun made him squint. He smiled to himself and found, much to his surprise, that he was whistling something that sounded like a jig and, totally alien to him, he was checking his phone every few minutes to see if he had any new texts.

***

London, Same Day

Nia woke to a pitch-black room. She was momentarily confused as to where she was before she fully remembered she was home. She was still struggling a little with jet lag. The red digits on her bedside clock registered eight thirty a.m. She turned on the radio and listened to the BBC news. She slipped on a nightie and a well-worn dressing gown and went downstairs.

The house was quiet, dark, and cold. Nia cranked up the central heating and made herself a cup of coffee before sitting down. She'd been on a location shoot for a month and she now wanted to get back into what approached her regular routine. She was aware of a vague excitement, the amorphous kind a child nurtured on the run up to Christmas. She took out her phone but then put it down, too needy she thought. She dressed quickly; running shirt, sweatshirt, yoga pants and went to her gym. Once there, she ran on the treadmill as a warm-up before a cardio-boxing session. She stayed and chatted to a few of the session's participants as they downed smoothies in the gym's social lounge, they were mostly stay-at-home mums. She had little in common with the group and, although she often grew tired of the cyclical chatter around schools, children's sports team and demanding husbands, they provided a social connection to a lifestyle very different from hers. It was a glimpse into a life that Nia once wanted although would never admit to. They were friendly, Nia was friendly, but she didn't consider them friends. Not the type of friends you go out for a drink with, share stories, swap secrets, or ask for advice. Nia had few such friends.

Nia drove from the gym and showered at home. She had renovated her bathroom and had an expansive walk-in shower with multiple shower heads. She stood luxuriating in the hot water allowing the steam to ease the muscle tiredness and tension from her workout and the previous day's flight. Once out of the shower, she checked her phone and was disappointed that there was no message from Tom but then remembered she'd been quite definitive about her contacting him. She wanted to text him but was still wary. Instead, she called her agent with Tom still very much on her mind.

Nia was going to meet Jane, her agent, for a mid-afternoon coffee in a chic, bohemian cafe. Nia was early, as she often was, she ordered a flat white and found a table that was conducive to conversation. She watched the door for Jane. Jane was more than an agent; she was probably Nia's longest and closest friend. A young mum entered with a toddler in a high-tech pushchair with moon-rover wheels. The mum unfastened her coat and Nia noticed the large, heavy baby bump beneath. The mum instinctively put her hand on the bump and smiled, and Nia remembered the same sense, the same feeling of life moving and growing under the touch of your hand. Then Jane entered with a loud hello and extravagant wave.

Nia and Jane had been together for over two

decades. Jane was a posh Home Counties girl, now in late middle age. She always dressed in immaculate tailored suits worn with colourful silk scarves. Hair was always perfect and as blond as a Swede's. Big, owl-like glasses, usually in a shade that matched her scarf, gave her a wise, thoughtful demeanour. Jane's voice was like a market barker's run through sandpaper. She had always been maternal towards Nia. She had never married, had no children, and Nia had always suspected that Jane was a very quiet and private lesbian. Nia also felt that Jane was always slightly disappointed in Nia for not having the A-lister career than once appeared to be in the offing. Still, Nia knew, Jane had stuck with her through some difficult times and had fought for good roles.

Jane continued to keep Nia busy and had helped her adjust to the vagaries of the acting profession. She had convinced Nia to take character roles, guest starring gigs, advert voice overs, and audio book narrations. There was almost always some job waiting in the wings. Jane greeted Nia like an aunt would a niece. Over coffee, they chatted about the Canadian job, whether there would be an option of a sequel. Jane noted rumours of potential roles and work options and suggested some scripts to read and auditions to go on. Nia half listened and made notes on her phone. She wanted to work and work constantly for she was aware of how cruel the industry could be for actresses of a certain age. She also wanted to work because she had little else to fill her days.

Nia had waited long enough in the conversation to ask Jane for a favour, hoping it wouldn't appear as Nia's top priority. Nia asked whether Jane could use her contacts to find one of those ex-army types who advised TV and film productions on the proper way to do military things, to provide some background on Tom Price. Tom was, she thought, a guy in his mid-forties, fit decent looking, witty and smart, straight, she had noticed the way he looked at her, yet single. There was a reticence when he talked about the army. She could tell he'd been hurt, physically, the limp, and probably emotionally. She was concerned that he had baggage and, God knows, she had enough baggage for any relationship. Jane was surprised.

"Anything you want to let me in on?" Jane asked.

"Just some guy I met," Nia replied over her coffee cup. "Just wanna make sure he's not some kind of bullshitter."

Jane slowly nodded, not fully believing Nia.

Coffee meeting done, Nia did some grocery shopping before going home. Jane called her as she was putting a few groceries away. The military advisor Jane had reached out to did indeed know of Major Tom Price. A decent bloke was the astute summation. Something of a hero, actually, an earned gallantry award, a Military Cross. A guy who was loved and respected by those who served with him until a helicopter accident ended his career and nearly his life. Rumours of a breakdown.

Nia put the phone back in her pocket. Overall, she thought, an okay report and very much what she had expected. Nia was an astute reader of people. Jet-lagged, she went upstairs and laid on her bed. She took her phone out of her pocket as it was uncomfortable. With the phone in hand, she decided to Google what an MC was. She was surprised by what it took to earn the award and had difficulty seeing Tom as a guy who had received such a medal. Her phone went on the bedside table. Nia felt guilty that she had somehow betrayed this chap she'd just met, when was that, yesterday? She felt sad about the sense he had experienced some kind of breakdown, which cycled back into guilt for snooping. But she told herself, that he was sure to Google her, and she'd be exposed, quite literally, and what would he make of what he found? Fuck it, she told herself, there's something here that needs to play out. She leant over to her bedside table and picked up her phone again.

***

Tom's phone beeped with an incoming text. He felt a wave of electric excitement wash over him. He was as desperate with anticipation as a teenager. 'Nia' his phone read. He opened the text.

"Hi, it's Nia."

YES! He said to himself. "Hi Nia." He typed.

She was glad to see him respond so quickly.

"You get back to your barge ok? ☺"

Tom saw the joke. "Yes, the narrowboat was waiting patiently."

"I enjoyed our chat yesterday," Nia continued, then took a breath and typed.

"I was just wondering; did you Google me?"

Damn, straightforward, he thought.

"Yes," he responded.

He's honest, she thought.

Tom was a little alarmed. Nothing and then… his screen showed 'Nia is typing'.

"And Major Price… do you still want to see me again?" Please, please, please, the voice in her head repeated somewhat to her own surprise.

Major Price, Tom thought, she had done some background research herself. He typed, "And, I very much want to see you again." And then added, "Soon." She was relieved.

"How about Saturday? I'm in a one-off play for charity. You could pop to the theatre and we could have dinner after," Nia texted.

"I'd like that," he replied.

She sent him the details about the play, the theatre, and possible dinner options. The sign offs were formal. Concern melted away but then Nia wondered whether she should have added an X. Tom smiled as he put his phone back in his pocket.

Almost as soon as he had stopped texting Tom was shockingly aware of two issues. He didn't have a way to get back to London easily and he didn't have date night type clothes. He called Rachel. She was delighted that Tom was acting alive for the first time in a long while. She immediately agreed to help him out on both fronts. She'd loan him the Land Rover and accompany him to a tailor she knew in Shrewsbury to buy a suit.

Chapter Six
London, November 26th

Tom drove to Watford Junction Tube station and parked the borrowed Land Rover; he had decided to take the underground to the theatre district. Tom purchased his return ticket from an automated kiosk. He moved to the platform and entered a carriage and took a seat strategically allowing him to observe the entire car. It was almost empty. He settled into the seat near the window as the Tube train pulled out of the station with its customary tug, pull, clanking motions and sounds. The first part of the long trek through the city was above ground and, although dark, Tom watched the city lights emerge, and flicker and flash past his window. He had always liked London. It was always London he visualised when listening to military briefs on defending Britain, its people, and its way of life. He searched his phone for suitable music and decided on a cliché, the Clash's ubiquitous 'London Calling', then, something completely different with The Cars' 'Heartbeat City'. He changed trains at Harrow and Wealdstone and entered the Tube proper, at the Bakerloo line and journeyed through to Embankment.

As the train moved speedily through the bowels of the city, Tom listened to The Jam's 'That's

Entertainment' delaying listening to their 'Tube Station at Midnight' like leaving a sundae's cherry for last. He then played it twice and then let the Jam's greatest hits play out. Tom caught sight of his reflection in the window. Freshly shaved, shirt and tie, new suit. New everything, he thought, including attitude. He was nervous and excited, like a teen out on his first big date. He had packed a small overnight bag but had left it in the Land Rover. Idiot, he thought. He had no idea how the night would unfold. He certainly had hopes but he was also half expecting it to be an embarrassing drama where they shook hands, talked to each other too formally, and closed the night early without any warmth, leaving him to shlep back across the city and a dilemma of either heading home or finding a hotel for a lonely night. God, he hoped not. The very thought filled him with a gut-churning dread. He tried to lose the anxious feeling in his music. He pulled out his phone again and took comfort in the re-reading of Nia's texts.

After forty minutes the carriage shook slightly as the train braked and emerged from its tunnel into dazzlingly bright station lights. Embankment. It was Tom's stop. He stood, buttoned his grey wool suit and his overcoat then moved to the carriage's door, minded the gap, and stepped on to the platform and resolutely on to whatever the evening would hold.

Tom arrived at the theatre in good time. He found his ticket at the 'will call' booth, just as Nia had directed. He left his winter coat with coat check and found his way into the theatre bar. It was bright, lots of red and brass, Victorian decor, and a jovial atmosphere. Chic and stylish people were drinking, talking, and laughing. He made his way up to the bar, ordered a G&T, and was a bit flummoxed when the bartender listed umpteen gins that were available, most of which Tom had never heard of. He chose Gordon's. He took his glass to the side of the bar, almost with his back to the wall and observed the crowd before him. The light, almost playful, atmosphere helped him to relax. He was looking forward to the play and couldn't wait to see Nia again. Before he had finished his drink, a bell signalled that it was time for the bar's patrons to find their seats. Tom felt part of the crush of people as they almost, as one, moved into the theatre. He found his seat, front and centre, and felt waves of anticipation break over him like surf.

In the theatre's cramped dressing rooms, Nia looked at her reflection under the harsh light of the make-up mirror. The make-up artist had certainly lived up to his description, a true artist, she thought. Her reflection radiated youth and vigour. Nia was looking forward to the play, *Blithe Spirit*, and her role of Ruth. It was a play she'd been in many times, playing many characters, and she always liked it. Nia wanted to enjoy it. She had some jitters and she was wanting Tom to be in the audience more than she dared to hope. Nia knew where he'd be sitting in the theatre and she wanted to be sure to catch his eye. She took a deep breath to clear her mind and to focus on the role. The stage manager gave the cast their five-minute alert.

Nia felt the applause as she stepped on stage, relaxed, and she launched into her first lines. A little later she watched from the wings. She cast her eye on to the audience; there he was, front and centre, smiling. She wanted to confirm her remembrance of what he looked like. The short dark hair, greying artfully at the temples, the longish face, and square jaw, the kind mouth, sad eyes that still smiled. Nia took another deep glance at Tom and then moved across the stage to interact with another character. She was able to compartmentalise her professional and personal lives and she focused on the play, only fully catching Tom's eye when she bowed to the audience's applause at the end of the play. She winked cheekily at him.

***

Tom waited for Nia in the bar. The crowd that remained in the bar long after the play's end cheered when the actors came in. Tom had taken up his position at the end of the bar again, his back to the far wall. Observing. He saw the cast shaking hands, smiling, and laughing with friends and patrons in the bar. He watched the faces of the crowd around the actors and then he saw her. Then he saw only her. To Tom, she looked simply transcendent. She wore brown boots, jeans, and a baggy white shirt that looked like it was cut for a man, under a bright red wool wrap. Her hair was curlier and maybe a bit redder than it had been the last time he had physically seen her. She was smiling as she talked to people in the bar, but he noticed how the smile grew and her eyes blazed as she caught sight of him. He could tell that she quickly made an excuse to absent herself from her compatriots and made her way over to him. He carefully placed his drink on the bar and stepped towards her.

Tom didn't know how to greet her, panicked and put out his hand for a handshake. Nia laughed and instead hugged him and moved to kiss him on each cheek. Very actorly. They held each other deeply and closely, far too closely for people who had only really met once before. They melded together, their bodies responding through some intangible code of chemistry. They both instinctively knew that the other felt it too which further heated both their excitement and comfort. Nia liked the way Tom smelled; clean and masculine.

"Tom, it's so nice you came. What did you think of the play?" She asked with a genuine desire for a positive response from Tom.

"It was really enjoyable. You were bloody marvellous," Tom said.

Nia was pleased and she kissed him lightly on his lips.

"Thank you," she said.

"Err, thank you," Tom said, pleasantly surprised by the kiss. "I haven't seen many plays, especially in the West End. I should get out more."

"Yes, yes you should," Nia said and added, "Hungry?"

"Famished," Tom replied.

"Okay, let's get you out a bit more then. Let's get out of here and grab a bite."

It was late as they left the theatre and they walked hand in hand through the dark and emptying streets. They found a Thai restaurant that was still open even though the staff had begun to mop the floors. There were no other customers. The tired but kind waiter said the chef could knock up some pad Thai and Nia ordered a bottle of white wine. Nia talked about the play, her fellow cast members, Noel Coward, the small faux Italianate Welsh village of Portmeirion where Coward wrote the play, and Jamaica where Coward lived next to Ian Fleming his wintertime neighbour. She was clearly on a post-performance high, talking quickly, and delightedly to Tom's ear sounding more and more Welsh. He didn't really know this woman having spent, what, only ten or eleven hours with her, but he felt as if he had known her for years. And, in a strange way, he had. Having watched Nia on DVD, he now knew what she looked like when she was eighteen, twenty-four and thirty-eight. He had seen her laugh, had watched as she cried, had witnessed a variety of her hair styles, lengths, and colours. Now, he wanted to spend some time with the real her.

Nia took a long draw on her wine. Her face grew serious.

"So, you Googled me then." It was a statement.

He put down his chopsticks, "I did. Yes."

"And?"

"You've had a great career but I can only imagine how difficult things must have been to live in the public eye for so long."

"The British press," Nia began. "They love you when you're new and fresh and obsequious. Then they try to destroy you if they feel you pissed them off. And I pissed them off and then they can be so cruel."

She caught his gaze and held it.

"Tom, a lot of what is out there is not really me," she said with such an intense earnestness that Tom felt sorry for what she must have been through.

"Nia. I don't doubt it. I know the press can be shits and the internet is full of mistruths and lies. Look, we're both in our forties and we both know that we had a variety of experiences, been round the block a bit, and that we've lived lives before this time now." He tried to smile reassuringly. "I would much rather hear about you, your past, your present, and your future, from you." He paused, "But, I did also watch some of your earlier work."

"Oh my God, you did?"

"I did. I think you're a brilliant actor."

Nia half smiled. "Thank you, but it's important to me that I want you to know that a lot of the stuff on the web, in the papers and magazines wasn't me. Wasn't all me. It isn't me. Quite a bit of the stuff that's been written about me isn't true exactly," she said.

"I don't doubt it."

"I don't want you to think you're with one of my characters or the girl in some long ago and faded gossip columns. But I do want you to know a little bit about me."

"I really do want to get to know you," he said. "I'd like to spend time with you."

"Okay, but hear me out," Nia smiled wistfully. "I'm sorry, but I do need to talk through some of this with you."

There had been moments in the past like this; new guy, romantic dinner, flush with wine and anticipation, when Nia realised that her date wanted to be with 'Our Nia' or the 'Welsh Spitfire' not the real Nia. She had been hurt too many times.

"Seriously, you don't have to do this," Tom said earnestly.

"But I want to."

She took another gulp of wine.

"I grew up hard. I left home when I was seventeen. I feel as if I've really been on my own ever since. My parents were too busy fighting each other to even notice I was gone. By my late teens I was working regularly and had some decent money, a car, my own flat. I thought myself worldly and wise," she smiled, really to herself. "All at a time when lots of people make poor decisions. And, boy, did I make a few bad decisions. I took some bad jobs and turned down good ones, dropped out of drama school, and there were some drugs, booze, and there were men of course. Quite a few men." She rolled her eyes and waited for him to respond. He didn't. "And, a lot of my bad decisions were played out in public."

She took another sip of her wine. "I learnt some tough lessons on being taken advantage of and of being lied to. My bloody dad asked for handouts after I made a film or two. This from a man who only paid attention to me when he wanted a new sparring partner after my Mam was too bruised, or when he wanted the money I earned, from a weekend job at the make-up counter in Boots. He even sold some family stories when the press was going through the 'Our Nia' phase. Which I hated, by the way."

He nodded and she captured his eyes.

"I'm sorry," he said knowing it wasn't enough.

"No one hurts you as much as family," she continued, eyes beginning to swim with tears. "Or those we love. Some people can be so callous and calculating and it took me a few heartbreaks and a couple of marriages, and a whole lot of hurt to realise that. You have to understand that the level of self-absorption in my profession is at a different level." She held a hand above her head. "Stratospheric levels. Or…" she moved her hand down, "Or, people play games to see what they can get out of other people. There is quite a bit of poison in this profession. It took me some growing to recognise all this shit and find a way to deal with it. So, you see, I have a hard time trusting anyone." She stared hard into Tom's eyes.

He was sitting back in his chair. He wasn't sure if she wanted him to respond or whether she was daring him to leave. He decided to just listen. He watched her eyes. She looked down and he noticed her face soften.

"I, after the second marriage, I didn't want to get hurt again. I kind of shut myself down. I think I may have become too cold, too, too less open to feeling. My bloody profession had left me emotionally stunted. I wanted armour that was impervious."

She took a big drink of her wine and refilled her glass. Tom noticed the tears welling in her eyes.

"I don't know why I'm telling you this," she half smiled and gave a slight shrug of her shoulders. "But I feel we have a connection."

Tom nodded his agreement.

"I want to let you know that I'm not easy to be with," Nia continued. "I'm bloody minded and difficult." Nia laughed. She sat back in her chair and smiled coyly. "Some first date eh?"

Tom felt a sense of panic, worried the next thing she would say would be that there was no room for him in her life.

Nia leaned forward, "But I'd like to take a chance. I'd like to get to know you," she paused, and reached across the table for his hand. "Now, you know everything about me," she lied, "But I don't know anything about you."

Tom's relief was manifest, he felt his face flush. He smiled shyly.

"Okay. I grew up in Manchester. Mum, Dad, elder sister. Close to my sister, Rachel, great taste in music. Went to school, then uni at Manchester, followed by the army. A bad but mercifully quick marriage, then semi-retirement on the canals. A dog name Jack. A little writing here and there. And, I'd like to get to know you, too."

"Nice try," she said with a laugh. "But, not good enough. I'm an actor, remember, you'll need to tell me something with a little drama. Like… tell me about the love of your life."

He sat back and stared at her. She grinned back at him. He told her of his love for the Periwinkle and for Jack. She laughed.

"Still not good enough," Nia said. "What about your ex-wife?"

"Ah, her," Tom said "I'm not sure, looking back, if what I felt for her was love, real love. I'm not sure I've ever really had a love of my life," Tom stated. He told Nia that his wife had been pretty and fun, that there was romance but he was sure that she hadn't really loved him. That she had been in love with a kind of ideal. That she had enjoyed the army life and that she didn't mind his absences when he was posted because she filled her time with civic activities which had included numerous affairs. In the end he hadn't any problems letting go. It now felt like a distant, embarrassing memory; he didn't tell her that there were other memories more real, more vivid, more hurtful.

"So," she said. "We've had three marriages between us, and they've all been rubbish." Nia drained the last of her wine. "Where do we go from here?" she asked and her eyes shone.

Tom thought for a moment.

"I like to think that our lives are now," he said. "And they're whatever we make them."

She tilted her head back and laughed a full-throated laugh.

"No," she said. "I actually meant, where do we," she made a gesture circling them both, "Go on from this restaurant." Their eyes locked.

Nia knew her eyes glistered with desire and she hoped he could translate.

"Is there a decent hotel nearby?" Tom asked quickly. He had decided that he would be a hostage to his past no longer.

"Yes," Nia said with a smile. "There's a rather smashing little boutique place just around the corner."

***

The hotel was off a quiet Georgian square. It was well-appointed and discreet. Tom checked them in, and Nia kept her head down and turned away from the small, CC camera above the reception desk. The concierge and the night porter exchanged knowing looks. Tom was given a room on the third floor and he and Nia held hands without speaking as they took the lift up. Tom opened the room's door with the key card and held the door open for Nia. She moved into the room but turned to Tom and kissed him. She shut her eyes, felt the warmth of his lips, responding, felt his lips part. Tom put his hand gently on Nia's lower back and pulled her even closer. He felt her tongue tease against his lips, touching his tongue and sending an electric sensation through his entire body.

Tom pushed the door shut with his foot and together they moved like tango dancers towards the bed. They both collapsed on the mattress still deep in the embrace of the kiss. They finally broke to throw off their heavy winter coats. She kissed him quickly and then got off the bed.

"Let me freshen up," she said. Nia swayed her hips provocatively as she went to the bathroom.

Tom took off his shoes, suit jacket, and tie. He turned a bedside light on and turned the bright, overhead light off. A police siren wailed somewhere in the middle distance

In the bathroom Nia stripped down to her underwear, a black matching bra and panties. Not lingerie but appropriate and sexy. She had showered at the theatre and had chosen her underwear with care, she had thought, just in case. She breathed into her hand, Thai food and wine. Not great, but not terrible. She washed hands and face and brushed her teeth with a finger. She ran her hands through her hair and noticed her cheeks were flushed pink with desire. She stepped back and quickly observed herself in the mirror. The Pilates and cardio-boxing were paying off. For a forty-four-year-old, not a bad bod she thought.

She turned out the light and opened the door. Only a bedside light was on. Tom lay on the bed in shirt and trousers. She tried to stand naturally but coquettishly leaning against the bathroom door frame. His eyes grew large as he watched her. She had an hourglass figure, he noticed, with full curves beneath matching, sexy underwear. He could tell that she had done some gym time. He slipped off the bed and quickly unbuttoned his shirt, the cuff got caught around his wrist, and he yanked it off sending the button flying, he then took off his trousers and socks. He stood there in his pants, erection obvious. He smiled embarrassingly. Nice body Nia thought; natural, nicely muscled, fit, decent chest hair, quirky tattoo on left shoulder. Quite nice really. Then she saw the scars, not so much scars but a wholesale mangling of his right leg. She moved towards him, she knelt unselfconsciously in front of his right leg and ran her fingers over the angry scars.

"Oh my God, Tom," she said. She looked up into his face.

He reached down and held her face and she stood up. Their eyes locked followed by their lips again. They fell onto the bed. Hands pulled, tugged, and unlatched underwear as they tumbled into each other. They made love with a joyous abandon.

After it was over, they lay side by side holding hands. Nia asked him about his leg wound. They moved together and both faced each other. He reached out to her face and gently moved a lock of hair from over her left eye.

"Helicopter crash," he told her. "Quite a bad one. Some time ago now. Looks worse than it is."

She sensed there was a lot more but now wasn't the time to ask. She reached down and ran her fingers over the raised welts and knotted skin from his knee to his thigh. She lingered over his upper thigh. Felt him harden again. She threw back the sheets, pushed him onto his back, and straddled him. He entered her and she gasped a little.

"Let me do the heavy lifting this time," she said.

Tom woke early. He watched her sleep. He knew that he had never felt anything like this before. He had almost only just met her. He already loved the tilt of her nose, the lift of her breasts as she breathed, the sleeping pout of her lips, her hair, her smell. Nia stirred and opened her eyes. She saw him and smiled. She felt a warm sensation in her core.

"Coffee?" he asked. She nodded. Tom got out of bed, slipped on his underwear, and moved to the room's Nespresso machine and turned it on. His back was to her.

Nia observed him as he ran the machine, "That's a really nice arse," she thought. The scars on the back of his right leg coiled around this thigh like a snake. They looked as if they still hurt. He passed the first cup of coffee to her and made a second. He moved the curtain aside slightly and was surprised to see that the grey old city was adorned by a fresh dusting of pure white snow. Beautiful, he thought. He turned to face the bed. He watched Nia, propped up on pillows sipping coffee.

"You look lovely," he said. He wanted to tell Nia that she looked better naked in reality than she did in a nude scene he had watched in one of her DVD's but then thought he might come across creepy. Nia put her coffee cup on the bedside table.

"Come back to bed," Nia said and patted the space next to her. So he did.

The bedroom was light when they again woke. Tom went to shower, and Nia joined him. They washed each other, now intimately familiar with each other's bodies. They dressed in last night's clothes and checked out. The morning was cold, but they decided to walk rather than taxi out for brunch although neither was hungry. They wanted to have as much time together as possible. They walked arm in arm, hip to hip. A few streets brought them to a little local shopping area where they found a Pret A Manger. Nia liked the fact that Tom asked her what she wanted. Too many people in her life had always expected her to pay. She would describe herself as a rather loud feminist, but she liked a man that treated her like a gentleman would.

They sat side by side. Nia pointed to a middle-aged

woman wearing a baggy sweatshirt that was emblazoned with the slogan 'Proud fur baby mum'.

"That must have been a difficult delivery," Nia whispered.

"Itchy," Tom added.

Nia laughed hard. When had a man, anyone, made her laugh as much as this guy? Never. She thought for a moment, "Where are you staying?"

"Umm," Tom stammered. "I don't know. I did bring a go bag but I left it in the Land Rover. I wasn't sure what would, what we, how the night would play out. I was thinking, if it didn't... then I, if not too tired, would head home or find a hotel if tired."

"And," Nia asked. "How did it turn out, would you say?"

"It was the most, bloody marvellous, night of my life."

Nia laughed and then realised he meant it and then she was aware that it was true for her too. Fuck, she thought, this is crazy. I'm in my forties but feel like a spotty teenager with a crush. But she knew that she had never actually crushed like this before. She buried that thought.

They took a couple of selfies together outside of the Pret as a light snow descended then took the Tube across the quiet city to pick up Tom's go bag. Bag secured; they took the Tube back across the city to Westminster. They emerged from the Tube station to the iconic view of Elizabeth Tower and Big Ben. Tom pointed out where he was once stationed outside of the Houses of Parliament in the weeks after 9/11. He could still recall the excitement and fear of being on London's streets with live ammunition in his rifle and his possessing of an innocence that was soon to be lost. They walked across Westminster Bridge and down to the London Eye, its usual queues absent. They almost had a gondola to themselves and they stood against the large curved plexiglass as Nia pointed out London's skyline. She leant into him and he felt her warmth. They then proceeded back over the bridge and up to Trafalgar Square hand in hand. The city was surprisingly empty on a chilly Sunday afternoon. Both were wondering what they were doing but both were enjoying it. They stopped in a pub off the square to warm up and have a drink.

"On my God," Nia whispered. "I can't believe I'm wearing the same clothes as last night."

"I've got a change of clothes in my bag, happy to share," Tom said.

Nia laughed but couldn't settle. She suggested Tom stay in the pub and she would find a shop to buy some fresh clothes. The speed of Nia's departure worried Tom, he wondered whether she'd return. He was suddenly very aware of his surroundings. He didn't really know what had happened, he'd had almost no time to process or reflect or plan. It had been a whirlwind of excitement and emotions. He checked his watch and wondering how long it would be before he would know whether she was returning, or not. The thought filled him with dread. He went up to the bar, chatted with the barman, a young Canadian. Tom liked Canadians, good soldiers. He had served with a tough bunch in Afghanistan. The bartender poured Tom a pint and a white wine for Nia. Tom returned to the table and had taken a gulp of his beer when Nia returned clutching a red and white striped thin plastic carrier bag.

Nia's shopping expedition had been quick. She had simply popped into one of the area's ubiquitous souvenir shops. She bought a T-shirt emblazoned with a red classic Mini with a union jack on its roof, white socks with Big Ben on them, a large sweatshirt bearing an Oxford University coat of arms, and a pair of novelty knickers, a thong with the slogan 'Welcome to England' written across the front. Classy, she thought, and grinned to herself, should really be 'Croeso I Gymru', Welcome to Wales.

Nia sat at the small pub table and sipped her wine. She was happy. She always liked feeling desired and enjoyed the confidence that had come with age and experience. Tom made her feel more than desired. He was a considerate lover. Gentle when he needed to be, firm and commanding when required.

"Okay," she told Tom. "A change of clothes," and held up the bag and then added as an afterthought, "and a toothbrush."

"Nice bag," Tom said. "Vuitton?"

Nia responded with her deep throaty laugh. They

drank simultaneously and then held each other's eyes.

"Hotel and then some dinner?" she asked but it wasn't really a question.

"Sounds like a fine plan," Tom agreed.

Tom hailed a cab and Nia suggested a small European chain hotel. Tom guessed that she wasn't comfortable enough to suggest her house and he was fine with that. He was simply enjoying being with her.

Tom checked in to the hotel as Nia waited in the small lobby, overly interested in a vending machine stocked with things tourists may need but had forgotten to pack. She tried to look natural while evading a possibility of being recognised. A small lift took them up to the second floor and a room that was about the size of a college dorm room.

"Whoops," Nia said as they opened the door and stepped into the tiny room.

"Hey, I'm used to this," Tom said. "I live on a narrowboat."

Nia collapsed on the bed and took off her coat and shoes. She rubbed her feet, sore from a long walk, in boots designed for show rather than walking. Tom made a move as if to massage her feet. Nia pulled her legs up.

"Oh no, I'm sure they're stinky," she said. "I think I'll have a long, hot shower, and change into my latest outfit."

She moved to the bathroom door and turned to Tom, "Coming?" she asked, and she bit her bottom lip ever so slightly. Tom smiled and joined her as requested.

After, they lay in bed. Nia rested her head on Tom's chest and absent-mindedly ran her fingers through his chest hair. She then ran her finger over the tattoo on his left shoulder. "Tell me about this?" she asked.

"Soldier thing," Tom answered rather curtly. Nia read the signal and didn't follow up, yet. There were parts of this Tom that were still closed off and that made him interesting but alarmed her a little. Tom wanted to lighten the mood.

"Getting hungry?" he asked.

"I could eat," Nia replied. "If I remember rightly, there's a good chippy not too far away." Tom nodded his approval.

"But, before we head out, I need another shower," Nia said with a smile and got out of bed.

Tom watched her as she moved to the bathroom, appreciating her nakedness. He found her confidence incredibly sexy. Tom dressed in his change of clothes from his go bag: Chelsea boots, jeans, shirt, and sweater.

Nia came from the bathroom looking fresh and radiant.

"Nice sweatshirt," Tom said. "Had you down as a Cambridge girl."

Nia laughed.

"University of hard knocks me," she said.

Tom usually hated such expressions but guessed that in Nia's situation it was partly true.

***

The early evening was Dickensian dark as they walked through a park square and through a few half-heartedly lit side streets to the fish and chip shop. Nia had remembered to point out a couple of interesting blue plaques along the way. The fish bar was small, about the size of a terraced house's front room. It had two tiny bar tables each with two chairs hard against the glass front. Tom and Nia both ordered fish suppers from the Greek Cypriot owner who also owned an amazing moustache. They asked for cans of Diet Coke and sat at one of the tables. The window was greasy to the touch.

"Feels like a teenager's date," Tom said. "Most of mine were disastrous."

"Oh, I can't believe that, Tom. Smart, funny, and dashingly handsome."

He blushed.

Nia smiled reassuringly.

"I thought soldiers were all gruff and tough. You're an odd one Major Price."

"Ah," Tom said. "I'm not Major Price any more, you see. Just plain old Tom Price. Much less gruff and shouty." He changed the subject quickly, "What about your teenage dates?"

"Um," Nia said and looked through the window at their distorted reflections on the greasy film there. "Quite a few. Bad boys mostly. Guys with motorbikes, leather jackets, tattoos before they were cool, dead end jobs. Lads with no ambition only caring about beer, sex and rugby."

"Skilful though, all three at the same time."

"Especially in the back of a Ford Sierra," Nia laughed.

Their food was ready.

"On my God," Tom exclaimed after his first fork full. "This is incredible. How can anyone make fish and chips this good?"

"It's all in the moustache," Nia whispered.

***

They stopped off in a small pub on their way back to the hotel. It had an authentic bar, little changed from Victorian times. Lots of polished wood and brass and a small fireplace. It also had a lounge bar little changed from the mid-1990s, replete with a tiny karaoke stage with its own sound system. There were three other couples in the lounge, all in their fifties and sixties. A grumpy bar tender turned the system on and retreated behind the bar. Nia and Tom stepped back into the Victorian bar where they ordered pints of cider.

Karaoke music played from the lounge. One of the patrons began singing 'How Deep is your Love' in the style of the Bee Gees.

"Bloody Hell," Nia exclaimed. "He's good. C'mon, this may be fun."

They grabbed their drinks and went into the lounge

and sat at a table with one of the couples who introduced themselves as Glyn and Jayne. Jayne spelled out her name emphasising the "Y". Jayne stared at Nia. Conversation between the four couples was surprisingly easy especially after songs were shared, rounds were bought and drunk. Nia watched Tom chatting with one of the men, a former old soldier, and she overheard some shared conversation about the army. She witnessed their immediate connection, their shared experience. There was so much to this kind, sweet man that she had yet to discover. Then she realised that she also shared an immediate connection to Tom, but she was troubled, was this just a mad, fun weekend type of fling or would she invest the time to push the connection deeper? She wasn't sure.

Each patron in the small lounge bar took turns on the stage. A few more joined them from the bar. They ran through the classic American song book, then Beatles, Motown, and seventies pop. Nia sang 'Don't Cry for Me Argentina' and the entire place went quiet in awe. She was an actor, she was Welsh, of course she could sing. Nia forced Tom onto the pub's small karaoke stage where he surprised her, and the other patrons, with a decent voice and an ability to entertain as he worked his way through a Smiths classic. Remember, he told her, that he had found many ways to engage with the soldiers under his command. He should have been an actor, she joked.

Jayne, who had earlier recognised Nia, turned to

her,

"You got a nice one there Nia. Kind eyes," she whispered. "Never thought your man, oh what's his name the big actor, good-looking bloke. Never thought he had kind eyes."

***

Nia stared into Tom's eyes as they lay on the small and hard hotel bed. Yup, she thought, kind eyes but still with a hint of sadness there. They both closed their eyes as they kissed deeply. They kissed until their collective desire demanded more. Nia removed Tom's sweater and shirt and then she pulled off her sweatshirt. Tom realised that she wasn't wearing a bra. Her hard nipples were obvious through her T-shirt of the Mini with the union jack. She knelt on the bed and unzipped his jeans and felt him harden in her hand. She pulled off his jeans and pants. She intimately massaged him for a moment and then stood on the bed and, wobbling a little, pulled off her own jeans.

Tom looked up from his prone position and laughed when he saw her thong. She twirled around as if on the catwalk. Tom leant up and grabbed one of the thong's thin straps with his teeth. Nia put her hands through his hair as he lowered her thong using only his teeth. She wobbled and collapsed on top of him laughing.

Chapter Seven
London, Next Day

Nia woke with no idea of the time. She had been driven from sleep by a crushing anxiety. She felt as if she had woken from a nightmare, struggling to catch her breath. As her eyes became accustomed to the dark, she looked over to Tom and watched him sleeping beside her. She had fallen deeply and quickly for him. Perhaps too quickly she thought. He was too nice for her, perhaps too needy, too… her thoughts continued as she began to self-sabotage. She was trying to rationalize; she didn't have time for a relationship, for any emotional attachment that persisted for more than a few sweaty nights of lust and desire. Everything she loved at some time; family, Goldenboy, the baby, she had lost. She didn't do meaningful connection. Any more.

The morning broke as grey as Nia's mood. They checked out and found a diner for breakfast. They talked over a couple of cups of coffee. Tom didn't want their time together to end but couldn't ignore Nia's distraction. She was a little more formal, cooling, perhaps, he thought, it was because they had to part. Nia walked Tom to the nearest Tube station when it was time for him to leave. Their conversation began to feel forced and Tom noticed that Nia walked with her head down as if concentrating only on her feet.

"I would like to see you again," Tom said trying to avoid sounding needy but knowing that he probably did.

Nia wanted to say, "Yes", but she held back and, instead, kissed Tom gently on the lips.

Tom responded to the kiss but was troubled by Nia's deflection. Conversation began to whittle away. Tom was already feeling the ache of leaving Nia. Nia was trying to swallow the anxiety that was bubbling in her gut. She used her Oyster card to accompany Tom down onto the platform.

Tom tried again, "I could travel down next Friday if you're free?"

Nia panicked.

"I've got a busy week," she said automatically. "There's the audio book to finish, I'm preparing for an audition, and then there's a location shoot I need to prepare for."

"Okay, when would you be free?"

"I'm not sure when I'll be free again," Nia replied somewhat disingenuously. "So, let's play it cool, for a week or two yeah?"

Tom nodded but felt the ground beneath his feet fall away.

"I'm not sure what cool means, Nia," he said genuinely surprised.

Nia felt like she'd throw up.

The Tube train pulled in. She kissed him gently on the lips.

"Please, just go Tom," she said "I'll text you later."

He boarded the train and turned to face her as the carriage's doors closed with their pneumatic hiss. Tom thought she looked lonely yet lovely as she slipped away and out of his vision. Nia stayed on the platform as the train disappeared into the dark tunnel of the underground. She sighed, shook her head slightly, turned and headed for home. She felt an icy wave of nausea grip her.

As Nia passed a crowd on the platform, someone shouted, "Oi Nia, give us a kiss then darlin'."

Nia put her collar up, her head down, and walked away.

***

Shrewsbury, Later the Same Day

Tired from the weekend, the drive from London, and the emotional bombshell on the Tube's platform, Tom sat silently, lost, at his sister's kitchen table, mug of tea in hand. He was despondent, troubled by the change in Nia. He had tried to think of what went wrong, and when. He knew he was romantically clumsy, out of practice. He hadn't had a proper relationship for years. Rachel had orchestrated a few dates after he had come out of the army, none were successful. There had been a few relationships since then, but most ran their course after a few days and few nights. None had any of the connection that he had experienced with Nia. He was at a loss.

Rachel's husband, Owain, came in from the evening milking and joined him at the large, well-worn oak table.

"Thanks for looking after Jack," Tom said.

"No problem, she's a good dog. I like having her around. She's a good ratter."

Tom looked down at Jack circled up in front of the Aga. This sweet, friendly, dog was still hard-wired to be a hunter-killer.

Rachel brought a fresh pot of tea for the table and joined the men.

"So, how was the trip?"

"It was good," Tom said trying to hide his hurt.

Tom looked down at his tea. It had been good, so what happened?

Rachel misread Tom's reticence.

"Oh my God," Rachel said. "You shagged her, didn't you? You shagged Nia Williams."

Tom blushed.

Later, Rachel drove Tom and Jack back to the boat. She felt Tom's melancholy.

"I don't know what happened," Tom told her. "It had been brilliant and then it just changed, she just changed."

"Oh Tom," Rachel said with genuine sympathy. "I'm so sorry."

Rachel wanted Tom to open up and to embrace life again. She'd seen glimpses of the old Tom since he had returned from Canada and knew it was because of Nia, but why did it have to be her, she thought, why couldn't it have been someone ordinary woman he met in a canal-side pub?

***

London, Same Day

Later that evening Nia curled up in her favourite chair, warmed by the study's Adam fireplace and her cup of cocoa. She was reading a script. Her potential role was of a 1960s' hospital matron hiding her homosexuality as other nurses and young doctors discovered the freedom the sexual revolution brought for straight people. It was a good, supporting role, but the matron was another dowdy, repressed middle-aged woman and Nia was thinking she was getting typecast. She was distracted and couldn't concentrate. She put the script down. She thought of Tom. Tom who did not think her dowdy. Tom who had taken her breath away. Why did she feel it so necessary to send him away and to do it so cruelly?

Nia knew she had so carefully crafted a life where she was insulated, protected, and safe. She had accepted that the price to pay to avoid the emotional pain that had once ripped at her insides was to avoid the connection, the attachment to anyone who could hurt her. It also meant that she denied herself opportunities for deep emotional relationships. It was a simple, bitter calculus. And, there was that dark voice in her head, that sometimes sounded like her father, telling her, punishing her, that she didn't deserve happiness. She liked Tom, felt that there was something, something special, but she wasn't ready for the investment that could result in any more heartache. They had a fun, evanescent weekend but best for Tom if he wasn't pulled any deeper into her world. Best for her, she thought.

Nia tossed and turned throughout the night in her cold house. At four a.m. she decided that she'd text Tom and let him know that she wasn't ready for a relationship. She worked on the scene in her mind and played it out like the good actor she was. She'd simply tell Tom that she wasn't too serious about relationships, that her career was her major motivation, and she had a lot of work coming up. Too busy for a romance. She hated it; it was all true but it was also a lie. She typed the scene into the text box but didn't send it. Something stilled her finger as it hovered over the send key.

***

November 28th

Nia went through her day with the text still loaded on her phone. She ran on a treadmill at her gym until her lungs ached. She cardio-kickboxed until she almost vomited. She leaned into the gym shower's hot stream of water until another patron asked if she was okay. Nia had had lots of affairs so why, she wondered, was this one so different? She knew the answer, and it scared her. She changed at the gym; Dr Martens, yellow leggings, heavy blue dress, black bomber jacket, scarf, hat and gloves. She even applied some subtle make-up. She went to meet Jane for coffee and sympathy.

The bohemian cafe was all but empty when Jane breezed in, late as usual. Nia was sitting with a coffee that had already grown cold. Jane looked her perfectly coiffured self. Her glasses were orange to match the orange and blue silk scarf that brought a flash of colour to her understated grey wool suit. Jane sat down, and Nia looked up from stirring her coffee. Jane could tell something was wrong.

"I think I need some time away," Nia began.

Jane peered over the rim of her glasses, "Aw fuck, Nia dear, you just returned from Canada. What on earth is wrong?"

Nia just simply told her that she had broken up with a new guy, Tom. It was news to Jane that Nia considered anyone a 'new guy', but she wondered about Nia's earlier interest in some background information on Tom Price.

"The soldier?" Jane asked.

Nia nodded.

"When and where did you meet him?" Jane continued.

"On the flight from Canada and he's no longer a soldier," Nia answered. "He's a great guy, sweet, generous, funny."

"English lad?"

Nia nodded.

"And good looking?" Jane asked.

"Yes, ruggedly handsome."

"English guy diffident?"

Nia didn't grasp the question, "What?"

"You know, cool — but not trendy cool," Jane extrapolated. "Like E.M. Forster said, it's not that Englishmen can't feel, it's just that they are afraid to. They think it's bad form, or something."

"No, not Tom. He was so authentic, full of feelings. In fact, he made me feel…" Nia stopped and looked down. Jane noticed Nia's eyes welling. "He made me feel."

"Nia, darling," Jane sighed knowingly. "It's you who is frightened of feelings. I have known you for twenty years. You do this all the time, you meet a chap, shag them, and before you know it, you shut yourself away or you walk out. I know it's your self-defence mechanism, so why is it different this time?"

"I don't know," Nia attempted to fool herself, gave up, looked directly at Jane and said:

"He was so different. He made it different this time. He made me laugh and he brought me…" Nia's voice broke, "joy."

Jane was stunned.

"Fuck Nia, seriously? You haven't felt like this since…"

"I know and it scared me. I just don't know what to

do. I can never trust these guys so… so all I could think about was running away."

Jane who usually eschewed physical contact reached across the table and held Nia's hand.

"If you want some advice from an old broad," Jane said, and Nia nodded looking down into her coffee. "As much as you want to, as much as anyone wants to, we can't control the future. You're the toughest woman I know but you're a coward, Nia. You don't need to shut yourself down or lock yourself away. You deserve some… what did you call it, joy. Have you broken it beyond all recognition?"

Nia looked up through her fringe, "I don't think so."

"Then, kiddo, I'd suggest you go get him back," Jane stated. "Maybe you should give him a chance to earn your trust."

Nia said nothing.

"Now," Jane continued. "What did you think about our lesbian matron?"

***

Nia walked aimlessly back from the cafe. The afternoon chill bit at her cheeks and she wound her scarf to just below her eyes, pulled down her hat, and thrust her hands deep into her coat's pockets. She shivered still. She popped into a bookstore to get warm. Nia liked books, really liked them and often joked that she liked them more than people. She began browsing shelves; starting on the new releases, autobiographies and biographies, checking to see if they were about anyone she knew. Then she moved on to history shelves then through to the travel shelves. She ran her fingers across the spines of books along the length of a shelf, and then stopped. She pulled the book her fingers hovered over off the shelf, *A Weekender Guide to the Canals of North Wales*, it sounded like the guides Tom mentioned he wrote but the author's name was different. She flipped the book over to find a picture of the author; it was Tom. Why was he writing under an assumed name? Military thing she thought. There he was, rugged, hand on tiller at the stern of a narrowboat, slightly embarrassed smile, Jack Russell at his feet. Okay, she told herself, I really do like this guy. It's time for me to take a chance.

Outside, a light snow blew around through the soupy dark evening. Nia sat in her favourite comfy chair with her knees up underneath her. The fire warmed the room but still she nestled under a hip blanket. Billie Holiday played on her stereo. Nia placed her cup of tea on a side table she'd once picked up in Petticoat Lane. She had earlier arranged a number of canal guidebooks on the beloved table's worn surface. She had been surprised at the amount and variety of canal guides. Who knew there could be so many, she wondered? She took a sip of her tea and watched the snow gently falling outside, lovely she thought, and hoped, there would be enough accumulation to build a snowman, or a snowwoman. She wondered how cold a canal boat would be in this weather. She thought about Tom on his boat. Nia picked up the first thin brightly coloured book.

Nia enjoyed books, and she read voraciously and well. She read Tom's book greedily. She enjoyed his eye for detail and his prose. She was aware that he wrote easily with the same sense of self-deprecating humour he displayed in person. An anecdote about a pompous boat owner made her laugh out loud. She liked the way he wrote. Nia ran her finger over Tom's picture. She held the book and smiled. I just spent an incredible weekend with this guy, she thought. Incredible enough for him to be her lover? That didn't feel right, my fella, she determined sounded better. She smiled, but her smile faded quickly as she wondered whether Tom would be receptive. She hoped he would be. Nia pulled out her phone. She had deleted her earlier composition and although confident that her bridge to Tom could be repaired, she was, nevertheless, a little nervous as she simply typed. "I'm so sorry. Had a wobble. I really do want to see you again... I'd love to see you again. Friday? I'll explain. Please write to me." She read her text and added an 'X before she hit send.

***

Llangollen Canal and London

Tom's phone chimed with a text alert. 'Nia' the phone read. An icy sensation gripped at his stomach. His desire

109

for her had only been heightened by the sense of her sudden unattainability. He held the phone for a moment knowing that this was one of those moments, a crossroads in life, that could spell happiness or sadness. Tom opened the text, read her words, read them again and smiled to himself as all concern melted away. He was thrilled that she had signed off with an 'X'.

***

On the canal the snow turned to rain and the temperature climbed. The rain and miserable weather limited Tom's boating, keeping him in the marina. Tom went through his daily routines with Jack and the Periwinkle with a new lightness after receiving Nia's text. He caught up with some of his writing but found himself frequently distracted with thoughts of Nia and memories of their two nights together. He found himself smiling as thoughts of her entered his mind unbidden. He now knew she was mercurial and unpredictable. She was a risk he was willing to take. He rationed his Nia DVDs and it became part of a new nightly routine. Dinner done, cabin warm, Tom would settle in with Jack nestled next to him to watch a TV series, special, or an episode where Nia made an appearance. He looked at his phone, often, to see the picture he took of Nia in the snow outside the Pret. He uncharacteristically checked his phone frequently for any texts and the ping of his phone alerting him to an incoming text made his heart race.

In London, Nia went through her week on autopilot. Her work on the audiobook, a rather stilted historical fantasy about the Romans in Wales, was good. Nia was always professional and quite liked audiobook work. She worked hard prepping her reading, she read through the book multiple times, she developed the accents for the different characters, made sure she pronounced town names correctly, but it was a tiring experience. The narrating itself was exhausting. She would leave the studio with a sore throat, and sore back, and tired of the sound of her own voice. However, she didn't share some of her fellow narrators' complaints that it was a lonely business; just you and a mike and an engineer, Nia actually liked the solitude of the studio. After one long session, she went straight from the studio to meet up with her one close, small circle of friends for drinks. They asked her about the location shoot and how she looked different somehow. They asked her had she lost weight, changed her hair, using a different foundation? When someone joked it must be a new guy, they all laughed. Nia smiled but kept quiet.

Tom followed up on Nia's request for him to write to her. He wrote naturalistically about a day on the canal with Jack. His words painted pictures of the countryside and the flora and fauna that passed by the journeying narrowboat. How the sun looked through morning fog. How a full moon looked from the Periwinkle's bow moored on a woody cut, quiet and alone. And then he subtly switched to his recent memories of London and Nia. He had counted the miles that separated them and the hours that stretched before them until they would see each other again.

Nia waited until she was comfortably on her favourite chair before she opened Tom's email letter to read it. She was moved by it. It made her want to spend some time with him and his dog on the Periwinkle. She smiled with the knowledge that he felt as she did. After reading and re-reading the email, Nia couldn't wait until Friday to see Tom, she Face-Timed him. She was pleased when Tom took her call.

"Tom," she began, her eyes down. "I just want to tell you I'm so, so sorry for how I was on Sunday morning. All of a sudden," Nia looked directly into her laptop's camera. "I felt that we had... had suddenly become serious and, to be honest, I was not ready for it. As you know, I'm not good with relationships. I'm sorry for what I said and for what I didn't say."

Tom was so relieved and smiled broadly. "That's okay. We can take it slowly if you'd like." But he really didn't mean it.

"I really like you, Tom, but let's take it how it is. Whatever happens, yeah?" Nia said.

"Okay, whatever happens," Tom agreed. "But what were you sorry for... not saying?"

Nia was quiet for a moment although she continued to stare through the screen into Tom's face.

"That, that I really like you Tom," she said. "But,

Tom, you must promise never, ever to lie to me."

"Absolutely," Tom said quickly. "No lies ever."

Nia smiled, "I would really like to see you again. Can you pop into London on Friday?" she asked.

Tom said he could, and Nia said she'd make some arrangements. Both Nia and Tom felt liberated and happy, and the conversation moved to their respective days, the weather, the news, and, surprisingly, football teams. She recommended some of her work to watch, but only when he asked. They talked of books and music. Through all the disparate subjects they touched on they were really discussing the connection that they had made. It took them ten minutes after saying goodbye to finally end the call.

Chapter Eight
Washington DC, December 1st

The road that snaked up the low hills on the outskirts of the smart Washington DC suburb felt like a country lane. It was a dark night and the road's verges were heavily wooded; although, here and there, DC's lights could be glimpsed twinkling through the trees. Konstantin Vukovic always enjoyed this stretch of his commute. It always reminded him of childhood and family holidays on the Crimean coast. It was only nostalgia; a longing for his Russian homeland had long since ceased. Not that he didn't love Russia, he did, a point he had always made clear to his CIA handlers. His love for Mother Russia was the very reason why the former GRU major had offered his services to the Americans. He despised Putin. The American money, the fancy house and car, the interesting job, and the new identity were simply fringe benefits. The CIA had been good to him and, after he had finally defected, they had secured a role for him as a Russia analyst for the NSA. Vukovic found the work satisfying. He enjoyed the job and, as usual, had worked late and was commuting home in the dark.

He hadn't seen the police car behind him until its flashing red and blue lights brightly appearing in his rear-view mirror startled him. He looked down at his speedometer, thirty-five miles per hour in a thirty zone. "*Blyad*," he thought in his native Russian, "fuck," and slowed down immediately and pulled onto the road's grassy verge. He reached into his jacket pocket for his NSA ID and hoped his tale of working late for national security would inspire enough empathy for the cop to dismiss him with a warning but no ticket.

He watched the police officer get out of the police cruiser. The cop was so small she had to be a woman, he thought, and a petite one at that. He dropped his car's window as she approached and watched her in his wing mirror. She's confident, Vukovic thought. The cop leant against the driver-side door and lowered her head to look at Vukovic through the open window. Pretty too, thought Vukovic, as the cop held him in her gaze. He noticed wisps of red hair that hadn't been fully tucked away under her hat. The cop smiled and the Russian saw her small, straight, white teeth before he saw the suppressed pistol pointing through the open window. The assassin shot Vukovic in the chest. The impact forced him back and to his right. He hung in his seat belt, moaning, with his chin on his chest. The assassin placed the end of the suppressor close to his left temple and shot him in the head. She knew from the blood and viscera that splattered over the passenger seat and window that Vukovic was dead.

The assassin calmly opened the driver's side door and raised the window. She placed the gun in Vukovic's hand with his finger on the trigger, pointed the gun through the open driver's door and pushed Vukovic's trigger finger so the gun discharged for a third time. Vukovic's hand would now be covered in gunshot residue and his finger prints would be clearly on the pistol's grip and trigger. She knew any decent forensics team would determine the death wasn't suicide, but it would create further confusion and possibly stall the investigation.

The assassin returned to the police cruiser and drove into the city. She parked the car on a dark street away from any traffic or CCTV cameras. She turned her police jacket inside out, so it became a red bomber jacket. She placed the police utility belt and hat in a garbage bag and exited the car and walked a couple of blocks. The assassin dumped the garbage bags in the grease bin outside of a fast-food shop and took off her latex gloves. Inside the store she ordered a Coke and fries and then signalled for a prearranged Uber. The Uber's driver was an unsmiling Russian. An émigré coerced from time to time to assist the SVR when they required additional support around the metro DC area.

The assassin entered the car and the driver nodded to a backpack and small spinner bag placed on the car's rear seats. The assassin opened the bag and took out a blouse and jacket and changed clothes. From a toilet bag she took out a hand mirror and bright red lipstick. The driver would later burn the assassin's gloves, police shirt, and jacket.

The Uber patron who got out at Dulles airport wearing black combat-like jeans, white shirt, blue college sweatshirt and a thin, black North Face quilted jacket looked nothing like a DC police officer. She shouldered the rugged looking traveller's backpack, put on a broad peaked baseball cap, wore large, tinted glasses, and tucked her hair up under the cap. If a passer-by were to notice anything about her it would be only, perhaps, the fiery red lipstick she wore. She approached the Delta check-in desk, showed the gate agent her Irish passport and collected her ticket in plenty of time for the eight forty-five p.m. flight to Dublin.

After going through security, she retrieved a pay-as-you-go phone from the backpack and texted Kamenev that the job was completed successfully. Kamenev replied, offered his congratulations on the successful conclusion of her business meeting and noted that he would be in contact about a business meeting in London. In a stall in an airport toilet, the assassin snapped the phone and, after, she distributed the broken bits across several of the airport's rubbish bins. She kept her head down whenever she was aware of a camera or even the possibility of one.

***

London, Russian Embassy, Two p.m.

In his office, Kamenev finished the encrypted message updating Moscow Centre on the progress of the DC mission. He was pleased with the outcome and continued to be impressed with the competency of his team, especially the little Irish assassin. He thrilled with the knowledge that Moscow's reach had penetrated deep into the heart of the enemy. He hated traitors and was pleased to play a part in hunting them down and bringing them the justice they deserved. Of course, he understood that it was an FBI traitor who had sold information to the SVR that resulted in the identification and tracking of Vukovic. An American traitor was useful, but a traitor, nevertheless. Kamenev secretly hoped that when the FBI traitor's utility was done, that they would receive whatever justice the Americans could mete out. In his book, traitors working out of a sense of shared ideology were one thing, those turn-coats who operated for money were the lowest of the low, but he was happy there were such people.

Kamenev's tummy rumbled. He looked up at his office clock, time for a late lunch. He grabbed his coat and headed out. He had grown fond of a little local pub's lunch of beef and ale pie. He walked with a lighter step; a pub lunch, a nice pint, and the death of a traitor, it was a good day.

Chapter Nine
London, December 2nd, Six p.m.

Nia had booked a hotel room. She wasn't quite ready to bring Tom into her home just yet, but she was close. She packed an overnight bag with care. She had planned an entertaining weekend. Tom drove in, parked, and caught a Tube train at the, now familiar, Watford Junction. He liked the first part of the train journey, above ground, watching London go about its life and business from the comfort of the train seat before the life of the city was replaced by the blackened Victorian brick of the Tube. Tom changed to the Central Line at Harrow and Wealdstone listening to his music for a further forty minutes before the train pulled into Convent Garden and his date with Nia.

Nia had asked Tom to meet her in the Duke of Wellington pub just east of the old market. He was early but she had been even earlier. Tom could see her waiting in the pub through its broad, street facing windows. He stopped on the street and watched her for a moment. He was so relieved. He knew that he had never felt the depth of emotion that he now held for Nia. He was anxious to see her again, to hear her voice, to make her laugh, to touch her body. He watched her a little longer as she sipped a red wine, she was self-possessed and self-contained exuding a confidence, some would say diffidence, that he suspected was a self-defence mechanism.

Tom entered the pub and saw Nia to his left sitting on a high stool, her winter coat on another stool, reserving it for him. She stood up when he came into the pub. She was elegant in grey suede boots, jeans, a lavender shirt, and blue cardigan. They embraced and Nia pulled Tom to her and held him closer and tighter. Tom touched her cheek and they kissed.

"Hi," he said.

"Hello, Mr Price," Nia said formally with a giggle and held out her hand. He took it and shook it politely. They both laughed.

Tom took off his Barbour and scarf. He was already warm. Nia noticed his small rucksack.

"Packing light," she laughed.

"Always," he responded.

They talked like old friends and any nervousness on reconnecting quickly dissipated. He bought her another wine and a Peroni for himself. They held hands and Nia leant over, wobbling on her the high stool and Tom kissed her. They got lost in each other. After another round of drinks, the pub filled with a happy and obstreperous Friday night crowd. Nia only had eyes for Tom as the little dramas of life played on around them. It grew too loud to have a comfortable conversation and Nia nodded towards the door and Tom signalled agreement; it was time to go.

Nia took him to a small subterranean club for tango dancing. She was good, of course, she had learned to dance for a few of her roles. Yoga and Pilates kept her limber and she moved fluidly. He was rubbish but enjoyed the feel her body so tight against his that he could feel the muscles of her thigh press against his as their sweat co-mingled. They moved across the dance floor together, alone among the crowd. After their dancing was over Nia took him through the city to a quiet wine bar where Tom, feeling peckish, ordered a meat and cheese plate for two that turned out to be the most expensive he'd ever encountered. Together they ate and glowed with wine and new romance.

They taxied back to the hotel, happy and tipsy. In their room, Tom unpacked his rucksack while Nia drew a bath. She invited him into the large marble bathroom. There, she had lit some candles, the bath bubbled appealingly with the aroma of lavender essential oils, while a bottle of champagne chilled next to two flutes. She stepped towards Tom and pulled up his cotton sweater. She unbuttoned his chinos and pulled them down to his ankles. Tom started to speak but Nia simply hushed him. He stepped out of his trousers. Nia stepped back and unbuttoned her shirt and let it fall behind her. She rolled her jeans down and off her legs. She wore plain white panties with lace edging and matching bra. Tom removed the rest of his clothes and held her in his arms. He unlatched her bra and gently removed it. Her nipples had budded with desire. She sat on the side of the bath and Tom pulled her panties down, delighting in the arch she made with her body so he could ease them down over her bottom. He kissed her knees and then slowly made his way up higher to the inside of her legs. She parted her legs as he reached the top of her thighs. He kissed her there and she moaned with delight. Nia reached down and stroked his hair as he continued to intimately kiss and stroke her sex. After she climaxed, they made love on towels laid out on the marble tiles. Then they lay together in the bath drinking champagne. Nia's back was to Tom's chest while he ran a hand through her thick hair, although neither said anything they were lost in similar thoughts.

The next day was a cold crisp winter day suffused with the kind of light photographers made their careers on. London, being a great walking city, Tom and Nia walked countless streets, saw countless monuments, old and new. Nia enjoyed seeing the city, her city, through Tom's tourist eyes. They made crude jokes about some of the ancients on the walls of the National Portrait Gallery. Nia pointed out a few portraits of people she knew or had worked with. Tom explained some archaic military rules the soldiers outside Horse Guards were required to follow. On that day, London was a city for lovers.

Nia had arranged for them to attend a play at the Wanamaker Playhouse. The playhouse was adjacent to the Globe Theatre, the large, instantly recognisable, facsimile of Shakespearian theatre which had closed for the winter. The Wanamaker was a smaller indoor theatre but still resembled its Elizabethan forebear. Tom dressed in smart blue cords and the same country check sports jacket he wore when he first met Nia. Nia watched him as he knotted a green knit tie over a plain white cotton shirt. What a good-looking fella, she thought, but so unlike so many of her actor friends he's never really embraced it. She dressed in a heavy green serge dress that accentuated the warm red highlights in her hair. It was low cut and fitted snugly around her breasts and hips. It was a style she liked.

The play was enjoyable, striking an intimate and romantic tone as the two main characters, storm separated lovers, were finally reunited through scenes that required the whole theatre to be lit by candlelight alone. Nia and Tom stayed, postproduction, to have a drink with the actors, most of whom were acquaintances of Nia. Someone shouted "Nia" with an accompanying camera flash. Nia had smiled, but Tom, standing a little back, as he always did, with sightlines to entrances and exits and on the crowd before him, noticed that her smile wasn't genuine. When Nia genuinely smiled her eyes sparkled, fine lines crinkled out from the side of her eyes, and her lips parted over her top teeth. Nia made her way through the crowd that had begun to circle the leading actress. Nia noticed Tom holding himself apart and joined him.

"Come and meet the play's lead," Nia said. "An old colleague."

Nia's old colleague was instantly recognisable, an actress in her ascendency. She was loud, funny, and rude.

"Well," the actress began as Nia approached. "We are honoured to be joined by the enigmatic Nia Williams."

The crowd cheered with sincerity.

Nia looked surprised and pleased. The actress held out her two arms and pulled Nia towards her.

"It is unusual to see you out and about Nia."

"I had heard that you were brilliant in the play and wanted to see it and you for myself," Nia responded generously.

The actress nodded an appreciation towards Nia and noticed that Nia and Tom were clearly an item. "And, who is this gorgeous man with you this evening, Ms Williams?"

Nia introduced Tom and he noticed the quizzical glance that passed between the two women.

"Nice to meet you, Tom," the actress said. "You're not an actor so what is it that you do for a living?"

"Oh, I write a bit," said Tom.

"Oh fuck," the actor laughed. "You'll need to get a real job if you are going to be with our Nia."

The crowd laughed and Tom looked towards Nia and she smiled back at him and raised an eyebrow.

"What do you write?" the actress continued with genuine interest.

"Oh, travelogues," Tom said. He was about to add

the word 'canals' but the actress interrupted:

"Oh, anywhere sexy and exotic?"

"Yes," Tom said quickly. "Wales."

The actress laughed a thin, high but genuine guffaw while looking first at Nia and back to Tom. The actress held Tom in her gaze for a moment, winked, then she returned to holding court.

Nia grabbed Tom's hand and sighed with a sense of relief. She moved through the crowd introducing Tom to some of the coterie of actors and acquaintances. Many were friendly but Tom noticed a collective look of surprise they almost all shared. He asked Nia about it. She thought for a moment and was struck by her own realisation,

"I don't usually do this, attend these public things any more. And, when I do, it's usually alone," she told Tom. She was bemused. She hadn't introduced a boyfriend since the early days of Goldenboy. Boyfriend? Was Tom her boyfriend. And, why wasn't there a better term for boyfriend for people in their forties?

She wondered whether she had introduced Tom to acquaintances to make him feel more comfortable and confident after her Tube station wobble or to signify the depth of the relationship to herself. Maybe a bit of both, she thought. They moved to the bar area as the event began to wind down. Nia looked at Tom and grasped his hand.

"Wanna get out of here?" she asked.

"Only if you do," Tom replied gallantly.

***

Outside the theatre the winter night was still and chilly. Once again, the normally thriving metropolis felt empty. North across the Thames, St Paul's Cathedral was lit up so dramatically that it appeared almost supernatural. They were drawn to it and walked across the Millennium footbridge and up to the Cathedral almost in unspeaking awe. They stood in front of Wren's masterpiece holding hands before turning for the Tube station. They took an almost empty Tube train back close to the hotel. It was a short walk from the station to the hotel. Nia pulled on Tom's arm as he opened the hotel's entrance door. She asked him whether he would like to come home with her rather than stay at the hotel. He knew that this was an important symbolic step for Nia, so he said that he'd love to see her home.

The hotel's concierge ordered a taxi. He had become more helpful when Nia agreed to still pay for the night's reservation. Nia and Tom entered the broad cabin of the classic black cab and Nia gave the driver her home address. Tom carried his rucksack and Nia's large overnight bag.

Nia lived in a town house off one of London's innumerable Georgian squares. It was a solidly established area not fashionable enough, yet, for sports stars and oligarchs. Nevertheless, as they stepped out of the taxi in front of the imposing three story façade Tom suddenly realised that Nia wasn't short of cash. This wasn't the home of a struggling actor. Nia opened her front door and Tom dropped the bags off in the entrance vestibule. Nia pointed down the corridor, noting lounge and dining room to the right, small toilet, then kitchen and breakfast nook towards the back. She took Tom up to the second floor with its guest bedroom, where Tom was momentarily crestfallen thinking that it was for him, and then a study which he noted held a beautiful fireplace, an Adam he wondered, and lots of books, then another bathroom. Then up narrow stairs again, third floor with its spacious bathroom, master bedroom, and an office-cum-guest bedroom. Nia turned on bedside lights and sat on her bed.

"Lovely," Tom said.

"Thanks, I've put a lot of time and effort into it."

"I meant you," he said.

Nia laughed and lay back on the bed and Tom moved across the room and kissed her.

Tom unbuttoned Nia's dress, pulling it gently off her body. He undressed her slowly, teasing her with kisses. They made love, tenderly and passionately. After, they drifted off to sleep content in each other's arms.

Morning's diffuse light etched its way across the bedroom as Tom woke to see a beaming Nia in her dressing gown carrying a tray of breakfast into the bedroom.

"I thought I'd let you sleep while I fixed some breakfast," she said.

"Hhmmmm, Nice. I like the service you get here," Tom joked. "Better than the hotel."

***

They spent the remainder of the day at Nia's home. They settled into the warm study on the cold and grey winter's afternoon. Tom was touched and slightly embarrassed to see his canal guides on Nia's reading table.

"Insomnia?" he asked nodding to his books. Nia giggled.

"Why the change of name?" she asked.

"Errr, military thing," Tom confirmed. "My name appeared in the press a few years back when I was, umm, picking up a medal. Thought it best not to necessarily advertise that the canal guy and the medal guy are one and the same."

Tom browsed the bookshelves and picked a well-reviewed thriller. Nia was curled up on her chair with a history book. He sat in the leather wingback near the fireplace. Nia looked up from her book.

"You write well," she enthused. "I didn't study English, but I've read a lot of scripts and have a decent sense of what's good writing."

Tom thanked her. They talked of favourite authors,

of books that had made differences in their lives, and films made from books. Then they settled in and read in companionable silence.

When it was time for Tom to head back, Nia once again walked with him to the Tube station and down onto the platform. This time, however, they kissed passionately and deeply. Nia asked Tom whether he could visit again, and they arranged a time and place to meet on the following Friday. The audiobook job meant that, for that week, she had almost regular work hours. The Tube train arrived too quickly for them. She watched Tom's train disappear into the tunnel and felt an immediate emptiness.

Tom thought of Nia through his entire trip back north. He was suddenly aware that she had given him a reason to move on with his life. He hadn't had as much fun on the town since… before the war, he recalled. And it wasn't just fun, Nia made him want to live rather than just exist. He stopped at Rachel's to drop off the Land Rover and to pick up Jack. Tom was made to sit through a cup of tea and a good-natured grilling from Rachel. Owain, from behind his newspaper, suggested Rachel leave Tom alone.

Tom cleared his throat and turned to Owain.

"Owain, you have lots of guys — plumbers, roofers, tractor guys, yeah?"

Owain nodded.

"Do you have a Land Rover guy?" asked Tom.

"Err, yes," Owain replied, putting his paper down.

"I'd like to get one. Gently used. Probably something with a short wheelbase, a Defender 90 perhaps."

Owain and Rachel exchanged glances.

"What colour?" Rachel asked.

"Doesn't matter," Tom answered.

Rachel looked towards Owain and raised an eyebrow.

Later, Rachel drove Tom and Jack back to the marina.

"Nia?" Rachel asked simply.

"Is wonderful," was all Tom replied.

Rachel attempted to watch Tom's face as she drove, trying to also keep an eye on the road ahead. She thought Tom's face reflected a contentment that she hadn't seen in him for years. Still, she had a concern.

"Be careful little brother. She's already binned you once. She doesn't have a good track record at this sort of thing."

Tom faced Rachel. "Oh, and I do?" he replied.

"Well," Rachel said turning briefly to Tom as she drove. "There was the Marina Girl."

Tom laughed at the reference. He'd had a disastrous short-lived liaison with the divorced daughter of a marina owner. It ended badly and resulted in the loss of Periwinkle's permanent berth.

"I'd like to meet Nia Williams," Rachel said. "Will she ever come up for a visit?"

The thought of Nia at the farm being given the third

degree by Rachel didn't thrill Tom but the thought of Nia on the Periwinkle did completely.

Back at the farm, Rachel put the car keys on the table where Owain was still reading the Sunday paper.

"Tom seems good," Owain announced, not really looking up. "Better somehow."

"Yes," Rachel said as she moved to the sideboard and picked up the photo of Tom in full uniform. She remembered exactly when the photo was taken just after Tom officially received the MC. He had begun to change then, still the kind man he always was, but struggling. His sadness was palpable. Rachel had now witnessed further change in Tom since his meeting Nia, more positive change. But it was Nia Williams, how could that relationship work? She worried for Tom.

"I hope it will last," she said, really to herself. "I really do."

***

Periwinkle

Jack and Tom settled into an evening on the boat. Tom's phone dinged with a text. Nia. Some friends were hosting an early Christmas dinner next Saturday, would he like to join them? Tom replied he'd be delighted. He'd like to meet some of her friends, he was already aware that she had a small circle of those she truly considered friends. He thought automatically of the logistics behind a trip to London, maybe with his new

Land Rover.

The week went slowly for Tom. The weather closed in and kept the Periwinkle moored up in the marina. It was the second marina that Tom had called home. He wrote a little, less than he wanted to. His guidebook editor was trying to convince him to write a book length work, perhaps a contemporary revisiting of L.T.C. Rolt's journey and thoughts in *Narrowboat*. Tom read quite a bit and he made a few playlists for himself and for Nia. He walked Jack and ran when the weather allowed. His right leg ached with the declining temperature. He bought a Land Rover from Owain's guy and arranged a parking space at the marina. He thought about Nia a lot.

Tom drove himself and Jack in his newly acquired Land Rover to Rachel's on the Thursday night. He planned on a dawn start Friday. He had a nine a.m. date, in London.

***

London

Nia's week was never routine, but her work on the audiobook gave her a temporary sense of a regular week. She hit the gym almost daily and met Jane for coffee. Jane let Nia know that she had the lesbian matron role if she wanted it. Nia read. She met Ben and George for a walk and again wondered whether she should get a dog. Nia made time to meet her friends for drinks. Her small circle of friends had been mostly established in the post Goldenboy years. They were a tight clique of five, all actors or media types. They were supportive but not demanding. Their work schedules and lifestyles meant that their get-togethers weren't calendared but occurred more organically whenever two or three were in town together. Nia wasn't a core, but they accepted her, cared for her, and they understood her pain and loss. They were surprised when, after one glass of wine, she did indeed say that she could owe her glow to a new guy and briefly described her relationship with Tom. It was if she went through the week keeping one eye on a clock willing it to be Friday morning.

***

Friday morning

Nia was early. She stood by the Tower of London's gatehouse entrance She wore a black beret and black gloves and put her heavy winter coat's collar up to combat the wind whipping over the Thames to her back. She waited for Tom with excited anticipation. Nia yearned to see him, to hold him, and to be held by him, then she saw him as he walked down the access road from Tower Hill. His limp was now familiar. He wore his boots, jeans, a leather jacket, wool gloves, scarf and hat. She watched as he caught sight of her and as his face broke into a broad smile and he picked up his pace.

She went to meet him almost at a run. They hugged and then kissed. She had planned another adventure day in the city.

"Right then," Nia commanded. "A tour of the Tower." She linked arms with Tom and they walked over the Tower's long-vanished moat and into the grounds.

Later, they taxied to Nia's house after a busy day in the city. As Tom unpacked his small rucksack, he retrieved and presented Nia with a small gift. It was obviously a book and Nia removed the gift wrapping with care.

"Instead of flowers," he said.

It was a copy of Rolt's *Narrowboat,* the rather odd autobiographical canal travelogue written just before the start of the Second World War. Tom said that many canal aficionados believe the book precipitated the rebirth of leisure cruising which, in turn, led to the massive renovation and revival of the UK's canal system. She smiled and quickly flipped through it. She stopped at a few of the book's illustrations. Tom noted the importance of the book but also said that it wasn't one of his favourites. Nia liked the fact that he had given her a book; he was already very familiar with her likes, dislikes, and proclivities.

"I have an ulterior motive for giving you this book," Tom said.

"Oh, and what's that?" Nia asked looking up from the book.

"It's an invitation to spend some time with me on my boat."

Nia smiled. "I'd love to," she said genuinely. "And, I think I'm going to be free starting Thursday."

Tom smiled.

"Okay then, that's a date," affirmed Nia. "Now, let's get ready for dinner with my friends. Just to prepare you, they are going to be loud, and will probably ask you lots of personal questions that will verge on the rude and vulgar."

"Sounds wonderful. I can't wait," Tom lied.

***

Nia's friends were as she described and Tom had been well prepped. The friends were all a little younger than Nia. Amanda, Constance and Orla were actresses doing mostly stage and TV work. Amanda, who had a recurring role on a police procedural, was a household name. Constance probably drank too much. Orla had voracious appetites generally. The fourth friend, Penny was in media PR. The restaurant was quiet and exclusive with the right amount of atmosphere, light and music. Tom was immediately struck by how posh Nia's friends appeared but wasn't sure whether they were all to the manor born or whether it was misperception, perhaps one supported by their drama school accents and elocution lessons.

The food and service were excellent. Tom was his

quiet, charming self and Nia was clearly comfortable with her old friends. Wine flowed and the women grew louder and more expressive. Tom noticed how the women interacted with Nia, respecting her experience and signalling some suspicion towards Tom. He didn't mind, it's what good friends do, he thought. He noticed too, that although Nia was part of the group, she was not of it.

It was late by the time coffee was served. No one wanted the evening to end.

"Let's go dancing," Amanda suggested.

"Tango?" Tom asked, and Nia laughed at the private joke.

Orla looked at them both trying to decipher if there had been a hidden sex reference.

"No," Amanda said. "Regular club, decent music."

After a quick Google of venues, they taxied to a Shoreditch club known for its eighties' vibe and music. The kind of music Nia knew Tom liked. Once there, it was easy to find a seat in the only half-filled club. Tom choosing a booth nonchalantly after a quick visual tactical sweep of the surroundings. Tom took drink orders and headed up to the bar. All the women watched him go.

"He's lovely," Constance remarked. "Where did you find him again?"

Orla asked whether he had a brother or a sister. The group laughed even though jokes around Orla's pansexuality had become a bit of tired old trope.

Tom made two trips with the drinks and then he sat back in the booth with his G&T. Nia had a vodka and slimline, for old time's sake, and he watched and listened to the old friends continue to talk and gossip. But mostly he watched Nia. He watched how her eyes sparkled, how her lips parted over her teeth, how an occasional heavy curly stand of hair would fall over her left eye, how she would absentmindedly move the hair tucking it behind her ear, how she caught his eye and smiled.

Tom enjoyed the stories from the theatre world, of naughty things that happen on TV and movie sets, who was screwing who, it was a window into a world he didn't know but one, through Nia, he now had a minor role in. He liked the group's shared reminisces of a collective past as he felt it gave him access to another part of Nia.

The opening chords for the Smiths' 'This Charming Man' began. Nia looked at him and nodded to the dance floor.

"C'mon," she said and reached out for his hand.

Nia's dancing was fluid and unselfconscious while Tom's wasn't, but they began to move well together occasionally touching and spinning within each other's orbit. Nia's friends watched from the booth.

"I don't think I have ever seen her like this," Amanda said.

"Me neither," added Penny

"Ah, *l'amour,*" Constance said.

Orla guffawed, "Nia doesn't do love." But as she watched Tom and Nia on the dance floor, said, "You think so?"

Constance and Penny both nodded.

"I don't think Nia's grasped how lonely she's been," Constance continued.

"Although I think what she's feeling on the dance floor hasn't quite registered with her yet either," Amanda offered sagely. "That she can't put that emotion," and she nodded towards Nia and Tom, "into words."

Tom and Nia stayed out on the dance floor as George Michael's 'Careless Whisper' began. More couples made their way out to the dance floor including Penny and Amanda. Nia swayed with the music and sensed the lights dimming as the dance floor became diffuse with lavender light and the spinning reflections from electronic mirror ball projectors. Tom reached out and held her by the waist and they slow danced holding each other. Nia could feel Tom's leg muscles taught and tight against hers. She held her face against his chest and then looked up into his face. His eyes were closed. She mouthed, "I love you, Tom Price."

Tom liked the darkness that crept across the dance floor. He loved the touch of Nia's body against his, the feel of her waist, the smell of her hair on his chest. He shut his eyes to prolong the moment, to isolate just the two of them. He felt her move and he opened his eyes; she held his hand away from his body as she twirled under his arm and moved backwards into him. Her back was to his front and she held his hands on her hips. She subtly but purposefully ground her bottom into his groin.

Chapter Ten
London, Autumn 2001

Nia was terribly drunk. Her head had started to throb with too many vodka and tonics and the bass heavy house beat booming through the club's speaker system. She could feel it reverberate through her body. She was hot after dancing. Tired after a long, difficult week on set and in her personal life. She had ended any communication with her family, just tired of the constant hurt and disappointment. She looked across the club, through a haze of lavender lighting, mirror balls, and dry ice to the dance floor below. There he was, Goldenboy; Nia had aggrandised the tabloids' nickname making it her own. Even as drunk as he was, he exuded cool, beer bottle still in hand, dancing with two or three women while others appeared to be circling him, predator like. God, Nia thought, he knows he could leave the club with any of those girls. So many, guys as well as gals, just wanted to shag him. Yes, Nia recognised, he's so good looking but he knows it. You can't have a face like that, eyes so blue, hair so golden and curly, and the body of a Greek God, but with a bigger dick, and not be a bit of a prick. He saw her and waved his beer bottle and smiled with unnaturally perfect and dazzling white teeth. But he's my prick, she smiled back.

She sipped her vodka. A man Nia had never seen before sat down next to her in her booth. City type, smart suit, attitude.

"Hi Nia, baby," he started.

"Fuck off," Nia said. Her eyes were like flint.

The man looked hurt and angry and opened his mouth to respond but thought better of it and left. Nia downed her vodka and needed a pee. The toilets felt cold and the music more diffuse. She splashed cold water on her face. There was a knock on the door.

"Nia, it's me." She opened the door and Goldenboy pushed his way in.

"Get out," Nia said. "It's the ladies' loo."

"Don't care. You got to try some of this," he said. He was stoned and held out a little baggie with white powder.

He pushed her into a toilet cubicle, placed some cocaine on the back of his hand and snorted it. He placed some more on his hand and proffered it to Nia.

"I don't want to," she said. "I've given it up, remember. Bloody kicked it."

"Come on, pussy. It'll keep you going 'till dawn. Come on." He pushed the back of his hand against her nose. Nia snorted deeply. Her nostrils burned, her headache ceased, her pupils dilated covering almost her entire irises.

"Fuck wow," she said.

Goldenboy grabbed her by the arm and they made

their way back on to the dance floor. She shut her eyes and let the music wash over her. She was re-energized and became part of the music as she danced. Nia felt Goldenboy's taut, gym toned body close to hers but then sensed him drifting away. She moved across the dance floor not caring. She opened her eyes and saw Goldenboy deeply kissing one of the other women at the dance floor's periphery. Nia shut her eyes again and felt the music move her around the dance floor.

***

Outside the club, a group of soldiers in civvies, but noticeable because they all sported the same obvious haircuts, waited in the queue to enter. They'd been there some time and they were getting chilly and pissed off as the bouncers allowed newcomers in ahead of them. They were getting restless. They wanted a good time after long days on post-9/11 anti-terrorism duties. A large black bouncer wearing a loose-fitting suit approached.

"Sorry lads," he began with a sincere smile. "We're only letting in couples at the moment. If I were you, I'd move on."

There were collective groans.

"Okay, lads let's find somewhere else," said one of the group, slightly older. "I'll buy the first round."

There was a ripple of approval from the group.

"What about a tat sir?" asked an already heavily

tattooed squaddie.

"Jones, I'm not going to buy a round of tats," said Second Lieutenant Tom Price. "What would all your mothers say?"

The group laughed.

"Nah, sir," continued Jones. "You said you'd get a tat with the lads after deployment."

Price smiled, "That I did, but standing outside the Houses of Parliament doesn't count as a deployment in my book. At least, not yet. Come on lads, there's a pub around the corner. Beer's getting warm."

The group pushed off shoving each other and laughing. They were happy young men feeling invincible and immortal.

***

Afghanistan, Spring 2006

The rubbish-strewn dirt road through the tiny hamlet was supposed to have been cleared and made safe. Lieutenant Tom Price had drilled his soldiers not to treat any road as totally safe, to watch where they stepped, to keep eyes peeled for wires, to be aware of any suspicious locals watching a stretch of road, or anything that looked out of the ordinary. Such vigilance took its toll. His men were physically and emotionally exhausted and concentration always slipped at the end of a long mission. Today's patrol was winding down and thoughts were already turning to the relative safety of their Forward Operating Base and the bunks, cold beer, and Skype phone calls home that were waiting.

Corporal Nick Jones was a good soldier. He loved the army and, like many a poor boy from the inner cities with little family to account for, had found a sense of kinship with his comrades. He was close to his platoon commander, Lt. Price, whom he would have followed to the gates of hell. Jones had made it a personal mission to get Price to agree to getting at least one tattoo. Jones liked his ink. He was lost in his thoughts, thinking of his next leave when he felt something spring under his left foot. He felt the explosion engulf him in flame, dirt and pain.

Jones was thrown in the air and landed in a broken pile. He looked down to where his legs had been and where his blood was already staining the sandy soil around him. Price ran to Jones and used his own field dressing to attempt to staunch wounds that were unstaunchable in the field. Price and the platoon's medic tied tourniquets on both of Jones' thighs. A Medivac helicopter had already been radioed for.

Jones looked up at Price with fear.

"Jones, you're going to be okay, do you hear me," Price said.

Jones grabbed Price's bicep with his right hand and Price noticed Jones' left hand was missing. Jones was breathing rapidly and was covered in blood. Price knew that Jones was bleeding out and there was nothing they could do for him. Jones' eyes fluttered and closed.

"Stay with me, Nick," Price commanded. "The chopper's coming. Stay with me."

The medic tied yet another tourniquet on Jones' left arm.

Jones cried out in pain and fear and his eyes opened.

He focused on Price's face.

"Aw fuck, Lieutenant," Jones gasped through pink stained teeth. "I think I've bought it, haven't I?"

"Nonsense," Price lied. "You'll be fit for purpose in no time." Price tried to smile reassuringly.

"Do me a favour, Tom," Jones said with a smile through a grimace. "You gotta get yourself some ink. Not a proper soldier if you don't."

"Only if you come with me too, Nick," Price replied.

Jones closed his eyes, he appeared to sigh deeply, and then died in Price's arms.

Chapter Eleven
Nia's House, December 9th

Nia made cafetière coffee while Tom showered upstairs. Her phone dinged with texts from her friends, mostly about Tom but Amanda asked Nia where she had learnt to twerk. Nia giggled. Tom's mixture of embarrassment and excitement on the dance floor had inspired a lustful romp as soon as they had returned to Nia's house. They had fumbled with their clothes as soon as they were in the home's vestibule and Nia, half naked, had pulled Tom into the lounge and they made furious love on the carpet. She warmed to the memory as she sat at the table with her coffee. She heard Tom moving upstairs and she felt comforted. Her cold, quiet, and empty house was no longer any of those things.

She sipped the coffee and thumbed through the Rolt book. She liked that Tom had bought her a book and she had already begun to think about books she could, in return, present to Tom. She hoped it would become a tradition for them. She heard Tom whistling as he came down her stairs. He limped heavily into the kitchen with his hair still wet.

"You okay," Nia said with genuine concern and nodded to his leg.

"Oh yes," replied Tom. "Just a little achy this

morning," he rubbed his scarred thigh. "I must have been in an odd weight bearing position." And then he remembered just exactly what had stressed his leg the night before. He smiled sheepishly.

Nia realised too and smiled back. She stood up from the table.

"Ok tiger, how would you like some eggs for breakfast?" Nia asked.

***

Llangollen Canal. December 14th

The early winter cold snap had been replaced by more classic seasonal weather: leaden skies, grey days and almost continuous drizzle. It was miserable weather but not too miserable now to keep Tom and his boat moored up. Tom took Periwinkle back north through the Llangollen canal. He watched the heavy grey clouds tumble and rumble to the west where he knew the mountains of Snowdonia would soon experience a deluge. He also knew that if the clouds weren't spent over Snowdon, then the drizzle he was now experiencing would become a heavy pounding rain. As it was, Tom had the canal almost to himself. There were almost no hire boats out this late in the year and most continuous cruisers had moored up for the season. This was a stretch of the canal that he never grew tired of. He enjoyed the solitude, the tranquillity, and the beauty of the canal and its adjoining countryside. He had traversed this stretch of canal numerous times and it never failed to take his breath away. Here, the natural beauty of the Ceiriog and Dee valleys was interspersed with the engineering genius of man, personified by the canal itself and its iconic tunnels and aqueducts. Tom was hoping the weather would be kind enough to allow Nia this experience.

Jack joined him on the little stern deck. She barked good naturedly at some ducks who quacked in response. It was the only sound Tom had witnessed, apart from the comforting, rhythmic *put-put* of the engine below his feet, for some miles. His voice sounded strange when he spoke out loud to his dog.

"Jack, my girl, we need to train you to make tea."

Tom moored up at Llangollen's narrowboat basin. He took the short walk into the little village to resupply the Periwinkle's small fridge with food and drink, bought fruit and vegetables, and, thinking about what would make Nia more comfortable, some fresh-cut flowers. He took advantage of a small and quiet launderette and washed some clothes, towels and bedding. He tidied the already spotless boat in preparation for Nia's visit. There had been guests on the Periwinkle; Rachel and Owain were frequent summer visitors, and there had been the rare romantic partner, but this was different. He was aware that Nia had a track record of shying away from relationships and guarded her privacy and her vulnerability. But by allowing Tom, literally, into her personal space she had emotionally opened herself to him. He wanted to reciprocate by welcoming her into his home. Tom Face-Timed with Nia and confirmed her arrival time at Crewe's railway station.

At Crewe, Jack waited patiently in Tom's Land Rover at a parking spot close to the station's entrance. Tom was on the platform, waiting less patiently for the train from London. He desperately wanted to see Nia again, to hear her voice, feel her laugh, to touch her, breathe her scent. He already couldn't remember what life was like without her.

The Virgin express train was on time. A number of travellers alighted at Crewe. Tom scanned the crowd and saw Nia step down from a first-class carriage. She had a large spinner bag with her. He watched as she appeared to hesitate as the platform crowd, most just off the train, thinned out, moving on to their next trains or off the platform and on to points home. She wore new hiking boots, designer combat type trousers, a colourful boiled wool Norwegian sweater and a navy pea coat. She put on a red knitted hat. She began to move down the platform when she saw Tom. Her smile moved him. They met on the platform and kissed deeply, oblivious to the travellers that moved around them.

"I'm so happy to see you," Tom said. "So glad you made it up here."

Nia hugged him again and her dark eyes shone. She carried her now well-thumbed copy of *Narrowboat*.

"Ummmm," Nia said, "God, I love how you smell."

Tom laughed. "How was the trip?"

"Smooth actually," Nia answered. "Spent most of the time reading the Rolt."

"What do you think of it?" Tom asked.

"Fascinating," began Nia. "But he's a bit opinionated, isn't he?"

"Quite. Some of his observations about people haven't aged well."

"Like bargees being a different race?"

"Yes," Tom laughed. "Like bargees being a different race."

"Is narrow boating still like this?" she asked pointing to a particularly romantic illustration.

Tom smiled. "Yes," he said simply. "It can be. But it can be rather chilly, especially these days, and some people feel the whole thing is too cramped. Are you ready for this?"

She nodded.

"Okay, let's go and meet Jack and the Periwinkle."

Nia was genuinely excited.

Nia liked Jack immediately and the feeling was mutual. Jack continued to lick Nia's hand as the actress positioned herself in the Land Rover's front seat. Nia also liked the Land Rover.

"Nice wheels Tom. Yours?"

"Just got it," Tom announced almost proudly. "I can keep it at the marina's car park even when I'm off cruising. It'll be a bit of a pain having to, sometimes, shuttle between boat and car but the benefits will outstrip any of those issues."

Nia was aware that Tom's purchase had more meaning than just the getting of a vehicle.

"By the way, you mentioned you like cars, what do you drive?" Tom asked.

"Oh, something a little speedier," she answered obliquely.

"Then you should have driven up. The country roads around here are a driver's dream."

"Ah, too many speed cameras for me," she said. "Maybe next time."

***

Tom had moved the Periwinkle back to Llangollen as a starting point to give Nia, arguably, one of the best short canal trips in the British Isles. The drive from Crewe would normally take a little over an hour but Tom took a little longer route so they ran parallel to the canal for a bit. They stopped in a little border village and had a late lunch in a half-timbered Elizabethan inn that was dog friendly.

The late afternoon grew grey and cloudy and Tom had turned on the Land Rover's headlights by the time they pulled into Llangollen. He parked at the narrowboat basin's car park, a grassy field, stone hard with winter temperatures. He carried Nia's bag, which was surprisingly heavy, and Jack ran on ahead. The marina spread out before them like a shallow bowl. Tom pointed out a couple of the boats whose owners he knew, but there weren't many boats tied up along the floating pontoons at this time of year. Tom and Nia walked up to a smart green narrowboat. The Periwinkle.

"Home," Tom said.

He held her hand as they walked on the floating pontoon moorings to the boat's stern. He continued to hold her hand to steady her as she stepped up on to the small stern deck. He unlocked two small doors, opened them, and slid open the roof cover which would allow them to walk down the stern cabin's three steps without ducking. He turned on lights and Nia could see a small tidy bedroom cabin. On the cabin's left, tight against the wall, was a double bed. A small cabinet at its foot. The walls and ceiling were a warm toned wood. There were windows either side of the cabin and small shelves stocked with books on either side of the windows and at the head of the bed. A few paintings, watercolours Nia thought, were screwed flat on to the cabin's curving walls. Nice, Nia thought, cosier than she expected.

Tom placed her bag on the bed. The bag looked huge.

"Oh my God, where do you keep all your stuff," Nia said alarmed at the lack of drawers and closets.

Tom had cleared out two of the cabinet's drawers for her and showed her a little wardrobe at the front of the cabin for coats and boots and another in the corridor that ran from the bedroom to the galley kitchen. The bathroom was on the left of the corridor. Tom showed her the small bathroom and demonstrated the odd way to flush the toilet and the need to pump out the shower when in use. The bathroom was spotless. She went to the tiny shower.

"Ever get two people in this?" she asked with a smirk.

"Once," Tom answered. "But she was very small."

Nia laughed.

"And pretty?" Nia asked with a cheeky smile.

"Oh yes, stunning."

"Okay, you can stop right there," Nia said with a giggle.

Tom showed her through the rest of the boat. Nia appreciated the fact that he had filled every space with books. There were some fresh flowers in a vase on one of the galley kitchen's small counters.

Tom made a fire in the boat's Morso pot-bellied stove. After the fire had taken, he went to the galley and made some tea. With mugs of tea in hand, they sat in the front cabin talking, Nia expressing genuine interest in all things canal. Tom answered her questions about his boat and the canal as best he could. Then Nia noticed the small collection of DVDs resting on a bookshelf, recognising them instantly as her work. She was touched. She stood up and started looking through the DVDs.

"On my God, Tom!" she exclaimed. She pulled out one of the DVDs. "Oh My God," she repeated. "This has a nude scene."

"Errr," Tom stammered a little embarrassed. "I discovered that."

"Tell me, Mister Price, are you some kind of pervert?" Nia laughed. "Seriously though, Tom, what made you get these?"

"Well," Tom took a gulp of his tea, draining it. "I was so sorry that I hadn't seen any of your work before that I wanted to acquaint myself with it."

"And, what did you think then?"

"Nia, you are very good. Your talent is obvious from your earliest stuff on and Jack's a big fan too," Tom said.

They both laughed. Nia felt a sense of pride.

"Talking of Jack," Tom added. "It's time for her walk. Would you like to join us?"

Nia nodded, "Absolutely."

They walked down the towpath past the shut cafe and souvenir shop and took a right turn down a steep hill into the village proper. There was a light misting rain rolling in from the mountains to the west. They walked across the village's ancient bridge and watched the Dee's water below rush, churn, and dance. Nia looped her arm in Tom's as they walked back. The mist became rain in earnest and the temperature dropped. By the time they walked back up the hill and along the towpath to Periwinkle's mooring, Nia was wet and chilled.

***

Jack lay on one of the cosy chairs enjoying the stove's warmth while Tom made dinner. Chicken was sautéing in a pan with shallots and a wine reduction sauce. Tom chopped mushrooms. Nia was showering and getting warm after the cold and damp walk. She dried herself in the bathroom, applied some subtle mascara and then slipped out of the bathroom wrapped in a towel and moved quickly the few feet down the corridor to the bedroom cabin. She closed the door. She made sure the curtains were fully closed as she slipped out of the towel, stepped into lacey lavender panties and matching bra, and then dressed simply in jeans, a white designer T-shirt, and, as she was still cold, an Aran sweater. She checked herself in the cabin's mirror, nodded to her reflection, then she moved down the narrow corridor from bathroom to kitchen. There, she asked whether she could help, secretly hoping Tom would say no. He suggested she open the bottle of wine, which was a chore she gladly embraced. A bottle of red was on the counter. She opened it with expert ease and poured two generous glasses and went over and hugged Tom.

"Music?" she asked.

"Try the iPad."

She touched the tablet's screen and found the music icon. She looked at Tom's playlists and stopped at the one labelled 'Phone Songs'. She turned to Tom who was stirring dinner in a large pan. It smelled lovely, she thought.

"You have a playlist of songs about phones?"

"Don't we all?" Tom asked. "Try it, it's brilliant."

Nia shrugged and hit play. ELO's 'Telephone Line' started.

"Classic," said Tom.

"Clichéd," said Nia. "But good."

Tom added a few more coal briquettes to the lounge cabin's stove. The cabin warmed sufficiently for Nia to pull off her sweater. She leaned against a kitchen cabinet and took a long draw on her wine. Dinner simmered.

"You know, I don't know this part of Wales at all," Nia said. "It's lovely though isn't it? The view from the bridge in the village, wow. And the hills, and that one with a castle on the top. I'm from the south, Cardiff way. Don't get back very often but have even done some filming there. Did an episode of Dr Who in Cardiff once. It's filmed there now."

"I always liked Dr Who," Tom attempted to interject.

"Kinda booming now, Welsh TV. Would have loved to have been able to be in some of the recent Welsh dramas," Nia continued. "But I don't speak Welsh. Have to speak Welsh as they film in both English and Welsh." She laughed, "I'm babbling. I'll stop."

"No, don't," Tom said. "I like it. It's like music."

Nia laughed her loud throaty rasp. "No one has ever told me that my voice sounded like music before."

"Then, nobody's really listened to you before,"

Tom said.

Tom opened another bottle of wine to have with dinner. The small table was set simply, and Tom quickly served the food. Nia took a tasting bite and was immediately impressed with Tom's culinary skills. They ate and talked. Nia loved how the conversation flowed naturally. She felt free to be her authentic self, not worried about how she appeared, she enjoyed telling her stories or discussing opinions with this sweet man as he genuinely listened to her. It wasn't the kind of listening, she knew, that a guy may have picked up from a GQ article on how to impress women, but real listening that reflected genuine interest. Nia liked his stories but noticed that he was still guarded about facets of his army career and experience. He was beginning to share more things with her, but she still felt he was only allowing her to peel back one layer of onion skin at a time. As he talked and as he listened, she was finding his charm almost irresistibly attractive. They finished the meal with coffee and whisky.

Nia excused herself and she made her way, a little unsteadily, to the bedroom cabin. She returned to the dining table holding what was obvious to Tom as an exquisitely wrapped book. "Please," Nia began. "Open it."

Tom took the book and unwrapped it. It was a first edition of Philip Hoare's biography of Noel Coward. He noticed that there was a flyleaf inscription: "Tom, who attended *Blithe Spirt* and revived mine. Love always,

Nia."

"Wow, thanks," Tom said. "It's lovely." He was touched by her inscription.

Nia put her empty glass down on the table and leant back in her chair.

"Time for bed?" she said raising an eyebrow coquettishly.

They quickly and haphazardly cleared the dinner service. Tom tucked Jack into her bed in the lounge cabin and closed the door to the rear cabin. Nia lay back on the bed and stretched her arms over her head. Her hair spilt around her on her pillow.

"Take my clothes off," she said.

Tom found her self-confidence incredibly attractive.

"Yes, ma'am," he said. They were both tipsy. He climbed on the bed, straddled her, and gently eased her T-shirt over her breasts and then her head. He sat back on his haunches. Her breasts filled the lacy lavender bra lasciviously. He moved down and unfastened her jeans' button, and unzipped her fly, she arched her back as he pulled the jeans over her bottom and hips, then down and off her legs.

"Another matching bra and panties," Tom stated. "Damn it, woman, how many knickers do you have?"

Nia giggled and laid there on his narrow bed on his narrowboat. Tom thought she was the most beautiful woman he'd ever been with. She opened her eyes. What was he waiting for? He pulled his T-shirt over his head.

"I want to imagine you like this always," Tom said. He slipped out of his jeans and underpants in one move.

Nia laughed, "What about this way?" she said as she unfastened her bra, a front loader, and wriggled out of her panties. She lay there totally naked. Tom moved his hands down her body in gentle stroking and massaging motions. She responded to his touch. He kissed her on the lips, she teased him with her tongue. She reached down and held his erection and moved it against her body so he could enter her.

They lay side by side, each enjoying the warm afterglow of satisfying sex. Their skin touching and sticking to each other. "That was lovely," said Nia.

"Thanks, you make it sound like a cup of tea," laughed Tom.

Nia giggled and pulled the sheet partway off her body. "Blimey, it does get hot in here."

Tom turned on to his stomach, resting on his elbows and leaned over and kissed her lightly on her lips. "I love your body," he said.

She laughed and made some mime movements. "My body is my tool," she said in an exaggerated French accent. She pulled the sheet off her body completely.

He laughed and kissed her, "Ah, it's a nude scene."

She guffawed. "Well, I don't do them any more. But, when I was young, and pretty, and had perky boobs, and a flat tummy…"

"I love your boobs," he said, and moved over and

159

kissed each of her breasts gently. "I love your tummy too." He moved down her body and kissed her stomach, her navel, and started moving down lower but she grabbed him by his ears and pulled him back up.

"This is nothing like acting," she said. "Those scenes are so rehearsed, so choreographed, that you don't think about how you move, it's like dancing."

"I like dancing," he said.

She guffawed and reached for him. "Yes, but you're really rubbish at it."

Tom laughed. "Is there anything that I am good at?"

"Yes," Nia said with a lascivious grin and a dramatic pause. "Making tea."

Tom gently hit her with his pillow. Nia bounced up and hit him back with her pillow. She straddled him and gently bounced the pillow off his chest and head. She felt him harden beneath her. It excited her. Tom eased her over his erection and she pulled him into her. They made love again slowly as the boat rocked gently at its moorings.

***

Tom was in the Periwinkle's small but efficient kitchen making breakfast. Jack curled up on her bed in front of the Morso stove. In the stern cabin, Nia curled under the bed's duvet enjoying its warmth. She felt ridiculously happy. She had so carefully guarded her emotions for so long that the depth and suddenness of her feelings for

Tom continued to scare her. As Nia listened to Tom as he moved around the kitchen, gently talking to Jack, and humming unselfconsciously to yet another of his quirky playlists she was irresistibly drawn to him.

She slipped on her dressing gown and moved down the small corridor to the kitchen. Tom was making fresh coffee, toast and scrambled eggs. She went up to him and, from behind, wrapped her arms around him. She placed her cheek against his back she shut her eyes.

"Tom," she began earnestly. "I think I've fallen in love with you."

Tom stopped his cooking and stood silently for a moment and then, without turning to face her, responded,

"No thinking for me. I'm sure I love you Nia." Then he turned to her; they kissed while the scrambled eggs burnt.

***

The Periwinkle slowly nosed her way eastward through the thin Llangollen canal. With no other boats on the canal, the narrowboat made good time. Nia stood on the stern deck enjoying her first time on a narrowboat and taking in the view of the misty Dee valley down to her right. As the canal approached the basin at the little town of Trevor, Tom steered the Periwinkle through a narrow bridge that led to a sharp right turn.

"Okay," he said with a smile. "Get ready for the

best but also the scariest trip across any aqueduct on any British canal."

Nia beamed and gave him a thumbs' up.

"You may want to stand on the left," Tom said. "There is going to be no railing on the right side of the aqueduct. You could simply step off the boat into thin air and down to the valley floor something like one hundred and twenty feet below."

"I wouldn't want that to happen," Nia smiled.

"Neither would I."

The canal narrowed as the mouth of the Pontcysyllte Aqueduct neared. The aqueduct had been in operation since 1805 and it continued to inspire awe given its radical design: the canal ran through a cast iron trough supported by eighteen high stone arches which gave it an elegant and light feel. It was the longest aqueduct in the UK and the highest in the world.

Tom slowed the Periwinkle as the narrowboat entered the twelve-foot-wide trough. The towpath was on the left with a fence between the path and the abyss. Tom gently steered the boat to the right side of the aqueduct and all Nia could see off the side of the Periwinkle was sky and space.

"Oh my God," she exclaimed. "It feels like we're flying. But really, really slowly."

Tom smiled. "You want to take the tiller?"

"You must be nuts."

"Not really," Tom said. "This is really easy. Just keep it straight. Even without someone at the tiller, the boat would continue to move forward like a slot car on a toy racing track, although the boat would continue to bounce off the canal sides."

Nia nervously took the tiller, her face etched with concentration.

"Has anyone ever steered a boat off the aqueduct?" Nia asked.

"No," Tom said definitively. "You can't. There's enough of a lip on the trough to keep the boat in the canal."

Nia visibly relaxed and smiled. "I love this, Tom. It's brilliant."

Later that morning, with the Periwinkle moored up Tom, Nia and Jack settled into the narrowboat's front cabin to watch a DVD of one of Nia's early films. Twenty odd years previously, Nia had had a supporting role in a low budget mock Hammer comedy horror film, the double entendre named *Vampire Moon*. It was one of those films that had lots of fake blood, ear splitting screams, lots of fake breasts and a few real ones, including Nia's. Nia's character was an over-sexed village girl who, although warned not to stay out late, does, and runs into a handsome young stranger. In the throes of lovemaking, the stranger's love bites turn real and Nia's village girl, amongst blood and nudity, is transformed into a vampire. The film just made its production costs back at the time and was instantly forgettable; but had now earned cult status and was now going to be shown at a British Film Institute Brit horror movie retrospective. Nia had been invited to attend the BFI event and she had asked Tom to join her. It would be an evening gown and black-tie type of event. She wanted to watch the film with Tom before the public viewing.

Nia, from the corner of her eye, watched Tom as he watched the movie. He laughed at the appropriate parts, showed shock at the clichéd gotcha moments, and appeared to appreciate her acting ability. He mouthed "Wow" and raised an eyebrow during Nia's pivotal nude scene. As Tom watched the film, he felt a sudden melancholy, not for anything he viewed on screen but from a sense of loss for not being with Nia in the past. It was a ridiculous, unrealistic feeling, and he knew that, but the ache was there like a regret.

Later, Nia noticed Tom was quiet as they walked hand in hand down the towpath. He had promised her a late lunch in a canal-side pub. Jack ran on in front.

Tom's pace slowed.

"What?" Nia asked.

"Oh nothing."

"No, there's something," she said. "Was it the film? Oh my God, was it my nude scene?"

"No, it's odd. It's just that I feel like I spent an hour with the you when you were twenty or so."

"Silly," she said. "That wasn't me. You know, I'm not really a nympho vampire." And then added with a dramatic flourish, "That's acting darling."

"I know," Tom said smiling. "It's just that I would have liked to have been with you then."

Nia stopped walking.

"No Tom, I don't think you would have liked me then at all. I was difficult. I was a little bit damaged and didn't realise it."

"Oh, I don't know," Tom began.

"No, look, I know. You would have hated me, and I would have hated that you were in the army for a start. More so after the wars began. Forgive me, but I couldn't help blame the military as well as the dicks in Whitehall. I was out protesting those damn wars. I was a member of 'Stop the War'. I hated all the 'Queen and Country' bullshit the media and generals were spouting."

"Nia," Tom said quietly. "That's fine. I wasn't a massive fan of those damn wars myself."

"Yes, but you fought in them, didn't you?" Nia said as more of an accusation. "For the feckless stupid government."

"Yes," Tom said resignedly. "It was my duty. It was what I had signed up for, it was my bloody job after all."

Tom was surprised at the conversation's turn. As was Nia.

"Nia, it's odd to think, but as soldiers we serve the government, the people, but when the shit hits the fan, most of that serving stuff goes out the window and we end up fighting for each other and not for the prevailing political authority. And, the shit hit the fan pretty bloody quickly. It got really bad out there… really quickly. My job simply became just trying to keep my soldiers and myself alive."

"I'm sorry," Nia said. "I can't imagine. It's crazy to think at that time I was worried about dying on stage and you were worried about actually dying." She smiled but it was thin. "But the soldier stuff has got nothing to do with it. Actually, it would have been the whole nice guy thing."

Tom opened his mouth to respond, but Nia put up her hand.

"It's true Tom," she continued. "It's so fucking true," she smiled, wistfully. "I ate nice, kind guys up or threw 'em away or both. I just didn't find them interesting. It was bad boys for me. I didn't know it then but my sense of normality was messed up. I had been abused by my family and I was kind of being abused by the industry, with all its focus on beauty and body, and the boyfriends. Everybody lying to everyone all the time. There were plenty 'me too' moments before they were called 'me too'. I was responding badly. I was too self-absorbed; everyone I was with was too self-absorbed. And there were drugs. Self-absorbed people, booze and drugs, a potent mix. A bad mix."

Tom didn't know what to say, "Wow, well I know I can't compete with your past."

It was Nia's turn to be surprised.

"You don't have to, idiot," she said. "Two husbands, a slight coke problem, and a series of meaningless relationships is not a lot to be proud of. And, no one is asking you to compete," she continued. "The past is past, a foreign country, right? I was different then."

"So, you find this," he nodded down the towpath, to the Periwinkle, and then he touched his chest, "To be exciting and interesting enough now?"

"Aye, silly, I do."

She grabbed his face in both of her hands and stared deeply into his eyes, unblinking. "I do now. It's taken a lifetime to find you and we're different people than we were in our twenties and thirties."

He reached for her hands and pulled them gently down, rotating them so he held them lovingly.

She turned away and looked down at their interlinked hands.

"I love you," she said. "Madly. Like I have never loved anybody before."

She pulled their clasped hands to her breast, over her heart.

"I have a few regrets from that time, for sure," she said. "Quite a lot of regret actually," she smiled wistfully to herself. "We all have them I'm sure. Like you joining the army?"

"No, Nia" he said. "Sorry, I loved the army. I don't regret that." Why was she back to this conversation, he thought?

"But the whole reason for it, the violence, the killing on all sides?" Nia continued.

"I saw it as service to the country, protecting people like you."

"But its whole bloody purpose is to ultimately fight, right?"

Tom was ready to respond, but Nia continued.

"That job made you kill people, didn't it?"

Ah, there it was. He stopped; time slowed as he looked across the canal to the meadow that lay beyond. Tom noticed a pheasant strutting amongst stubble crop, while a small tractor was engaged in tilling the hard soil. His breath condensed.

He looked at her and saw the earnestness etched on her face. Normally, he would ignore the question, or deflect it, laugh, or walk away but he knew that he needed to open this part of himself for Nia.

"Yes," he sighed. "I did, but you know what was worse? Having men and women killed around me. Knowing it was my sworn duty to try to protect them as much as I could, with my own life if it came to that."

She waited for him to continue, but he didn't.

"And you don't regret it?" she asked.

"Why are you asking?"

"I don't really know," she answered. "But I need to grasp a sense of who you were, to understand who you are. Does that make sense?"

"Not really," Tom said. They stood looking at each other. Tom felt constrained by the silence, then said, "I regret the loss, the lives taken too soon, but not the whole experience."

"Even though it broke you?" Nia asked.

He was shocked for a moment. So, that's why she was pushing this line of conversation, he thought, and then with a dismayed realisation, was he broken?

"I'm sorry, I didn't mean to…" Nia began, and Tom noticed the fear in her eyes. "Oh God, Tom. That just came out. I don't think you're broken."

"No, you're right. I was a bit broken," he said quietly. He was worried that Nia would be scared off, but he determined to be open with this woman he had fallen irretrievably in love with. "Yeah, you're right," he continued. "I was deeply changed by my experiences. It all eventually got too much. It made me retreat into myself. You see, I was subsumed by all the pain and sadness that surrounded me. I couldn't shake it, it consumed me. It was too much. But you ask about regret, I don't regret it, because, you know, in a strange, rather fucked-up way, it has brought me to you. So, you see, I can't regret any part of that journey." He held her hand and pulled her in front of him, he smiled. "I was broken but you've made me whole again."

Nia smiled and her eyes were wet. Tears ran down her cheeks. She pulled him close and lay her head into his chest. She found his combination of strength and vulnerability authentic and, importantly, rather sexy. She smiled as she looked up at him and kissed him.

"You big sweet, sensitive lug," she said. "Let's find the pub and grab a drink." She released him from the hug and, still holding his hand, they made their way off the towpath, over a brick, humpbacked bridge that crossed the canal, up a slight rise and into the local pub.

Nia was sitting by a log fire when Tom returned from the bar with their drinks; wine for her, cider for him. Her cheeks were still damp and chapped red from cold wind and emotion. Jack stretched out in front of the pub's fireplace. She smiled up at Tom as he approached. He thought she looked so beautiful at that moment.

"I love you," Tom said. "I want to spend the rest of my time with you."

Nia smiled as her eyes floated in tears again.

"I so love you too. You, know, I was broken too," she said after taking a first sip of wine. "Broken for a long time. I just didn't realise it until I met you. You made me aware of how lonely I was," she said. "I felt like I was on some kind of autopilot. I was going through my life trying to avoid the mistakes of my past. You made me feel again, Tom."

She wanted to tell him why she felt robbed of her happiness, but it still felt too raw and what she felt for Tom was too new.

***

The next morning was another cold one. Tom's breath condensed as he went through the routine of checking and starting the engine. A low winter sun was bright while a thin layer of mist clung to the surface of the canal. It was quiet on the cut as the Periwinkle meandered through the soft countryside. A few cows dotted a field, a few sheep in another. Nia joined Tom at the tiller with two steaming mugs of coffee in hand. Tom pointed out some heavy ewes grazing their way towards spring lambing. They saw no other boat through the morning hours and were only kept company by the occasional duck couple or, as Nia pointed out, a ducky threesome, a thruple, she called it. Such an arrangement was not uncommon in the acting world, she noted to Tom, and she named the additional hen 'Orla'.

At lunchtime, they moored opposite a field of sheep and one large, proud ancient oak tree. Nia made a quick lunch as Tom tied up the boat. They both liked these moments of routine domesticity. Nia had dressed warmly in boots, wool trousers, jumper, gilet, Tom's beloved waxed jacket and her red hat, gloves, and scarf and took the tiller during the early afternoon trip as the canal meandered lazily around the slow gentle contours of the countryside. Tom was impressed with her ability. The logic behind steering a narrowboat was simple, move the tiller right to turn left, move it left to turn right and use the control lever to increase or decrease speed. The combination of tiller and throttle would turn a fifty-foot-long boat through sharp corners or through a tunnel or a bridge opening only six inches wider than the actual boat with surprising ease. It usually took some time to be a decent helmsman, but Nia was a quick study. They chatted companionably on the stern with Tom pointing to interesting landforms and the occasional glimpse of interesting wildlife. Nia, genuinely interested, asked about the history of canals and the people that used to work on them.

Tom took the tiller as they passed an informal marina of weathered and battered boats, live-aboards, owned by people at the margins of society. These were not the well-maintained luxuriously appointed narrowboats of the well to do, those occasional cruising bankers, lawyers and doctors. Nia thought the rusting, fading boats, in what she called the bargee town, looked like something dystopian like Mad Max on the canals. Good people, Tom noted, people just trying to get by.

Nia took the tiller again and pushed the throttle control to increase the engine's revs and the Periwinkle sped up, but almost imperceptibly.

"Pedal to the metal, baby," Nia said.

Tom laughed.

Nia enjoyed her turn at the tiller. She slowed down to pass a moored boat and shouted a hearty 'hullo' to the boaters along with a customary wave. As the Periwinkle rounded one sharp corner and moved under an ancient masonry bridge, they heard the soft and muffled sounds of boys playing some kind of sport from across a number of fields. In the middle distance they could see a rugby game being played at an independent school. Snobs, Nia thought dismissively, thinking about Goldenboy's privileged and entitled background. She wanted to tell Tom more about her past with Goldenboy, about the lost baby, the lost years but she still held back.

The winter sun changed to the soft, enveloping grey that almost felt like shade. They had timed the trip well and moored up at a small town's two-hundred-year-old canal wharf. They changed into running gear and, with Jack along, took off down the towpath for a jog. Tom had altered his running schedule with Nia aboard knowing that after a day's cruise the engine would have warmed water enough for two showers, with Nia's shower being noticeably longer. They ran back down the towpath and out into the countryside, Jack running ahead or taking off through the hedgerows only to join them from the rear with a crazy catch-up sprint. Nia was a fluid runner; again, it was another of her professional skills, this one utilised to keep herself in shape. As they ran, Nia noticed how pronounced Tom's limp was and how he occasionally grimaced through some discomfort. They reached a turnaround point. Tom held her by her waist and they kissed.

"I'm having a lovely time," she said. "This," she nodded to the canal and the fields that stretched around it, "Is bloody enchanting. I never knew it existed like this. I now see why you love it."

"It's so peaceful it's restoring," Tom replied. "Now, race you back to the boat."

After showering, Nia volunteered to cook dinner and Tom headed into the little town to purchase a few more essentials and a bottle of wine. The wharf was still and silent as he returned. The canal black and smooth as slate. The Periwinkle was one of the few moored narrowboats that were lit. As he approached, he could see Nia through a window busy in the boat's galley. He stopped and watched her. Her being in his boat still took his breath away, she exuded a happiness as she moved from sink, to counter, to cook top. Tom noticed she was either talking to Jack, to a phone on speaker, or to herself. Or, he reconsidered, she was singing along to one of his playlists. He smiled. All that was important to him was here. At that moment, he was the happiest he had ever been.

Chapter Twelve
Russian Embassy, Kensington, December 20th

The Russian Embassy was quiet. Most employees were enjoying some extra flexibility around the Christmas festivities. Kamenev was almost alone as he worked late. He enjoyed the relative quiet of the embassy at night and it also enabled him to access the offices and computers of his embassy colleagues. Moscow Centre hadn't
specifically ordered him to surveille his own compatriots, it was simply in his nature to do so. Aggressively personally and professionally ambitious, Kamenev was always attempting to find anything that could be used as leverage for himself or for the FSB in their struggle with the SVR for primacy. During especially quiet nights, he made sure a trusted FSB man monitored the embassy's CCTV and internal security systems while another secured staircases or hallways allowing Kamenev to do his snooping. His few weeks in London had turned up little; an SVR surveillance specialist who had saved a stash of voyeur pornography acquired from the job, and some draft emails from the Rezident urging Moscow to cancel Kamenev's mission.

Both helpful pieces of information.

Kamenev poured a hot cup of tea from his samovar. The FSB's file on Daria Kirov was open on his desk in front of him. Another traitor, he thought, an enemy of the state masquerading as a journalist. He examined some file photos of her although he already knew her face well. He felt that she was pretty; small, thin, short dark hair and even darker eyes set on high, sharp cheekbones. But he didn't feel the stirrings of desire as he once did. The helicopter accident had damaged more than his face. He put his feet up on his desk and opened the SVR watcher's porn file and clicked through a number of the photos. He felt nothing and returned to the Kirov file. Neutralising Kirov would be his third successful operation and would mean a promotion, perhaps his own Rezidentura. He licked his lips in anticipation.

***

Llangollen Canal and Rachel's Farm, December 21st
The morning was one of those sunny winter mornings all bright and blue sky that made the chilly bite of the temperature all the more surprising. The Periwinkle was the only boat on the canal as it slowly nosed out of the wharf. Tom skilfully reversed the boat to a watering stop and filled the boat's water tank as Nia held the narrowboat calm by its centre rope. The plan for the day was a trip down the cut to the Shropshire market town

of Whitchurch, moor up at its reclaimed small wharf and grab a ride with Rachel or Owain to the farm for dinner. Once underway, Nia took the tiller and Tom went inside to make cups of tea.

The journey was uneventful. Nia and Tom talked constantly at the tiller with Nia occasionally popping inside the Periwinkle to get warm. They encountered a swing bridge and Tom moored up and he and Nia, along with Jack, walked down the towpath to raise the bridge. Tom returned to the boat and gently moved past the bridge which Nia, still on the towpath, lowered and then ran back to the boat. Tom warned her about the dangers of running on canal verges especially near locks and swing bridges as a hidden bollard could trip the runner leading to a nasty fall on the towpath or into the canal itself. Nia answered with an, "Aye, aye, captain". After a couple more swing bridges, which they took turns in raising and lowering, Tom nosed the Periwinkle into a sharp right turn into Whitchurch's small basin. Once again, the Periwinkle was one of very few boats moored up.

Nia wanted to run again, so they ran along the path that followed the route of the old canal into the outskirts of town, then up a slight rise, around the town's ancient parish church, and back down to the narrowboat basin. After their showers, Tom and Nia dressed casually for dinner at Rachel and Owain's. Nia wouldn't admit it to Tom, or herself, but she was nervous to meet Rachel. It wasn't only that she hadn't met a lover's family

177

member, formally, since Goldenboy, it wasn't even that she was aware of Rachel's important role in Tom's life, it was the simple desire to connect to someone close to Tom. Nia wore jeans, a little less tight than usual, brown boots, a lavender shirt, untucked, underneath her Aran sweater. As the forecast was chilly, she wore a Berghaus quilted coat.

***

Dinner went well. Rachel was surprised as to how natural, thoughtful, and witty Nia was. She quickly became aware that Nia's connection to Tom was obvious and deep. Dinner over, Owain took Tom out to see a new piece of farm equipment. It was a move that Rachel had prearranged. With the boys out of the house, Rachel brought tea on a tray to Nia at the dining room table. Nia would have preferred coffee post dinner but hadn't said so. She knew that Rachel was quite an authority at the farm and in Tom's life.

They chatted about the cycles of the farm and some of Nia's work. Rachel laughed at the appropriate stories and punchlines and Nia felt that they were connecting.

"Why is Tom still barging?" Nia asked. "If he loves boats so much why isn't he sailing the coasts?"

Rachel laughed.

"It's because he's actually a terrible sailor. He gets nauseated watching the sea on TV. There aren't many waves on a canal," she replied. Then, more earnestly,

"Tom is a lovely guy," Rachel said. "He's had a tough go of it for a few years now but he's more like his old self again, and I think that's due to you Nia." Nia smiled almost shyly. Rachel continued, "But I don't want you hurting him." Rachel's stare was chilling.

"I don't intend to," Nia began defensively. "I really, really like him."

"Like him how much?"

"I've rather fallen in love with him."

Nia's declaration surprised Rachel, who gawped a little. The words surprised Nia too, they sounded rather loud, but she liked the way they sounded. She liked the way they felt not so much in their production but in her core. In her soul.

"Quite a bit actually."

"But," Rachel stammered. "But you don't know him."

Nia sat back in her chair feeling affronted, she made a gesture with her hands, "Well, do we really know anyone?" She felt stupid as soon as she said it. "Sorry," she said. "You're right, but what I know of the Tom I have been with is that I want to spend all my time with him."

Rachel leant forward, "Look, Tom's been through so much over the last fifteen years or so and he's kind of shut all the pain, his and others, inside. He's been going through life on autopilot. Did he tell you our parents died when he was still in sixth form?"

Nia shook her head.

"Oh my God. I knew they had both passed away, but he never really mentioned when," Nia answered.

"It was unexpected, a train derailed injuring about thirty passengers and killing two of them, both our parents. Just incredibly shitty bad luck. I had just finished uni and was working at the time. I was able to live at home with Tom while he finished his A levels. He was so quiet about everything, wouldn't let me in. He went off to university and I think he had a good time, but I was never really sure. In his second year he joined the OTC. I think he found something there, in the camaraderie of the military, that became his family."

Rachel took a drink. She captured and held Nia's gaze.

"But, his experiences in Iraq and Afghanistan forced him to retreat further into himself, I think. He's been trying to be only in the moment, finding a kind of peace on his bloody boat and losing himself in his earbuds living his life to a soundtrack. Seriously, have you seen his playlists? He even has one 'songs about food'."

Nia laughed, "We actually listened to it making breakfast. His including Bob's Marley's 'Jammin' was inspired."

Rachel laughed, "You're not the Nia I thought you were."

"Good thing?"

"Yes, good thing. Good for Tom. I love my brother and I just want him to find happiness."

"I want him to be happy too," said Nia. "I think I can make him happy, but there is the part of him that he won't let me into."

"Okay, I know," Rachel said sceptically. "He hasn't let anyone in really. He's only shared bits with me, and I got more information from the army doctors and his old CO. When he was just out of the army, he was having a really bad time, I thought it was nightmares and stuff. Owain knew that the grandfather of a neighbouring farmer had served in World War Two. We thought it would be a good idea to get the old man and Tom together for a chat. Well, it turned out the old farmer had been a para, not only that, he was among the first to land in France on D-Day. They sat together," she pointed, "There in front of the Aga for hours telling war stories. But then I overheard Tom ask the old man, who was ninety-five, when did his nightmares end and do you know what the old boy said?"

Nia shook her head.

"The old boy said, 'Never'."

Rachel noticed the look of concern that clouded Nia's face.

"I could tell Tom was bothered by it," Rachel continued. "But after a couple of days mulling things over, he told me that wasn't his issue. It wasn't nightmares…"

"Is it PTSD?" Nia asked

Rachel looked down at her hands and then straight into Nia's eyes, "No. Not really. I think he just reached his capacity for handling tragedy and sadness. He was emotionally spent. He was always a kind and gentle boy, an empath if you will, it just got to be too much for him."

"Was it the helicopter crash? Did it affect him, more than the physical injuries, I mean?" asked Nia.

"I'm not sure, but it gutted him emotionally as far as his time in the army was concerned, although the leg injury alone would have ended his army career. I think the crash was the straw that broke the camel's back," Rachel sighed. "He never really fully recovered from it, if you ask me."

***

Six years Previously

Tom's recovery was harder and longer than the doctors thought it would be. Tom's femur had been shattered and, once the Chinook's metal had been removed from his leg, new metal in the form of orthopaedic plates and screws had painfully replaced it. His right leg ended up a centimetre or so shorter than his left. There were, also, symptoms of the latest in a series of concussions and he was aware of an ennui that grew on him like moss on a tree. Mobile but limping, he was granted leave and ordered to go home. It was a problematic order as Tom didn't have much of a home. There was Rachel and Owain at the farm, his own small Manchester house, a beloved classic Mini Cooper, and very little else. Even before he could go 'home' he was determined to complete one more important military task.

Tom travelled to Liverpool in full uniform. Departing the railway station, he took a taxi to an unfamiliar address. He found the house he was looking for and knocked on the unfamiliar front door. He heard someone approach from the other side and he instinctively straightened his uniform. The door was opened by a smartly dressed, fit woman in her mid-fifties.

"Mrs Roberts?"

"Yes?"

"I'm Major Tom Price. I wanted to, um, I wanted to let you know that I was with your daughter when she died. I wanted to personally express my condolences to you and your family."

Mrs Roberts, held his eyes for a moment then with a sigh, "Then, you'd better come in then."

Mrs Roberts held the door open as Tom stepped over the threshold. She led him into a small vestibule that opened into a nicely appointed sitting room. Over tea and home-made Victoria sandwich cake, Mrs Roberts asked Tom to tell the story of the helicopter crash that took the life of her only child. Tom had recounted the events of the evening numerous times to army intelligence, RAF crash investigators, and families of other dead and wounded. This time, however, his throat tightened and, unbidden, his eyes filled with tears.

"Please, take your time, Major Price."

When he told Lieutenant Roberts' mother about her daughter's last moments he was silently weeping. He felt awful that a grieving mother had to console him. Later, he washed his face in the Roberts' downstairs bathroom. He used the mirror to straighten his cap, and again smoothed the front of his uniform. He looked at his medal ribbons and felt a phoney. He knew that he was done with this life.

***

London, December 22nd

Nia put the kettle on, enjoying the familiarity of her kitchen and her things. She had headed home to London to prepare for the BFI event and to make some last-minute arrangements for Christmas day. Tom was heading down the next day. She sat at her kitchen table with a hot coffee and opened her phone to see that Tom had sent her a link to some playlists. She liked Tom's playlists although her musical tastes differed, having been formed by the mid-1990s' Brit pop scene. She had memories, some fuzzy and altered, some mirror clear, of hanging out with some of the era's bands. She liked a lot but not all of Tom's selections, but she also appreciated his subtle sense of humour and irony in his choice of tracks. She saw that he had linked two new playlists, one named 'Welsh Music', and one he had simply labelled 'Nia'.

She opened the Welsh songs, saw groups she had expected; Manic Street Preachers, Catatonia, Maria and the Diamonds, Stereophonics, Tom Jones, Bryn Terfel, a few unexpected; John Cale, Andy Fairweather Lowe, and Paul Young's 'Wherever I Lay my Hat'. She texted Tom. "Hey, Paul Young isn't Welsh. I know, I even met him once."

Tom responded, "Ah, but the bass player, Pino Palladino, is Welsh. Great vocals, sure, but that version is driven by the bass."

She listened to it again. Yeah, okay, I can see that, she thought.

She refreshed her coffee and sat down and moved to the link for the 'Nia' playlist. No one had burned music for her since the late 1990s; she found herself excited with the anticipation to see what Tom had curated for her, about her?

The first track was Nick Drake's 'Northern Sky'. She had never heard the song even though she had once acted on stage with Nick's sister. The song was, perhaps, the most beautiful she had ever heard. She teared up and played it again. "What the fuck," she thought. "Being moved to tears through a song. I'm never like this."

***

Tom made the now familiar trip down in the Land Rover and then across London via the Tube. They met at the

Duke of Wellington pub just off Covent Garden and, after a drink, Nia took Tom across the street to the London Film Museum for a James Bond exhibition. They both enjoyed the exhibition's collection of Bond related vehicles. They shared a pot of tea in the museum's cafe and they argued good naturedly over Bond's problematic relationship with women. Tom feeling that the films objectified women, Nia pointing out, that from an actor's perspective, many of the female roles were solid ones. Nia was recognised by a patron and asked for an autograph.

"You would have been a great Bond girl, Nia," the patron stated.

"Thank you," said Nia generously, ignoring the 'would have'.

She leant into Tom, "There's hope yet. Me and Daniel Craig. Yummy."

They took the Tube south of the Thames. Nia knew the way, walking Tom through some dark and close streets to a traditional Italian restaurant she knew well. The small restaurant was still family owned, and still decorated with red and white chequered tablecloths, iconic Italian prints on the wall, chubby bottles of Chianti served as candle holders, and bunches of plastic grapes garlanded the room. A cheap and cheerful Christmas tree had been placed in the corner. It was, as Nia noted, a step back in time to an era when small restaurants such as this, often run by former Italian prisoners of war who remained after the peace, provided colour, spice and flavour to the bland and over boiled regular British faire. As Nia promised, the food and wine were excellent and the laughter that emanated from the kitchen simply added to the elevated level of happiness both Tom and Nia were experiencing. Tom told Nia that his ravioli was the best he had ever had. Nia smiled, pleased that Tom had enjoyed the meal and this experience with her. They held hands across the table as they finished their bottle of a ruby rich Primativo.

It was late and raining when they settled the meal's bill. The restaurant owner offered to call them a taxi but both Tom and Nia were content with stretching their legs after their dinner. The streets were dark and slick with the rain. As the warm lights of the restaurant faded behind them, Nia held Tom's hand a little more tightly.

"Maybe we should get a taxi," she said.

"It's only a couple of streets," Tom replied. "We'll be fine."

They turned right into a small street. The high stone walls of the Victorian church to their left, darkened by over a century of city grime, cast a fog like darkness across the entire street. One streetlight buzzed bravely but only dimly about halfway down the narrow road. A boarded up, ready for demolition and redevelopment, brown concrete two-storey1960s' block of flats ran down the right-hand side of the street. Tom tried to imperceptibly increase their pace; he had heard an additional pair of footsteps behind them. His military training was alert to the fact that the street was an ideal landscape for an ambush. Then, he noticed a figure emerge from the deep shadows of the church wall in front to them.

"Fuck," Tom said, and he slowed his and Nia's pace.

"What?" Nia asked with barely disguised fear in her voice.

Tom steered her towards the streetlight as the two men approached. One from the front and the other one from behind. "Could be nothing," Tom said. He watched as the men clearly moved towards them, one reached into his bomber jacket's inside breast pocket and pulled out a hunting knife.

"Get behind me," Tom growled in command.

Nia turned to face Tom, she had never heard him speak like that. She noticed that his jaw was clenched and jutting, his cheekbones appeared to elongate, and his usually light and warm eyes were cold and dark. Nia got directly behind Tom watching the men approach over his shoulder.

"Awright, mate," the first man without the knife said. "How about giving me your wallet, phone, and watch?"

"And the whore too," the knifeman said as he closed to about a yard in front on Tom. "And any jewellery too." He moved the knife in his hand, holding the blade down while making axe-like chopping motions. Amateurs thought Tom, but even amateurs

188

could kill easily. He slowed down his breathing, he heightened his senses, watching every move the knifeman made while also being acutely aware of the second mugger's position.

Nia felt Tom switch his weight and turn slightly sideways to face the knifeman who smiled showing drug-rotten teeth. In a blink of an eye, Tom pivoted on his strong left leg and kicked out with his right catching the knifeman just below his left kneecap. The knifeman yelped in pain and stumbled forward as Tom grabbed his forearm and then the hand that held the knife. As in one fluid move, Tom bent the knifeman's wrist and extracted the knife from his hand. He then pulled the man forward unbalancing him, spun him around into his quickly approaching compatriot. Tom shifted his weight again, pulling Nia behind him. The second mugger recovered and swung a haymaker punch at Tom's head. Tom sidestepped easily and punched the man in the throat. The man collapsed to both knees with both hands at his throat grasping. Tom moved his feet quickly and, seemingly effortlessly, brought his right knee into the man's nose. The man slumped over backwards and lay still and twisted on the damp pavement, blood quickly pooling under his shattered nose. The former knifeman grabbed Tom by the shoulder and tried to spin him around, but Tom used the momentum to bring his left elbow into the man's temple, sending him thudding to the ground. Tom knelt and put his right knee over the man's chest and grabbed his head with both hands

189

pulling it forward and over his chest. The mugger, only semi-conscious from the elbow strike, cried out in pain.

Tom heard his name being screamed. He looked at the man's face between his hands realizing that he was within a few centimetres of breaking the mugger's neck. He let the head slip out of his hands. "Tom!" Nia screamed again. "Enough."

Tom stood. He looked at the two unconscious, broken men lying under the dim streetlight. "Shit," he thought. He knew that his training had taken over. His response had been honed through years of such training in unarmed combat. It had all been a bit of fun in the gym back at base, but it had become all too frighteningly real through too many tours of duty.

"Tom," Nia said. "Let's get the fuck out of here."

"No, I think I should call the police," Tom said still watching the men on the pavement.

"Tom," Nia said as she held Tom close. "It will be complicated. The police are more than likely to arrest you than those two pricks. Let's go. C'mon."

She pulled Tom and they began to move down the street picking up pace. Nia had almost broken into a jog and she reached behind to grab Tom's hand. Tom stretched out his hand to meet hers and then realised he was still holding the mugger's knife. He threw it over the high church wall.

Nia snuggled into Tom as they sat on the Tube train. She rested her head on his shoulder. Tom looked ahead still in a half fugue state. "I'm sorry," he said quietly.

"For what," Nia asked.

"For that. I was… was too much."

Nia reached up and gently touched his face.

"It's the training you see," Tom said looking down at his hands and then to Nia. "Whether it is commanding a troop or individually, you're taught to respond quickly with as extreme a level of violence as you can. It's reflexive."

"Tom," she said sweetly and quietly. "You were protecting me from two men, drugged out of their tiny minds, and one with a knife. You did what you had to do and, and," she paused, "I kind of like the fact that I have a big strong fella who can look after himself."

They were quiet for a moment. They held hands and held each other's gaze as the Tube train gently jostled them together.

"I liked the restaurant," Tom said.

Nia laughed.

"One of my favourites," she added. "But next time we go, we should go during daylight."

They both laughed and Tom kissed Nia softly at first and then, as she responded, more firmly.

Tom and Nia slept late. Nia made brunch with an unaccustomed nervous energy. The BFI event would be a big one for Nia. She had withdrawn, almost as much as it was possible for a constantly working actor, from the public gaze. She seldom went to gala events, award shows, opening nights or premiers. On the rare occasion she did, it was to support one of her friends and, even then, Nia attempted to make herself invisible and usually made a polite and early departure. Somehow, she thought as she sipped coffee at her kitchen table with the BFI's invite propped up in front of her, the lightness and happiness she felt with Tom had inspired her to agree to this one.

Tom joined her in the kitchen with a yawn. She smiled at him. He was wearing one of her large flannel dressing gowns, but it looked more like an embarrassingly tight kimono on him. He poured a coffee, he motioned with the pot to see if Nia needed a refill, she nodded. Tom topped up her mug. "I'm tired," he said with another yawn. "It's the adrenaline you see."

Nia looked at him not quite comprehending, "Adrenaline?"

"Err, the muggers," Tom said as he sat opposite Nia. "The fight. It would have jump-started a flow of adrenaline, the fight or flight response… "

"Well, I'm glad you didn't fly without me."

"But, after a fight, after the danger is quelled, the adrenaline dissipates leaving you wiped out. We had guys over in Afghan and Iraq who would, back at base, crash out for twenty-four hours after a fire fight."

"So, it was the fight then, the adrenaline, and the tiredness?" Nia asked.

"I think so, yes," Tom answered earnestly.

"And not last night's incredible sex then?"

They laughed and Nia reached across the table and

192

entwined her fingers with Tom's.

"Thank you," she said. "And thank you for coming with me tonight."

"Nonsense," Tom responded. "I think it's going to be brilliant, because you're going to be brilliant."

***

Nia was in the master bathroom in front of the dressing table's mirror. She was nervous as she prepared, more anxious than she had been on opening night of all but her first play. Her hair was redder, and she was a couple of pounds lighter, both in preparation for the evening's BFI event. She stepped into a lacy black thong and then fastened a matching strapless bra that was skilfully and carefully engineered to provide enhanced push-up support. She stepped back and observed herself in the mirror. She was going for a bit of a wow factor tonight and it was coming along.

Vampire Moon was a seriously B-grade film, but it had been fun to work on and it had helped Nia's career, although it had deepened her typecasting as a vamp, literally. Nia looked back on the movie fondly as it opened career doors to more auditions, job offers, and an expanded social life. It had been a pivotal moment in her life, a touchpoint that led on to some good things but also some darker times. Looking in the mirror now she couldn't remember whether she had been truly happy when she made the film but she recalled the excitement and the thrill of that time. She smiled at her reflection with the knowledge that she couldn't remember being happier than she was at that moment.

Tom showered and shaved in the guest bathroom and changed into his rented dinner jacket. Nia had taken him to a good theatre costumer and made sure the suit fitted almost as if custom made. He looked at himself in the bathroom's full-length mirror. It reminded him of being in dress uniform. It was a realisation that just a few months prior would have precipitated a wave of nausea. He wasn't too excited about the evening. He had never liked crowds or formal events, but Nia had really wanted him to be with her and he wanted to be with her, wanted to be there for her. He was looking forward to spending the Christmas period with her. Tom went into the study and poured a glass of red wine. He knew that Nia was often invited to grand social events and that she hadn't been to many of them over the past ten years. But this one was special.

Upstairs, Nia slipped on a classic black sleeveless evening dress. It was tight and low cut, accentuating her hips and her cleavage. She dabbed Floris No 89 again, behind her ears and on her cleavage. She added an emerald necklace. It had a certain wow factor appropriate for the evening and for the film. Tom hadn't seen her ensemble yet. Nia came downstairs to the vestibule where Tom waited with coats. She stopped about halfway down the stairs and swayed sultrily from side to side, then turned around, so Tom could take in the full effect.

"Holy fuck," he said. "I think I have a stiffy."

Nia laughed her deep throaty laugh, "That's what I was going for."

"My God, you really do look fabulous, vivacious," Tom added.

"Thank you, I actually feel vivacious."

Chapter Thirteen
London, December 23rd

The British Film Institute Southbank, all big-box glass and steel, was stuck between the concrete brutalism of the Royal Festival Hall and the National Theatre, on, as its name suggested, the south bank of the Thames. Many a tourist would have walked past it on their way to the London Eye. BFI had laid on a car service and Nia and Tom were dropped off right in front of a red carpet in good time for the seven p.m. showing. Tom was surprised by the classic red-carpet entrance and with a respectable crowd and paparazzi.

"It's for the star," Nia whispered. "He became quite big after the film." She turned to Tom and smiled apprehensively. "It's show time."

She felt Tom pull back but held him tightly to her side as she stood on the periphery of the red carpet.

"It's your moment," Tom said. "I'll see you at the door."

"No, Tom, let's do this together."

Tom noticed Nia's smile was strained.

Nia took a deep breath and moved onto the carpet holding Tom's hand.

Tom was in awe of Nia as she worked the red

carpet, posing for photos, chatting with some of her old cast mates. He was amazed at her confidence and her self-possession, her radiating an easy but affected charm. The crowd shouted for selfies, or a direct smile, there were a few wolf whistles. The door was held for her and she waited for Tom now a pace behind her. Tom, rather embarrassed, quickly moved up the carpet to Nia's side. Photos flashed, and they entered the BFI.

Nia and Tom were escorted to the theatre's red seats. Tom relaxed when the theatre lights dimmed. A single spotlight focused on a rather academic looking academic who took to the stage to introduce the film. Nia reached over the armrest, found, and then held Tom's hand. She remembered the flight from Montreal and how far they had come since then, how much they had changed. Tom enjoyed the film, even though he had just watched it; it was more vibrant and visceral on the big screen. He was pleased for Nia as the audience 'ohhed' and 'ahhed' appreciatively. She squeezed his hand hard when her nude scene began.

"Love those giant, perky boobs," he whispered into her ear.

She squeezed his hand again and he squeezed back.

After the film's credits had rolled and the theatre's lights returned, Nia along with four other members of cast and crew took to the stage for a Q and A session. They were seated on comfy chairs around a low table. Generously filled wine glasses were placed on the table. The academic who now served as the Q&A moderator

197

had clearly developed a bit of a crush on Nia and directed the majority of questions to her. Tom thought Nia looked simply stunning sitting up the stage. He could tell from her accent that she was excited and the more excited she became, the more Welsh she sounded. Nia enjoyed the experience, she felt Tom's support from the seats, and noticed his big grin, she felt freed somehow and was animated, funny, and charming and less guarded than usual. The crowd responded approvingly. Nia got a standing ovation when she left the stage.

Tom re-joined Nia for drinks in the spacious private bar artfully decorated for Christmas. The bar was crowded with the guests and patrons. Jane emerged from the crowd and grabbed Nia by the elbow and pulled her along as she worked the crowd of old acquaintances and industry professionals. There was lots of fake cheek kissing and loud 'dahlings'. Tom instinctively stepped back to the edge of the room where he had sightlines to areas of ingress and egress and he felt more comfortable in a position where he could have eyes on the crowd. Nia's friend, Constance, came and stood next to him. She was already buzzed.

"Not comfortable Tom?" she asked with a slight slur.

"No, I'm fine. Enjoying the moment," he smiled. "Nia's moment."

Constance leant into Tom.

"Nia's looking really good, tonight," she said. "I

think you're good for her."

He nodded not sure what other response to make.

"You know that she's been hurt badly, that we all love her and want to protect her, right?" Constance asked.

Tom nodded slightly. "Aren't they the same, love and protection?" he asked.

Constance swayed a little.

"Yes," she answered.

"Then I'd like to try to protect her too," Tom said.

Nia joined them before Constance could respond. Nia grabbed Tom by the hand and held it down at her side. Constance excused herself to step outside for a smoke.

"Tom, come and meet my oldest friend, Jane," Nia said.

As Tom and Nia made their way through the crowd, an actor came up to Nia and gave her an intimate hug and kissed her full on the lips.

"Nia darling, so nice to see you out and about. We must catch up some time," he held her hands and stepped back clearly appraising her. "Fabulous dress and that body, you've been working out. Someone's a lucky guy."

He winked at Tom, and with another kiss on Nia's lips, he was gone, absorbed into the adjacent crowd. Nia looked at Tom nervously, "Don't worry," she whispered in his ear. "He's gay."

"Oh, really? Figured that," Tom said.

Nia finally joined Jane again. Jane was wearing a dinner jacket with a white silk scarf and white owl glasses.

"Nia darling, the room's abuzz. You've been brilliant, you clever girl," Jane greeted her with a real kiss on the cheek. "And, you look absolutely fucking fabulous."

Jane turned to Tom. Nia introduced them.

Jane smiled at Tom, "Nice to meet you. Have heard a good bit about you, Major Price. Nia tells me that you are good for her and I must say she has been glowing since she met you."

Tom wasn't sure what to say so responded with a simple, "Thank you".

"Nia's one of my closest friends," said Jane whose demeanour had become matronly. "And if you ever hurt her, I will have your balls." She smiled with phoney sweetness.

"She's just joking," Nia said.

"No, I'm not," Jane responded without the smile.

"In that case then, I will endeavour to keep my balls out of your hands," Tom said.

Jane laughed, "You do that young man. You just do that."

Jane turned to Nia, who was still slightly in shock, "Nia, there's someone here I'd like you to meet. They were very impressed with your performance tonight..." Jane grabbed Nia by the hand and moved her on to another group.

Tom stood there alone with a glass of indifferent champagne in his hand. He watched as people and groups moved and interchanged like dance partners. Tom caught Constance's eye in another group clustered around a high table. There was Orla with her arm around an unnaturally pale, tall, thin woman in a slinky dress that purposefully exposed a significant amount of side boob. Talking to the side-boobed woman was a face he half recognised. He knew he had seen the face before and trolled his memory for context. When no context emerged, he moved close to Constance and gestured for her to join him. When he felt they were out of earshot of Orla's group, he subtly nodded to the mysterious man and asked Constance whether she knew him. Constance stared at the man for a moment, then told Tom that she didn't recognise him. Seeing the concern on Tom's face, Constance said she would find out. She artfully moved towards a waiter with a tray of drinks and was soon absorbed into the group where Tom's man stood. Tom grabbed a fresh champagne from the itinerant waiter and watched as Constance chatted with Orla, Orla's companion, and then exchange a few words and a polite smile with the mysterious man. Tom made some painful small talk with a Czech art director while waiting for Constance to circle back. Tom excused himself from the art director as Constance grabbed him by the hand and moved him away from the mingling patrons.

"He's Russian, from their embassy," she said.

She noticed Tom's face change immediately. A

photofit of a memory took shape in Tom's mind's eye.

"Some kind of cultural attaché at the embassy here," Constance continued. "Name of Kamenev. Looks like he's had some facial injuries, burns perhaps."

"Fuck me," Tom said to no one.

"Do you know him?" Constance asked.

"I'm not sure," Tom answered honestly. Images of faces flashed through his mind like business cards in a Roladex. The name Zalkind screamed in his head. The Mi-17 helicopter crash must have been for real and Zalkind must have survived it with some injuries. A new name, new face, a new role but same evil bastard. Kamenev/Zalkind, as if suddenly aware of Tom's psychic hatred, looked across the groups into Tom's eyes. Tom noticed a cloud of concern cross the Russian's face.

Constance moved on to another circle of loud and happy people. Tom felt himself move as if electrically charged to the very periphery of the room. He didn't notice Nia as she joined him, but she sensed his apprehension.

"What's wrong?" Nia asked.

Tom nodded towards Kamenev still ensconced in Orla's group.

"I think it's someone from my past," Tom said.

Nia laughed falsely, "All these people are from my past."

Tom didn't laugh.

"Oh. Military past?" she asked, "Bad?" and Tom

nodded.

A few high tables away, Kamenev graciously made excuses and stepped away from his group. He took one last long look across the room at Tom trying to lock his facial features into his own memory. He didn't recognise him, but he was concerned. The British guy had a military bearing, had taken up tactical positioning to watch events in the bar, and had a limp possibly from military action. The Brit had no field craft, so he wasn't an intelligence operative but Kamenev was concerned enough to leave the event earlier than he had originally planned.

Jane approached Nia and Tom and pulled Nia away to be interviewed by a young, starry eyed reporter from the *Evening Standard*. Tom left the event room, took some stairs down and stepped into the utility bowels of the BFI. He found a small blocked corridor that he felt was relatively secure and called Jacques Gagnon. Gagnon answered on the fifth ring.

"Tom, not that I'm not pleased to receive a call from you, bro, but it's five p.m. the day before Christmas Eve. Tomorrow's a holiday here and I'm buried in paperwork trying to clear my desk. And, there's an office party to prepare for. Can we chat after Christmas?"

"Sorry Jacques mate, it is important. I think Zalkind's alive. He's calling himself Kamenev working out of the Russian Embassy here in London as a cultural attaché, probably cover for intelligence."

There was silence, Tom heard Gagnon's heavy breathing.

"Are you sure?" asked Gagnon. "You're not at some party pissed out of your mind?"

"Not pissed and not one hundred per cent sure. But, Jacques, I'm pretty certain. He's had some facial surgery. My friend said it looked like the type someone would have to cover burns rather than anything cosmetic. So, yeah, pretty sure it's him."

"Shit. Fuck. Okay. I'll do some digging here to see if we have any records we could piece together. I'll also see if your MI5 and MI6 can shed any light on this. My office party can wait while I try to do the digging but don't you do fucking anything, okay?"

Tom agreed and hung up. Gagnon put down his phone, opened a laptop and began searching for flights to Heathrow.

Tom felt lighter when he returned to the event room and its bar. It was Gagnon's problem now. Nia was finishing up with the interview. She called Tom over and held his hand again. The reporter asked who the handsome man was, Nia answered simply, "My fella." Tom liked the sound of it.

Nia whispered to Tom that she wanted to get her handsome fella home. Their sense of urgency to get coats and car service was only obvious to themselves. They dropped coats as soon as they entered Nia's house. Tom undid his bow tie and took off his jacket. He expected an almost feverish climb up the stairs to the bedroom. Instead, Nia led him up to the second floor and into the study. He took off his cummerbund as she closed the curtains. Nia lit the fireplace, dimmed lights, and poured two glasses of port. They clinked glasses. She took a gulp of her port then put down her glass and turned her back to him. She ran her hands through her hair, pulling it up as if in a makeshift bun. She lowered her head coquettishly. Tom downed his port and put his glass down next to hers. He moved behind her and brushed her exposed neck gently with his lips. Her skin goose bumped to his touch. He nuzzled into her neck enjoying the scent of her perfume and desire.

Tom began to unzip her dress. Slowly until there was enough slack to gently ease the dress off her shoulders. He kissed her shoulders from her neck to her arms. Kissing the ball of her shoulder he could see her face in profile, her eyes were closed, and her lips were slightly parted. He returned to her dress, zipping it down to her lower back. Nia moved her arms, so the dress slipped off and over her breasts. Tom kissed the hollow where Nia's back ran down to the band of her lacy black thong. Nia pursed her lips and involuntarily moaned ever so slightly. Nia's moan excited Tom and he pulled off his shirt and stepped out of his trousers. Nia began to breathe more quickly. He ran his hand softly down her spine and then out over her hips and around and down her buttocks. He unzipped the dress and it slipped over her hips and down to the floor. Nia stepped elegantly out of it. She remained with her front to the fireplace, her light olive skin glowing in the reflection of the fire's light and heat.

Tom ran his hands over her exposed buttock cheeks and back over her hips and then up her back moving slowly to her front and up to her breasts. He unlatched her bra and cupped her breasts from behind. Her nipples were hard under his palms. He removed his pants and then moved his hands gently down her body to her hips until his fingers slipped inside the thong's waistband. He gently pulled the thong down. Nia stepped out of the thong as it lay on the floor. Tom moved close in behind her and embraced her. He rested his linked hands on her tummy, and she reached down and pulled a hand up to her mouth. She kissed his hand and gently bit his fingers. Tom's other hand gently stroked her. Nia felt his erection against her buttocks. She held Tom's hands as she knelt down, and he followed behind her. She let go of his hands and leant forward allowing Tom to enter her.

Across the city, Kamenev sat at his desk in his embassy office running through the SVR, FSB, and GRU's picture libraries of Western intelligence and military personnel. He stared at pictures of face after face, "Just who the hell are you?" he said to himself.

***

206

Afghanistan, Bagram. Nine Years Earlier

The RAF Merlin helicopter's cargo bay was full of a variety of service men and women. Captain Tom Price felt like a sardine jammed into the cargo hold alongside twenty other personnel most of whom wore or carried full equipment. Like Price, most of the personnel were on their way to Bagram Air Base and, like Price, most were not fond of the older Merlin's lack of ballistic armour. Price didn't like helicopters. He was heading to Bagram for a series of intelligence briefings. His experience and insight were being sought for he had been in the country for a hell of a tour; encountering IEDs, suicide bombers, Taliban night attacks, al-Qaeda day attacks, vice versa, even hand to hand fighting where he had ordered his men to fix bayonets.

The Merlin flew low and fast over the surrounding mountains and approached the massive, former Soviet military base in a sharp arc. Bagram was now home to nearly sixty thousand allied service personnel including, at one time, Prince Harry. Price looked down at the sprawling base of hangers, control towers, an ugly mass of concrete walls and barriers, temporary huts, shipping containers, sandbags, and razor wire along with the usual detritus of large military establishments. The Merlin landed in a sandstorm of its own making and Price stepped off the helicopter's rear ramp into searing dry heat. The airbase was a hive of activity; fast jets were taking off the runway, Hercules and Globemaster transport aircraft were lined up like buses, and helicopters; Chinooks, Blackhawks, and evil looking Apache gunships, constantly buzzed through the airspace. Although in an active war zone, the base itself was relatively safe but Price kept his helmet close in case of enemy mortar or rocket attacks. Price was greeted by a coterie of British and American staff officers for an informal lunch at the base's Pizza Hut. The incongruity of the situation appeared to strike only Price.

Price attended an afternoon briefing on the increase in IED activity. The brief, led by a Brit intelligence staff officer, strongly suggested that the increase in the amount and quality of explosives was sourced from Russia. The Russian state intelligence agency, FSB, and military intelligence, GRU, still had contacts in Afghanistan and liked nothing more than to tie a whole series of NATO armies down in a war that was unwinnable. The Russians, as the Soviets, had experienced their own long and bitter struggles in Afghanistan and still had an intimate understanding of how to conduct operations there. They still maintained contacts and influence.

The briefing continued and the intelligence office projected an image of a face on to the room's small screen; GRU major, full uniform, left breast full of medals. The GRU was run, like the FSB, on a volatile mixture of ideology and paranoia.

"This," the briefing officer stated, "is Feodor Zalkind, currently attached to the Embassy of the

Russian Federation, Kabul. Some of you who have spent time in Kabul may have encountered him; charming man, speaks English perfectly, he's cultured and witty but a complete bastard. It is strongly suggested that he is playing a significant role in the northern arms trade and supporting AQ and Taliban insurgents. It's rumoured that he pays a bounty for dead coalition forces."

Price stared into the face on the screen, bastard, he thought. The briefing officer continued.

"If any of you have lost men or women to IEDs made with Soviet era RGO grenade or MON-50 mine components, this is probably the supplier. As most of you know, we can't touch him in Kabul or anywhere else when he's on official embassy duties. But chaps, if you ever encounter him in country, do us all a favour and simply slot the bastard."

The audience laughed politely. Price stared at the slide, committing the facial features he saw there to memory, determined never to forget that face.

Chapter Fourteen
Periwinkle, Christmas

The Periwinkle was moored up in the Llangollen narrowboat basin. Tom and Nia arrived at the boat around dinner time on Christmas Eve. They had driven up from London in the Land Rover only making a quick stop at the farm to pick up Jack and confirm Boxing Day arrangements with Rachel. Tom and Nia were both tired. Upon entering the Periwinkle, Tom turned on the lights of a small Christmas tree in the front cabin and lit the Morso stove while Nia unpacked groceries. Jack curled up on a chair, watching.

Nia brought Tom a glass of red wine and as he sat in the lounge's other chair, she sat in his lap. She took a sip of her wine.

"Thank you, Tom," she said.

"You're welcome, but what for?"

"For last night. It meant a lot to me that you came to the BFI event. I really had a good time and that was because of you. And for this." Nia motioned to the little scene in the cabin.

"Nia, there's no need to thank me for anything. Really, I should be thanking you for the last five weeks," Tom added. "They have been the happiest of my life."

Nia guffawed, then kissed Tom with wine wet lips, "Fuck, Tom," she said. "It's the bloody same for me."

The next morning, Christmas Day, was cold, wet, and windy. The Periwinkle rocked gently at its mooring.

Nia made coffee as Tom scrambled eggs. They kept brushing against each other as they worked side by side in the small galley until Nia wrapped her arms around Tom from behind, "Hmmmm," she said. "How do you always smell so…?"

"Eggy?"

"No, silly. So, warm and masculine."

"Because it's Christmas," Tom said.

"And, I can't imagine a nicer Christmas than with you here," Nia laughed, but then became serious.

"My Christmases growing up were usually pretty rubbish. So, I've never been one of those people who go nuts for Christmas. If I'm not working, I usually have a quiet day by myself with some good food, a good book, a bit of telly. Or, maybe dinner with Amanda and Penny or Ben. But it's never felt special. Just dinner with friends really. But today, but today is… different, it really feels like… like Christmas."

Tom grinned. He faced Nia and held her face gently in his hands and kissed her.

After breakfast, Tom and Nia walked into the village and attended Christmas Day services at the local parish church. Neither were regular church goers, usually only attending for weddings and funerals, but they both wanted a shared experience that was new for them as a couple. They sat, stood, and knelt when they were supposed to, they sang carols, chatted with some locals, and shook hands with the vicar at the end of the service. They held hands as they walked back to the boat through misty rain.

The Periwinkle's oven couldn't handle a Christmas turkey, so Tom had prepared two plump chicken breasts with all the traditional trimmings. They ate heartily, Nia stating that church must have made her hungry. "Let's have coffee in the lounge," Nia said. "And open presents."

Six wrapped gifts nestled under the small Christmas tree. Two each and two for Jack. Nia's gifts for Tom were wrapped exquisitely and expensively. She wanted him to open her presents first. Nia had commissioned a highly regarded watercolour artist to paint the Periwinkle crossing the Pontcysyllte aqueduct. She had paid a premium to have it ready and framed in time for Christmas. Tom was touched.

"It's beautiful," he said. "It deserves to go in a gallery but I'm going to hang it here in the cabin."

"I'm so pleased you like it. I had the artist make a copy that's going on my study wall, if that's okay with you?"

"Of course it is," Tom answered. "I love that you enjoy the Periwinkle and the canals. There's no way my gift can compare but, please, do go ahead and open your present."

Nia did so. Tom had bought her a Barbour waxed jacket. "Perfect for rainy days on the canal," he announced with the subtext clear.

They exchanged and unwrapped the books; a first edition of Ian Fleming's 'On Her Majesty's Secret Service' for Tom and Melvyn Bragg's Richard Burton biography for Nia. They opened Jack's presents for her.

They took Jack for an early evening walk along the towpath and Nia wore her new Barbour. They were alone on their cold and dark walk but were welcomed back to the narrowboat basin by the warm lights of the Periwinkle. Back on the boat, they settled in with generous glasses of port to watch a Christmas film on the cabin's small TV. Nia excused herself momentarily only to return to the lounge wearing her new coat.

"I love it Tom," She said. "It really is perfect."

"I'm glad you like it," Tom said.

Nia unzipped the coat, she was naked underneath it.

"Wow," Tom said. "Now, that's a Christmas present."

In bed, in that moment just as sleep embraced them, Nia and Tom, independently, thought themselves that it had been the best of Christmas days.

***

Rachel's Farm, Boxing Day

Rachel had sent the boys to finish the washing up and she and Nia settled into the farm's sitting room. She poured herself and Nia brandies as they sat down in front of the lounge's wide log fire. Jack, as was usual, curled up on the fireplace rug. Nia asked Rachel about the farm. It had originally been Owain's, Rachel told her, but she and Tom had bought additional land to make it a true family affair. Owain was a careful and proficient farmer so everyone's investment was paying off.

"So, Tom's a landowner?" Nia joked.

"In a way, yes," Rachel noted. "He owns about half of the farm."

Rachel watched Nia for a moment.

"Tom's not landed gentry but he's okay financially," Rachel said. "His army salary was decent, and his separation pay, kind of a pension, is healthy. Plus," she smiled, "he has hardly spent any money since his divorce, he's got solid savings, and he gets some income from his writing. And, as you know, he lives rather frugally."

Nia nodded although she wasn't sure what to feel… grateful for Rachel's efforts to, what? Make it clear that Tom wasn't a gold digger? She realised that some of her friends had hinted she needed to find out this exact information, but she was perturbed to think that Rachel thought Nia would be concerned about such financial issues. Nia swirled her brandy in its glass,

214

contemplating what to say.

"Rachel," Nia began and looked into Rachel's eyes. "Thanks for letting me know but please understand that I have no worries about Tom and money."

Rachel sensed Nia's discomfort.

"Look, Nia," Rachel said with a smile. "I'm sorry, I didn't mean to bring up any difficult subjects. And I certainly didn't mean to cast aspersions on you or Tom, far from it. It's partly because for most of my working life I was an accountant. I always see things in terms of assets, profits, and losses. Forgive me."

Nia smiled, making it obvious that the issue was already forgotten. Both women took sips of their brandies.

"Why did you leave your career?" Nia asked.

"I met Owain and loved the idea of moving to the country. I was so tired of the big job, big city rat race. Tired of the bloody heels and hose, of being a smart woman in a male dominated field. It was wearing to always have to work twice as hard for half the respect."

Nia nodded sympathetically and Rachel asked Nia about her encounters with sexism in the media industry. Nia laughed and said the whole industry is based on sexism. She recounted a story of an early visit to Hollywood. She had made several appearances on TV programmes and had been in a couple of British films where she had generated some positive buzz and recognition for her work. A US agent had seen *Vampire Moon*, which had picked up a small cult audience in the

US and had invited her to Los Angles for a business meeting. Nia had been young and excited, and the American agent was suave and smooth talking. He had welcomed Nia into his office with an incredible view of downtown Los Angeles through a panoramic window. The office was huge, and he showed Nia to a long and wide leather sofa next to two matching chairs around a low steel and glass coffee table. The agent got her a bottle of water and sat down, directly next to her.

The agent was charming, Nia continued with her story. The agent made her comfortable; he asked about her family, her training, her plans and dreams for her career. The more the agent talked the more Nia relaxed. Nia told Rachel that she felt herself settling into the agent's large sofa while he continued to ask her, about the roles she thought she would like to play. Then he asked her if she would continue to, as was obvious in *Vampire Moon*, feel comfortable with nude scenes. Nia said that with the right script, cast and crew that she didn't have a problem with nudity. Then the agent leant over and squeezed both of her breasts with his two hands almost as if he was honking horns. They're real, he had stated with evident surprise. Of course, they are Nia responded as she stood up and punched the agent in the nose. She flew home the next day.

Rachel laughed. "Nia Williams, I really like you," she said.

"I bet you say that to all Tom's women," Nia said with a cheeky grin. She felt that she and Rachel were really bonding.

"No," Rachel answered seriously. "No, not at all. I didn't even like his wife. Tom couldn't see her for what she was, bless him. Too nice again. It was a complete disaster. It was always going to be rubbish. I was so glad they didn't have a child together."

The words, even in a context beyond her, cut Nia. Rachel noticed the change in Nia's expression and the stiffening of her body language.

"Oh Nia," Rachel said. "I think I've said something hurtful."

"No," Nia stammered. "No, not really, but… yes in a strange way."

Rachel leant over and held Nia's hand, "Would you like to tell me about it?"

Nia didn't know why but she did want to tell Rachel.

"When I was married, for the second time," Nia began, "I became pregnant, accidently. I wasn't exactly happy about it, it wasn't a good time at all, but I decided to go ahead with it. My husband, the Goldenboy, was livid that I had let myself get pregnant. Like it was all my fault. He was worried that it would stymie our careers, especially his, and he was concerned about what it would do to my body, and so he gave me an ultimatum, the baby or him."

"What a wanker," Rachel said as she tried to remember tabloid stories about Nia and Goldenboy. She thought she remembered, but asked, "What did you do?"

Nia looked into the fire, "I tried to persuade him that we could make it work. I tried and tried and tried," Rachel noticed a tear run down Nia's cheek as she spoke, it shone in the firelight. "But he was adamant. I told him that I wanted to keep it, that we could be a family. He didn't want a family. He gave me an ultimatum really. Then he just walked away from me, from our baby."

"Oh Nia, I'm so sorry."

"I was so scared. My childhood had been absolutely shit, and I was worried that bad parenting could be genetic or hereditary or something. But then something clicked. I was so happy. I planned a new life and then, and then…" Nia began crying. Rachel moved over and hugged her. "My baby died. I, I felt as if I'd lost everything. I felt it was my fault too."

Nia hugged Rachel back, hard. She shook and sobbed until Rachel felt the dampness of Nia's tears wicking through her shirt. "Nia, Nia, Nia," Rachel whispered while she stroked Nia's hair with her hand. Nia looked into Rachel's eyes silently thanking her for precipitating a little catharsis.

"I haven't told Tom about any of this, haven't really told anybody."

"Oh Nia. You should tell Tom," Rachel said. "If he's going to be a part of your future, he needs to be part of your past too."

"Do you really think so?"

"Absolutely," Rachel replied.

"What about his pain?"

"This is different. Nia, I've known him all his life, and you are the best thing that has ever happened to him."

Nia wiped her tears and blew her nose. She smiled at Rachel.

"Did you try to have children after?" Rachel asked.

Nia was caught off guard by the question.

"Errr, no. There was no one in my life I felt that could inspire or even share that experience. Rachel, I've been hurting since I lost the baby. I felt I couldn't love anything again, that I couldn't even love myself after what happened."

"I'm so sorry. You deserve to be loved and to love, Nia. We all do," Rachel offered.

"I," Nia hesitated, "I think I am now."

"You are, sweetie. Still too early for future plans?" Rachel asked.

Rachel's bluntness was surprising to Nia, forcing her to go to thoughts she was burying.

"I think we're both taking it day to day. Seeing how it plays out," Nia said a little defensively.

"You know that there's still time, Nia?"

Nia was surprised. "Time for what?" she hesitantly asked.

"You're what now, early forties? There's still time for the whole relationship thing, picket fence, garden all that,"

"Well, I kind of have that now."

"Do you think you'd ever want children? There's still time for that too."

Nia was stunned by what she perceived as Rachel's insensitivity. It stung and hurt her especially after Nia had considered she had shared a moment of deep intimacy, of her exposing her deepest most vulnerable secret to Tom's sister. Rachel smiled reassuringly and squeezed Nia's shoulder as she stood and proceeded to clear away the tea service. Nia heard an outside door open a room away and heard the happy chatter of Owain and Tom's return. She stood and wiped her eyes again. "Fuck," she thought. "I do have time." But she also knew that there wasn't a lot of time, her biological window was shutting slowly but inexorably, but there was time. And, now, perhaps, just perhaps, there was a man. A man with kind eyes and, more importantly, a kind and open heart. Would he want children? Her mind went to so many different places, "He was nice to the mum with the toddler at the airport," she thought. "But he's never mentioned kids — but then why would he? And, fuck, he lives on a tiny boat."

Tom entered the room, still wearing the purple paper crown from his Christmas cracker, and went over and hugged Nia. He saw her eyes were red and puffy.

"Oh God," he said, "what did Rachel say now?"

Nia smiled and shook her head slightly and Tom understood that it was something that Nia didn't want to talk about. Nia smiled and squeezed his hand and changed the subject.

Later, as they prepared for bed in the room that was considered Tom's farmhouse bedroom, Nia explained that she had been momentarily upset over the discussion with Rachel over finances. Tom apologized, but, with a smile, explained that Nia didn't have to ever worry about him being a gold digger. As they settled into the comfort and warmth of the moment before sleep, Nia reached her hand down her body to her tummy. She let it rest there for a moment before turning to spoon Tom. She felt Tom's body relax into sleep as she attempted to banish thoughts of motherhood from her consciousness. She lay awake trying to think of other things. Tom twitched next to her. Nia had become accustomed to Tom's occasional physical and audible manifestations of his dreaming. He never remembered his dreams, but Nia could sense the way Tom would tense in the throes of a dream that he was probably back in Iraq or Afghanistan. Tonight, unownable to Nia, he was in Afghanistan, in theatre.

***

Afghanistan, Eight Years Previously

Captain Tom Price had been seconded to a small, tough detachment of Canadian special forces serving deep on the northern border. There had been rumours of arms for drugs transfers with the arms coming from Uzbekistan to be traded for the Taliban's raw opium. Opium bound for the Russian market. After a number of missions that came to naught, the group had received actionable intelligence and found themselves observing a small village at the mouth of a valley trailhead that wound its way up and through the mountains. The Canadians were tired, it had been a long slog through difficult terrain to get to this point and they were nervous, not quite trusting the intelligence they received from local friendlies.

The Canadian commander, Captain Jacques Gagnon, a tough Quebecer with the longest red beard Price had ever seen, was observing the village through night vision binoculars. He pointed towards the village and Price, who was lying prone next to him, focused his own optics. Through the green haze, Price could see a small group of armed locals emerge from the village and move towards a dusty field. Gagnon radioed his men who had been sent to flank the village. Unseen by Gagnon, Price, and the Taliban, the Canadian soldiers began to move towards the field. Through his night vision binoculars, Price saw the Taliban stop. They all turned to face north.

"Something's coming from the mountains," he told Gagnon.

They heard it before they could see it.

"A chopper," said Gagnon.

The Russian Mi-17 transport helicopter swooped down out of the valley at a nearly impossible angle just a few feet above the ground. Incredible manoeuvres all the more impressive in the dark without lights.

"Fucking Russians," Gagnon exclaimed.

The Mi-17 came to a perfect landing in the dry field. Both Price and Gagnon, having spent quite a bit of time in helicopters and hating them, recognised a skilled pilot at work.

"That's not the first time he's done that," Price said.

He began taking pictures of the events through his binoculars.

On the ground, the helicopter's crew were quickly conducting business with the Taliban. Price was able to focus on what looked like the Russian commander. He recognized the face from the Bagram briefing.

"Fuck," he said. "It's Zalkind."

Feodor Zalkind, sometime trade attaché at the Russian Embassy in Kabul. Sometime foreign service diplomat, but always full time GRU intelligence officer. The rumours of him supplying explosives for Taliban and al-Qaeda IEDs were now fact. The Russians liked nothing more than to make things difficult for the Western militaries.

"High priority target," Price noted.

"Let's slot the fucker," Gagnon said.

Down below them in the field, a Taliban fighter reacted as if he heard something. He dropped what he was carrying to the Mi-17 and unslung his AK. Price could hear shouting before the assault rifles bloomed fire and death. Tracer fire leapt across the field and valley side and then, suddenly the deep darkness was further rift by flares, the Canadians were caught in the open with little cover. A heavy machine gun from the Mi-17 opened up and rocket propelled grenades snaked from the field and the village to where Gagnon and Price knew their comrades were.

Gagnon radioed for air support while Price opened up with his own rifle trying to give the Canadians in the field some covering fire. The Canadians' chatter through Price's earpiece was loud and indistinct. Then, the helicopter's heavy machine gun swung towards him and Gagnon and bullets raked across the berm they had taken cover behind. It moved on as suppressing fire came from one of the Canadian groups on the ground. Back on the berm, Price sighted on Zalkind as the Russian was entering the Mi-17. He fired, saw the Russian duck, and saw a bullet hole emerge in the helicopter's aluminium skin. Zalkind closed the cabin door and the helicopter began to elevate. Price fired more times seeing his bullets strike the Mi-17 but to no serious effect. The helicopter continued to rise while its cargo door machine gunner laid down a constant stream of fire towards the dug-in Canadians. Price, angry and frustrated that he had missed Zalkind, fired at the machine gunner.

More Taliban emerged from the village adding to the suppressing fire. Gagnon ordered his men to fall back while the vicious fire fight continued. Price saw an isolated group of Canadians about to be outflanked and he ran down the berm to where he could see the nearest group of friendlies. He continued to fire his rifle, swapping magazines on the run. He slid into the shallow depression where the four Canadian troopers were lying. Two fully engaged with the enemy, one injured but alert, while the other soldier lay on his back, eyes fully wide but looking unresponsive. There was a lot of blood.

Taliban fighters approached through the Canadians' fire. Price aimed his rifle and fired. Nothing happened. He was out of ammo. He reached down to his holster and drew his Sig Sauer side arm. He flicked the safety catch off just in time to fire twice at the nearest Taliban fighter. Price saw his bullets strike and the Afghan crumpled. The Canadians drove off the other Taliban.

Price holstered his pistol and reloaded his rifle.

"Give me all the suppressing fire you can then fall back to the berm," he shouted. He grabbed the unresponsive soldier, threw him over his shoulder, and ran back for the berm. Puffs of dirt arose around his feet like deadly weeds. He zigged and zagged. He could see Gagnon firing and ran for him. He dropped the wounded soldier and ran back, zagging and zigging, for the second injured man. The Canadians in the depression gave him enough time to hoist the soldier over his shoulder and they joined him on the run back to the berm. Then Price heard jet engines roaring from the south and a couple of US Marine Harriers appeared. The Harriers' cannon and missiles drove the Taliban back to the village and the Canadians extricated themselves. They retreated to the prearranged emergency egress point carrying their wounded, and their dead, with them.

Gagnon and Price made official after-action reports. They had the photographic evidence that Zalkind was trading drugs for guns. Their superiors noted that the Russians reported a Mi-17, on a diplomatic mission, had gone down killing all on board, including one of their Kabul based attachés. They weren't willing to pursue the international incident any further. Neither Gagnon nor Price believed any of it.

Later, over beers at Bagram, Gagnon told Tom that if he ever bumped into Zalkind again he'd kill him to avenge the death of his troopers.

***

Kensington, London, Russian Embassy. Present Day
The former Major Zalkind, now Colonel Kamenev, was frustrated with his inability to find the face from the BFI. He had engaged a skilled SRV analyst to help try to place the Brit. They searched again through their photo file of Western intelligence and military agencies; individual faces, glossy eight by tens, photofits, faces in crowds at meetings and public occasions. None appeared to match his memory. Kamenev suggested the analyst search for friends and acquaintances of a British actor, Nia Williams. She had stuck in his memory from her role in the vampire movie which had been the

atrocious film's highpoint and from her presence at the BFI, all thick dark hair and impressive cleavage.

The next morning, Kamenev, bleary eyed, returned to the embassy after only a couple of hours' rest. Coffee in hand, he went to the analyst's station and was greeted with a big toothy grin, "I think I've found him, sir." Kamenev expected some computer photofit image and was surprised when the analyst, brought up the online morning edition of one of London's free newspapers. He enlarged a photo.

"Is this the man you are after?" the analyst, a studious young man from Irkutsk, asked.

Kamenev sat at the analyst's chair. There was Nia, big smile, camera flash reflecting off her emerald necklace and there behind her, nervous grin, was the Brit.

"Yes. That's him," Kamenev said. He turned to the analyst, "Well done, son."

Kamenev returned to the computer. And read the caption:

"Nia Williams, the Welsh Spitfire, wows at the BFI. Nia Williams, 44, made a rare red-carpet appearance at last night's BFI Southbank event. Nia, who just returned from filming in Canada attended with a new man in her life, Tom Price…"

The Russian zoomed in on the photo so that Tom's face enlarged. "Tom Price, my friend, who the devil, are you?" Kamenev said in public school English. He turned to the analyst. "Print that out," he ordered in Russian.

Kamenev made his way to the SVR Rezident's office. The Rezident was a grizzled veteran of the intelligence game. A former KGB officer, he was a short timer now on a glide path to a welcome retirement. He had been given the London Rezident's chair as a nod of recognition to his devoted service to the state. Service that began when Russia's intelligence agency had different initials, was all powerful, and all brutal. He missed the prestige and fear that the old agency had engendered, but he didn't miss the domestic and international brutality, he had never fully embraced the iron fist of state security. He recognised that the old violence and the cruelty had begun creeping back into Russian domestic politics and its foreign relations. He didn't like it and, indeed, it now confronted him in the seat across his desk as he leant back in his chair and listened to Kamenev's story. He knew Kamenev and Zalkind were one and the same. He was aware of Kamenev's past and knew that the FSB man was rapaciously ambitious. He also knew that Kamenev and his various teams of thugs had put men in the ground from Afghanistan to Chechnya, Syria to Istanbul, and from Sweden to England's Home Counties.

The Rezident had initially objected to Kamenev's posting as he objected to the mission and the man. He also hated the power shift in Moscow that resulted in the expansion of the FSB's power and operating authority at the expense of his SVR. The cagey old Rezident thought it incredibly arrogant and dangerous that Moscow would have ordered another direct action against a Russian dissident living in the UK. FSB arrogance. Madness, he thought, to do this so soon after the attempt on Sergei Skripal, the Russian double agent who had worked for MI6. Skripal and his daughter had survived being poisoned by a nerve agent, but an innocent English bystander was killed, and the dirty operation was exposed to the world's press and opprobrium. Yet the attack on Skripal, the Rezident recalled, had instilled a heightened level of fear among the émigré opponents of the Kremlin. Many had gone silent, others went deeper underground, a few brave souls maintained their vocal opposition of Putin and the Kremlin. Kamenev was looking to quiet such voices.

The Rezident was secretly relieved to hear Kamenev's report about being recognised at the BFI event believing, now, that it would end the scheme to kidnap or kill Daria Kirov, the influential émigré Russian journalist and activist. He was convinced that the plan was at an end. He looked at Kamenev smugly.

"So, what would you recommend as a course of action?" he asked.

"I'd like to find out more about this Tom Price. If he is someone from my past, my mission here could be jeopardised," Kamenev said. "I'd like to put the actress under surveillance and, when Price shows up to see her, put him under surveillance until we know who and what he is. I don't want anything to derail my task here. If he could cause a problem, then I propose that he be... removed from the equation."

"Is it, is he, that important?" the Rezident asked.

"It is that important," Kamenev replied brusquely.

The SVR man rubbed his chin; he had shaved poorly that morning. He couldn't disguise his apprehension.

"Okay, I can make a surveillance team available... but just for surveillance. Time and resources, being what they are, means I can't do any more than that."

"Thank you," Kamenev said almost with a sneer. "And if I require more than a bunch of watchers? If I need help... persuading Mr Price?"

The Rezident calmly leant over his desk and put his hands together almost in prayer.

"Colonel Kamenev, after the Skripal fuck up, the UK now watches our every move. Do you know that there are over half a million CCTV cameras in this city? We can't move without MI5 or Special Branch following us. So, there will be no... extra curricula activities in this case unless I explicitly say so, is that understood? Furthermore, I am going to call Moscow with my recommendation that the mission be cancelled or at least postponed."

Kamenev sulked. "Yes," and, after a pause, "sir. That is understood. I'll note in my report that SVR offered limited assistance in a matter that could be of utmost importance for state security."

The old SVR man again leant back in his chair and a smile cracked his face. "I will also be recommending that Moscow recall you for impertinence and behaving like a jackass with the English bourgeois elite."

Kamenev stood, "You do that, you old fool. I think you'll find that I have more friends in Moscow and at the Kremlin, than you could possibly imagine."

"Kamenev, I'm the Rezident here. Checkmate. Now fuck off… but do keep me appraised."

Kamenev left the office clearly in a huff. The SVR man got up stiffly from his desk and moved to the window and his view of London. He liked the city, he liked the people, he liked the food and drink and he would be sorry to leave. Sorry, also, to leave the role in the hands of upstart imperious arseholes like Kamenev.

Chapter Fifteen
London, Nia's house, January 10th

Nia woke to her alarm. As always, her house was cold. She lay in bed enjoying its warmth but missing Tom. It was a feeling that she knew would only deepen through the two weeks she'd be away on a closed TV shoot. She had been offered a role in a BBC drama to be filmed in Wales. Partly, Jane told her, on the strength of her appearance at the BFI event. She was a last-minute replacement for an actor whose Welsh accent had failed muster. Nia was also attracted to the part in the 1920s costume drama about the closed mindset in the Welsh village and its gradual opening in the shape of a dynamic teacher all the way from England. The charismatic teacher, still recovering from the horrors of the first world war, was the lead character. Nia would play the wife of the village's cruel and reactionary Baptist preacher. The preacher's wife would become a quiet ally to the teacher and his modernised curriculum but not the object of his affection. That role went, of course, to a much younger actress. Nia, in this case, didn't mind the obvious ageism at work. The script was good, her role meaty, and she knew the director was a good one. Nia had been alarmed that the lead role had gone to Goldenboy, but as there would be no on-screen romance with Goldenboy and, after chatting with Tom, she had accepted the role. She had spent a busy week alone learning her lines.

Nia had temporarily put aside the script for a guest starring role on a weekly detective drama playing a doting single mother whose only child goes missing. She would have several good scenes with the show's star who played a damaged but brilliant detective. Nia would be required to go through lots of emotions. There would be shouting, crying, desperation, and gut-wrenching tragedy. Her concerns that the script would stir up her own feelings of maternal loss were not shared with anyone. Tom didn't know of the pain and guilt she still carried. Rachel's advice to Nia to talk to Tom about the loss still resonated with Nia. She lay there, fuck, Tom should know, she thought.

She got out of bed with an audible shiver and put her heavy dressing gown on. Partly to jump-start another stream of thought she moved across the bedroom to open the curtain. As she did, she noticed someone move quickly into the square's small park across the street below her window. Nia could still see the damp footprints the person had left behind.

"Fucking paparazzo," she said out loud. "I do one public event and the bastards are back."

In the square's small park opposite Nia's house, the
cold and tired SVR watcher whispered into his hidden microphone and reported a confirmed sighting of the actress.

Heathrow

Gagnon was 'made' as soon as he made it through passport control. Being six feet five, rail thin, with a long red beard, and cue ball bald, and Canadian, he was always strikingly noticeable. Somewhere in the depths of a Border Force database, Gagnon's passport was flagged as belonging to a member of the intelligence community and passport control automatically notified MI5. The database system noted that Gagnon's visit was not official and, that the Canadian, against intelligence service standard procedure, had not informed any of the UK's security services. MI5 would need to call him in for a little sit-down chat. More troubling for Gagnon, was that he was also made by the SVR. The SVR look-out, who possessed a preternatural ability to remember faces, called the sighting into the Rezident's office at the Russian Embassy, SVR's London central. There, it didn't take the intake analyst long to confirm that Dr Jacques Gagnon, now of Canadian Military Intelligence, was in London. Kamenev would discover Gagnon's arrival when he went through the SVR's sights and sounds activity logs the very next morning.

It was clear to the SVR tail that the tall Canadian wasn't a trained or experienced field agent as he shadowed him across the concourse, through a large revolving exit door, and to the taxi rank. The Russian noted to himself that Gagnon had no field craft, that he must be some sort of analyst. The watcher called the embassy and they directed him to note the taxi's licence plate but to return to his general surveillance duties. SVR control knew that, if needed, the licence plate would give them the taxi company, the driver and, for either a few pounds or through some medium level skill hacking, they'd discover where Gagnon was dropped off.

Gagnon took a taxi directly from the terminal to his hotel. He paid for the taxi and got out onto the pavement, picked up his bag and turned to walk into his hotel. He remembered some field craft training and scanned the small lobby and didn't see any potential surveillance. He checked in and made his way up to his room. There he unpacked his bag, showered and changed clothes. He left his room and found the stairs and proceeded to go down to the lower level and through a labyrinth of corridors to an exit that opened on to a small service alley behind the hotel. He stood in the alley by a small skip taking in the surroundings and checking for a tail. He smiled to himself. He made his way down the alley and out onto the street.

Gagnon made his way through London's busy streets. He found a small supermarket where he purchased a burner mobile, a small paring knife, a bag of chocolate bars, and a half bottle of bourbon. He found a Pret A Manger, ordered a red eye, fired up his new pay-as-you-go phone and called Tom.

On the Periwinkle, Tom chatted with Gagnon but

didn't put the phone down at the call's end. He called Rachel and asked her to look after Jack as he had business in London. Rachel asked whether it was Nia related and Tom said it was a meeting with an editor. Tom didn't like lying, so he called his editor and arranged to meet to discuss the narrowboat book idea.

The next morning, Tom dropped off Jack with Rachel and drove south in his Land Rover. He stopped at a big-box store and bought his own pay-as-you-go burner phone. He called Gagnon with it to let him know his ETA in London. As Tom drove, he felt that he was cheating on Nia. This drive had been part of their romance, a rendezvous in the city had become a special part of his, and Nia's, life. But now he was driving to London to meet his old Canadian comrade in arms to discuss the life and death of a Russian military intelligence officer. Gagnon, on the other hand, had no such qualms. He was looking forward to meeting with Tom and to the possibility of enacting some revenge. He had slept well and had taken a run through the early morning emptiness of a slumbering city.

Kensington, Russian Embassy
In the same still greyness in the same city, Kamenev looked through the previous day's SVR, FSB and GRU reports. It was a quiet day and so the report of Gagnon's arrival at Heathrow had grabbed Kamenev's attention. He felt it couldn't possibly be a coincidence. He ran some quick background checks of the life and career of

Jacques Gagnon. Kamenev scanned the text on Gagnon's military service and his deployments to Afghanistan and Iraq.

"So, another old hand from Afghanistan eh?" he noted softly to himself.

He cross-referred his own records and his own after-action reports. He searched through publicly accessible UK and Canadian records, and through hacked Western military and intelligence service records. "Thank you, WikiLeaks," he thought. He re-checked the timeframes and knew instantly that they cross-referenced with his last missions in Afghanistan. He sat back in his chair and took a long draw on a cup of coffee. So, he thought, I'm guessing it was this Gagnon and Price who were in the field the night my helicopter went down. Instinctively, his hands went to his face, touching the scars and skin grafts. He pulled up pictures of the two men on his computer screen, both appeared younger, both fresh faced wearing slight smiles. "You bastards," he said softly. "You ruined my face, set back my career. Now you show up to ruin the mission that will make my career. That's not going to happen chaps. It's going to be time for a little payback."

It was time to move the official reaction up a notch, Kamenev thought. Two retired Western military officers who had once crossed his path are now in and around London. Kamenev decided to circumvent the Rezident. He picked up a phone and called Moscow Centre on a secure line. Ten minutes later, he replaced the phone in its cradle and smiled to himself. He now had two operations to manage. He was confident both would run smoothly to his and the Kremlin's satisfaction.

***

Thames House, Home of MI5, London. January 12th
The harried deputy director was looking forward to grabbing a quiet five minutes with a cup of coffee and a chocolate digestive. Maybe even a quick online peep at the football result even though she knew it would ruin the excitement of watching the game's evening rebroadcast. An officer, female, young, pretty, ambitious, a graduate from a red brick university, knocked on her door.

"Do you have a quick second, ma'am?" the officer, an intelligence communications analyst, asked.

"Sure," the DD said, with an inaudible sigh while subtly switching her screen from BBC Sport to a spreadsheet.

The analyst spread out three large grainy photos on the DD's desk.

"We just got these in from Holyhead, off of the ferry from Dublin." She pointed at what looked like three men in a car; a driver and the other two in the rear seat. All were clearly trying to avoid having their pictures taken.

"These two," she pointed to the men in the rear seat,

"Have come up hot." She paused for effect and looked to the DD for some affirmation.

"Go on," the DD encouraged indulgently. The DD tried to remember the analyst's name.

"Low level FSB heavies," the analyst continued. "The kind of thugs they bring in for dirty business. Not wet jobs but enforcing compliance through beatings and so forth."

The DD was now alert. It was not uncommon for the SVR, FSB or GRU to mete out punishment and retribution to those Russians living abroad who had displeased the Motherland. Even when those émigré Russians were supposed to be under the protection of their adoptive countries. The poisoning of Sergei and Yulia Skripal had happened on her predecessor's watch.

"Any other chatter to suggest why they're here and how did the Garda miss them in Dublin?" Patel, her name is Patel the DD remembered.

"No chatter yet, ma'am, but we're monitoring. As for the Garda, it looks like the Russians came in on a private flight and then went straight on to the ferry terminal. Still, they should have been flagged at least by airport passport control."

"I'll have a word with our Irish friends later as they clearly dropped the ball on this one. Let's not do the same here," continued the DD. "Private jet. I don't like the sound of that. Suggests speed which suggests something is up, Ms Patel. Let's find out what."

Patel nodded.

"The bloody Kremlin is always sensitive to criticism," continued the DD. "They're jailing and beating their domestic critics and even assassinating a few. And now it looks like there's an uptick in their international suppression campaigns; interfering with the domestic political elections of NATO countries, running fake news campaigns, and intimidating Russian nationals living in the UK and abroad. Do we think they have anyone in the crosshairs?"

Patel shook her head. "Nothing really, ma'am. Although the exiled journalist Daria Kirov is still very vocal and visible."

The DD nodded, "Still refusing official protection?"

"Yes, says she knows how to look after herself."

The DD snorted. "Typical arrogant Russian. Litvinenko and Skripal were experienced intelligence operatives and still Moscow Centre got to them rather easily, too easily I'm afraid." She held up the pictures again. Russian heavies. "Let's get a track on them; traffic cameras, CCTV, I want to know where they go, who they meet with, and why the bloody hell they are here? Grab a couple of analysts to help you and keep me informed. If they stop for a shit on the M6, I want to hear about it, understood?"

"Yes, ma'am," Patel said, rather excited by the assignment and the prospect of heading up a team.

Good kid, the DD thought, as Patel left her office. But what the hell is going on; FSB, FSK, SVR, GRU,

KGB, NKVD, SMERSH lots of changing initials but still the same bunch of brutal bastards.

"Not on my watch," she said to herself.

The deputy director returned to her computer and refreshed the football result. There was another knock on her door, "what now," she thought but switched the screen again and smiled as another analyst came into her room.

"Sorry to disturb, ma'am," the analyst, male, middle aged, pushing retirement, announced. "Not a big issue, perhaps, but we just confirmed that a Canadian Military Intelligence officer named Jacques Gagnon entered Heathrow yesterday and is staying at a London hotel."

"On official business?" the DD asked.

"No, ma'am, unauthorised and unreported as far as we can tell."

The DD thought for a moment, "Call Ottawa. Let's see if signals were crossed or if they know what the hell is going on with this Gagnon. And, get me all the info we and Six have on Gagnon. Especially, any Russian connection."

The analyst nodded and quietly left the DD's office. The DD sighed, "Russians and Canadians, what the hell is going on," she said to herself. "Coincidence? I think not."

Chapter Sixteen
Brighton, January 10th

Daria Kirov seldom took the same roads home. She alternated her routes and the times she travelled. She changed her home address frequently and no longer had a permanent office, preferring to work in coffee shops, pubs, and libraries with good Wi-Fi. She attempted to memorise the faces of strangers and car number plates, and was alert to persons or vehicles that appeared out of place. She wasn't just a highly observant journalist; she was considered by the Kremlin as an enemy of the state. Her reporting on Chechnya, the Ukraine, and domestic suppression had led to threats and intimidation, at least one beating, numerous arrests, and what she considered to be an assassination attempt through poisoning. Even now as she took her Honda CB300R up to forty miles per hour along the almost empty road meandering through an industrial park on Brighton's outskirts, she constantly scanned the road behind her through her motorbike's handlebar mirrors.

She was anxious to get home, at least to her temporary home, a small rented cottage in the Sussex village of Ditchling, after a meeting with her agent. Her agent had good news; a major British newspaper and a

French magazine had agreed to publish a new series of articles Daria was already preparing concerning the further revocation of press freedoms in Russia. An Irish daily was also expressing interest in publishing her work. The commissions would keep her solvent for the year but, more importantly, she thought, it would keep the issue of the Kremlin's increased authoritarianism in the forefront of the world's press. She felt rather pleased.

Daria stepped up a gear and took the 300cc bike up to fifty miles per hour as the road emerged into almost empty countryside. Although she was dressed warmly under her leathers she wanted to get back to her cottage and warm up in front of its small fireplace. The difficulty of motorcycle riding through a British winter was offset by the sense of personal security she felt on the bike. She felt more anonymous in leathers and helmet, liked the bike's immediate speed and manoeuvrability that gave her confidence that, if needed, she could outrun any car. She was alone for most of her eight-mile journey. Daria swung right at a crossroads in the tiny village of Tovey moving away from Ditchling, checking no one was behind her. Then she noticed a grey Ford Fiesta appear in her mirrors. She knew it could have only pulled out of the dead-end lane she had passed on her left. She was suspicious and accelerated so the Fiesta quickly disappeared from her mirrors. Daria pulled a fast right, leaning expertly into the curve. She accelerated past sixty miles per hour on the country lane leaning into a sharp left-hand hairpin and hit seventy on a straight. The country lane emerged onto a larger B road. Daria crossed it, again moving away from Ditchling only slowing down as she hit the outskirts of the small town of Hassocks. She zigged and zagged through a few outlying streets ensuring that there was no Fiesta on her tail before finally turning right on the connecting road that ran into her home village.

The rest of her short trip was uneventful. She reached her home and parked the bike behind the cottage so that it would be unseen from the road. She went inside her cottage and immediately upstairs. She stood in her road-facing bedroom observing the quiet street from behind the room's net curtains. No grey Ford Fiesta crawled past, just a tired-looking middle-aged man who didn't even glance at the cottage. Daria stepped away from the curtain. She sat on her bed, pulled out her laptop from her backpack and began to search for short term home rentals.

Lost in Hassocks, a few miles away from Daria's cottage, the driver of the Fiesta pulled into the curb to await instructions. He was one of four FSB drivers out that morning patrolling the roads leading into Ditchling. He had radioed in his sighting and then one of the other FSB drivers had picked Kirov up on the Hassocks to Ditchling road. Shadowed her, saw the bike slow down and was adroit enough to follow on foot to see Daria wheel the bike behind a cottage. The information had been relayed to the team and all but one began to program their GPS units for a return to London. One surveillance team would stay in the area. The Fiesta driver hit 'home' on his GPS and smiled to himself, "We got the bitch. Colonel Kamenev will be most pleased." He put his car in gear and he too drove away.

Russian Embassy

Kamenev ended the call on his secure desk phone and smiled with self-satisfaction. So, after weeks of searching, his team had finally found the slippery Kirov woman. She was another traitor, no surprise as she wore a traitor's name. Kamenev knew the story; Sergei Kirov, Stalin's chosen man in Leningrad, was assassinated by a mysterious gunman. Although Stalin denied complicity, it was he who benefitted from his potential rival's death, even using it to purge the party of those less than true believers. Kamenev smiled as his poured a cup of hot tea from the traditional samovar that graced his office credenza. He respected the work of Stalin and Stalin's secret police, the NKVD, a forerunner to his own organisation. The NKVD were devoted to the party, to the state, and especially to the man who ruled it and Kamenev felt a kindred spirit with them.

Kamenev was totally devoted to the former KGB man who now ruled from the Kremlin. Putin had returned a pride to the country and had won the country a new degree of international respect. Kamenev liked the feeling that Russia was once again a great power, one with influence, one to be feared and if the ephemeral trappings of democracy and a free press had been sacrificed to attain Russia's rightful place in the world, then so be it. Russians liked to be ruled by a strong man who possessed an iron fist. Ms Kirov, who had been tireless in her opposition to the Kremlin, would soon be crushed by that iron fist of the Motherland. The prospect gave Kamenev a sense of joy. There was a knock on his door and a small, pretty, red-headed woman entered.

"Sit," Kamenev said with a smile and motioned to the chair opposite across his desk. "I know you Irish are great lovers of tea, would you care for a cup?"

"Not if it is that Russian shite," the unsmiling assassin replied in a broad working-class Dublin accent.

Kamenev's smile slipped. He took the afront personally and wanted to slap the woman opposite him but instead took a deep breath, he needed this uncultured woman, she was one of the best.

"Okay," he said through a rictus-like fake smile. "Let's get down to business. The Kirov woman has been found and her literary agent may be interested in getting a meeting with you in your journalist guise. But, before that, I have another job for you."

"Oh yes," the assassin said with real interest.

"Yes, here in London. And I think you're going to like it," Kamenev said.

The assassin tuned her face slightly, "And why would that be?"

"Because one of the targets is a former British soldier."

The assassin smiled, "I would like that. I'd almost say that I'd do that for free, but I won't. I'm assuming this will be for my usual fee with the additional tariff for a quick job?"

Kamenev nodded. He watched a slight smile emerge at the sides of the assassin's almost clenched lips. He was more than willing to employ her and to work with her, but he didn't like her. He couldn't help but wonder what had driven this hard and unpleasant young woman to become a ruthless killer.

***

Gagnon looked at his official phone's screen after another incessant 'ping' of a text. It was his Ottawa office, Canadian Military Intelligence. He ignored the message, the latest in a number of texts and such emails demanding to know what he was doing and to get in contact with his home office or MI5. He buried the phone deep into a coat pocket and slipped out of the hotel's hidden entrance, put up his heavy winter coat's collar and eased his way through the small service alley. The FSB man who had observed Gagnon from the alley's dark corner called in his observation into the embassy. "Yup," he said to himself. "The Canadian's not a field agent."

Gagnon walked through some busy shopping

streets, found a Costa Coffee, he avoided Starbucks when he could, entered and ordered a double espresso. He found a seat and called Tom to reaffirm their meeting time and place. Gagnon had been more perceptive than his tail imagined. With his coffee in front of him on the cafe's small table he pretended to read the phone while surreptitiously observing the clientele in the busy cafe. Gagnon had thought he spotted a tail in one of the shop front's reflection. His furtive assessment of his fellow coffee drinkers confirmed it.

The Russian's field craft had been good, but Gagnon had spotted him. Most field agents maintained a tell. Gagnon spotted the Russian's. There is something about operating in the world of secrets, lies and deception that changes a person. It's like a weight or a worry or a nagging pain. People look different, their faces have expressions not in keeping with their surroundings, their gestures are unnatural or forced, they walk differently as if they are a poor teenage actor in a school play. They're often unsettled, agitated and nervous and they often appear to change, morphing into a variety of characters, gaits, even accents. Simple things can give them away; the way they look at their wristwatch, the way they pretend to read something on their phones, the way they smoke. At first, Gagnon thought the guy tailing him was maybe MI5, but the suit and the shoes screamed something else. They were too formal, slightly ill fitting, too out of place. Like the guy was foreign, not Canadian or American foreign, Gagnon knew, but middle European foreign. He called Tom back suggesting a change of venue for their meeting.

Gagnon continued to exercise his basic field craft as he made his way back to his hotel. He glanced at people he passed on the street suspiciously, seeing enemy agents in the faces of the uniformed schoolboys laughing at what they viewed on a phone, of the young Asian mum pushing a pram, on the face of the elderly postman done with his shift. Gagnon used shop window reflections and naturalistic backwards glances to check on his tail. He moved in and out of shops, he occasionally stopped to tie shoelaces. He was cautiously convinced that he had lost the original tail and not picked up a new one. Gagnon walked past the hotel's service alley, stopped, looked behind him, didn't see an obvious tail and ducked back into the alley. The access door was unlocked, and Gagnon slipped back into the hotel. He worked his way through the service corridors until he emerged in a public area.

The tall Canadian made his way to the check-in area and saw a concierge wearing a morning suit with golden keys on his lapel. Gagnon asked the concierge to order a taxi and have it pick him up discreetly. The clever concierge organised two taxis, one for Gagnon, the other to block any potential tail car. Gagnon laughed as his taxi took off and the second following taxi pulled out across the lane of traffic and stalled. Gagnon looked behind him and smiled again. With his back safe, he looked forward to meeting with Tom.

The taxi made its way through central and tourist London and out into an old, unfashionable neighbourhood. The taxi circled around the block, stopping on a quiet street in front of a small pub. A Land Rover Defender was parked on the other side of the street. Gagnon paid the taxi driver, added a large tip and entered the pub. He saw Tom leaning against the small bar, the only patron in the pub. They hugged.

"Jacques," Tom said.

"Good to see you, brother," Gagnon responded.

Tom ordered a beer for his Canadian ally and they moved to sit at a small, round table. They took long draughts of their beers and talked about Gagnon's flight, the worrying experience with the tail, and what tactics to take with Zalkind/Kamenev. Gagnon ordered another round and returned to the table with two pints in his hand, "I think I told you in Afghan that if I ever came across that Russian bastard that I'd give him the bad news, that I'd kill him," Gagnon said.

"Jacques, mate, but this is London. We can't go around slotting anyone here even if they are low life bastards like Zalkind," Tom implored. "I thought we could go to MI5 or MI6 and if that didn't result in some kind of action, then maybe the press."

"The intelligence services won't do anything," Gagnon tutted. "I know, because I work for one of them. I have a kitchen knife in my belt, if I see him, I'll go for him."

Tom looked deep into his friend's face and then smirked, "C'mon Jacques let's think seriously about this."

They drank their beers. Tom got another round. They ordered some pub food. They talked about Zalkind and they eventually agreed that they would call MI5 in the morning. If there is any slotting to be done, they decided, they'd leave it up to the spooks of Thames House. The topic of conversations moved beyond the Russian. Gagnon talked enthusiastically about turning his dissertation into a book. Tom responded that his next book would still be about journeying along British waterways. Another round relaxed Tom and he mentioned Nia and his depth of feeling for her. Gagnon expressed an interest in meeting her and wondered, half seriously, whether she had a sister. At last orders, they left, both a little wobbly, by separate taxis to different hotels. Tom planned to return in the morning to pick up his vehicle, probably after they had secured an interview with MI5. Tom's taxi dropped him off at his hotel, but Gagnon had his move past his hotel before dropping him off. Pleased with his rudimentary field craft, the Canadian doubled back around the street and entered the alley from the opposite side. He was buzzed and overconfident.

Gagnon was aware of his mistake as soon as he entered the hotel's service alley. Two men, one he recognised as his earlier tail stepped out of the shadows next to a full skip and approached him. The first man smiled but it wasn't genuine. Gagnon read his facial expression as a mask of deception but then it turned worse, it began to read violence. The man's smile had turned into a sneer.

"Dr Gagnon," the accent was Russian. "You'll be pleased to accompany me." He made a gesture that was clearly meant to suggest he was armed. Both Russians closed on Gagnon, crowding him, one was so close that Gagnon could smell his rather unpleasant breath.

"I'm not going anywhere with you guys," Gagnon said and pushed the first Russian. The man immediately approached again, and Gagnon lowered his six-foot five frame and headbutted the FSB man across the bridge of the nose. The Russian put his hands up to his face as blood gushed between the fingers of the cupped hands over his nose, he groaned and staggered into the alley. Gagnon turned quickly to face the second man who was reaching into his coat. Gagnon was surprised when the hand that came from the coat held an evil looking knife rather than a gun. Gagnon smiled and pulled the paring knife from a jury-rigged cardboard scabbard from under his belt at the base of his spine.

"You want to do this, fucker?" Gagnon asked, again smiling with a confidence he didn't really feel.

The Russian smiled back, showing surprisingly good teeth, and moved towards Gagnon. Gagnon felt himself being grabbed from behind. He immediately thrust his head back connecting again with the first Russian's already broken nose. This time, the Russian groaned in pain and went down and stayed down. Gagnon swung to face the knife man, saw the blade a moment too late and felt it sting across his chest. Instinctively he thrust his own knife somewhat blindly up and out towards his attacker just as the Russian tumbled into him. The Russian held him as if initiating a hug, and Gagnon heard a low grunt and gurgle and watched the FSB man's eyes appear to turn opaque with death. Gagnon let the Russian drop onto the alley's wet and dirty concrete.

Everything happened so quickly, Gagnon didn't have time to think. His chest burned and his hand returned covered in blood after he touched it to his breast. The knife wound on his chest made a deep breath painful, but he realised that he'd been lucky as the knife had glanced off a rib and had not pierced a lung. The Russian, however, had not been so lucky. Gagnon's knife strike had been quick, luckily accurate, and fatal. The Russian had fallen to his knees almost immediately and was dead by the time he toppled forward on to his face. Even as an analyst, Gagnon had received some field training, and even while he tried to clear his head, some of the training had taken over. He quickly went through the man's pockets lifting his wallet, phone, pocket litter and his watch. Gagnon moved to the first Russian, but he was coming around. Gagnon stood up and a deep breath reminded him of the pain in his chest. He decided to move. He needed to confirm his attackers had been SRV, FSB, or GRU, clean up, see to the

253

wound, from which he could feel the blood seeping through his coat, and inform the authorities.

Gagnon tidied himself up. He used his scarf as a crude chest bandage and, with a quick last look down the alley to where the Russians lay behind the skip, walked as nonchalantly as possible to a more populated and better lit street and turned and walked to the front entrance of his hotel. He passed the check-in counter and the patrons that always seem to be hanging out in the foyer as quickly and nonchalantly as he could. He made it to his room before collapsing onto the bathroom floor. He wound a towel around his chest and called Tom on his burner phone.

Gagnon sat in a hot bath whilst his blood pinked the water. He went through the Russian's wallet. He was relieved, the attacker's documents clearly suggested he was a foreign agent of some sort not some unfortunate mugger. Gagnon guessed FSB. The Russian's UK driver's licence was good but a fake, suggesting he had been in the country only a short time. Gagnon wondered why he had been followed, how did the Russian know his name, why had the FSB dispatched heavies, possibly trained assassins, from outside of its London station to case him? Given the clothes, it looked like the Russian had come directly from Europe.

Gagnon dressed the shallow knife wound and bagged his bloody and torn clothes and the towels he had used to staunch his wound. He called the front desk asking for a couple of additional towels. He planned to dispose of the most heavily bloodstained towels in waste bins outside of the hotel. He then packed his things. He felt dead tired. The adrenaline rush of the fight, of being alive, was dissipating, leaving him feeling smothered in fatigue. He went through the events in his mind as an after-action report. He had formed a sense of the narrative he'd share with MI5 when there was a knock on his door. He placed a towel over his wound and tightened a hotel robe around him.

He expected it was Tom. Gagnon reached for the doorknob, then hesitated.

"Who is it?" he asked.

"Room service, sir," replied a young female voice in a thick Scottish accent. "Dropping off more towels."

Gagnon looked through the door's peephole and could make out a young woman in a maid's uniform holding a stack of towels, a chambermaid's cart directly behind her.

He opened the door to the young woman who was small, pretty and red-headed and looked good in her tight uniform. She held a pile of towels in her arms. She had a sweet smile. As Gagnon approached, she squeezed the trigger of the suppressed Walther PPK/S she was concealing among the towels. The nine-millimetre bullet caught Gagnon high above the left breast. He fell back into the room. The woman moved in quickly, she kicked the door behind her, but it failed to catch and close. She approached Gagnon who was prostrate on the floor gasping for breath. The assassin was disappointed with herself. She had meant to shoot him in the heart but had missed by a centimetre or two. She dropped the towels and took aim for a shot to the head to be sure this time. Tom entered the room at a run and barrelled into the woman. She fell across Gagnon and rolled to her right before she sprang up on her feet still holding the gun. She fired at Tom without aiming. The bullet passed above his right shoulder and thundered into the plaster and brick behind him. She swivelled towards the Canadian and fired once again at the prostrate Gagnon. The big Canadian reflexively rolled to his right. The bullet dug into the floor a few centimetres from his forehead. Tom dove into the redhead's midriff and they crashed to the floor heavily together. This time, the assassin dropped the Walther. Tom saw the gun before she did and reached for it. As his hand grasped for the Walther the assassin kicked him in the stomach. Tom was still able to grab the pistol and he rolled onto his back bringing the gun up towards the red-headed killer. She dove, rolling again through the open doorway then turned and ran down the hotel's corridor and was gone.

Tom closed and locked the door and then knelt next to Gagnon. He felt for a pulse. Stronger than he had expected. He noticed the knife wound while using more towels to staunch the bleeding gunshot wound.

"My friend," Tom said. "What the bloody hell have you been doing?"

Gagnon grunted. Tom called for an ambulance and

the police. He waited impatiently for their arrival so Gagnon could get professional attention, knowing that he would undoubtedly be the police's prime suspect. His bloody fingerprints would now be on the Walther. He thought about calling MI5, he thought about calling Nia, but he made neither call. Two young but experienced paramedics arrived quickly. They knelt next to Gagnon and began working on him. Tom moved back allowing the paramedics to do their work, he noticed a tattoo on one of the paramedic's forearm's.

"Military?" Tom asked.

"Yes mate. RAF Regiment," the paramedic replied without looking up.

"The guy on the ground did four tours in Afghan," Tom said. "Take care of him."

The paramedic looked up, "No worries mate, we've seen a lot of bullet and stab wounds both there and here. He's in good hands." He gave a quick smile. "He'll pull through."

Tom felt a massive sense of relief. He sat on the floor with his back to the wall. He watched the paramedic's work on Gagnon and too many memories came flooding back. He smelt blood, cordite and desert. He hadn't noticed the police enter the room nor heard their first questions.

Chapter Seventeen
Russian Embassy, January 14th

Kamenev was puce with anger. He took a huge gulp from a tall glass of ice-cold vodka. He hadn't had vodka for breakfast since his time in Afghanistan. The evening had been a litany of disaster. His surveillance team had overstepped and precipitated a street brawl where the damn Canadian had killed one of the FSB men and beaten the other. Then his most trusted and experienced contract assassin, for the first time, missed her target and, worse, was eyeballed, reducing her future utility. Kamenev had spent the dark morning hours arranging the exit, via London's City Airport, for his walking wounded. However, he had cannily used the opportunity to appear to also leave the country himself. He had made sure he was seen entering the aircraft but a quick change into a mechanic's overalls, a wig and a peaked cap pulled low over his eyes had made him virtually invisible as he left the jet with other ground crew personnel. He travelled back from City Airport hidden in the back of an embassy Range Rover.

Back at his desk, Kamenev had spoken with Moscow Centre. Their anger and disappointment had been made abundantly clear. His career was on the line.

He was ordered to expedite the Kirov mission. Snatching her was no longer an option, the mission now was a straightforward assassination. It didn't need to be clever, kill her and get his team safely out of the UK. Her death would send yet another ripple of fear and anxiety among the Russian exile community and Moscow Centre would simply deny involvement. Kamenev was ordered to personally be on scene to supervise and then to return to Moscow immediately after the mission's conclusion.

Kamenev took another long pull on his vodka. A good solider, he would comply with orders. But, he thought, if his career was going to effectively be over, he would settle the growing score with Tom Price before heading home to Moscow.

***

Tom woke and momentarily wondered where he was. The room itself was typical of a low to mid-priced international chain. He had been in such rooms before and they all looked and felt the same. It was comfortable and utilitarian but stale. It could have been New York, Toronto, Rome, or even, latterly, Moscow. The only difference would be the vista that lay behind the curtains and the type of prints that could be found on the room's walls. After a night at the police station, Tom had been returned to his hotel at dawn and had grabbed a few hours' sleep. Sunlight emerged through the gap in the curtains illuminating the room's architectural prints of London landmarks. He ached for Nia. It felt odd for him to be in a hotel room without her. He felt even odder to have not been totally truthful with her.

Tom made a cup of coffee with the room's Keurig machine. He recalled the police station's desk sergeant furtively informing him that he would be contacted by the security services. He sipped his coffee and wondered what any potential meeting with MI5, or the security services, as they preferred to call themselves, would bring. He had encountered officers from the sister service, MI6, in Afghanistan and Iraq and Qatar. He respected them, they were all charming, but they were hard bastards and they played the game well. They'd had a lot of practice from the cold war, to hot wars, domestic terrorism, international terrorism, and the global war on terror. They had entered the twenty-first century with a renewed efficiency and greater degree of egalitarianism. There were still plenty of the public school, Oxbridge graduates and Guards officers but there was a growing cadre of men and women who had been educated in state schools, at red brick universities, and having served in less prestigious regiments. The new breed of professionals had been exposed to the bitter results of intelligence failures and had become harder men and women, more willing to get their hands dirty. Tom respected them but he didn't necessarily like them. They tended to be overzealous in their commitment to the mission at hand, collateral damage be damned.

The phone rang, pulling Tom away from his reverie to the bedside phone.

"Hello," he said.

"Major Thomas Price?" the voice said. "I'm Smith from err, from Thames House. I'm downstairs in the lobby. They sent me to pick you up."

"Okay," Tom said quietly. "Give me ten minutes."

Tom hung up. He was suspicious. He found and called a number for MI5. A recorded voice asked him to leave a message. Tom quickly finished dressing. He chose his blue cords, country sports jacket, a fitted white cotton shirt, and a blue knit silk tie. He slipped on a pair of brown leather Chelsea boots. He carried his heavy winter overcoat over his arm.

The lift descended quickly and opened out on to an overly ornate and pretentious lobby. Tom quickly scanned the lobby area. He spied at least two hotel patrons who were definitely not patrons. Shit, he thought, this is not a polite invitation. Tom spotted a man, waiting nervously near the large revolving door. He was older and heavier than the two other men, the more experienced leader. The man smiled nonchalantly and waved Tom over. As Tom walked through the lobby, he noticed the two men taking up a covering position. For the first time since Afghanistan, Tom wished he was armed.

"Morning Major Price," the man said holding out his hand. "I'm Smith. I'm from the Thames House."

"Smith, why the cavalry?" Tom asked nodding towards the muscle.

"Standard procedure, Major Price. I'm afraid we need to bring you in for questioning. You'll be a good chap, now won't you?"

The question was rhetorical and there was a slight menace to the phrasing. Smith pushed the revolving door and Tom got into the space, pushed hard and found himself in the street. He thought about running but the three men who were quickly at his side disabused him of the notion. A black Range Rover pulled up at the curb with a screech of breaks. The rear door opened as if it was operated by remote.

"Can, I at least see some ID?" Tom asked.

"Please, Major Price, just get in," Smith ordered rather than asked.

Tom found himself seated between two large men. He was so close that he could smell the men's deodorant. Tom regretted that he hadn't run for it, remembering the first few minutes of a capture are the best time to affect an escape. Fuck, he thought, as he sat between two MI5 men, if, indeed they were MI5 he thought. Could they be SVR, FSB or GRU? Gagnon, who was an intelligence officer, had run into trouble with some Russians and had opened his door to a potential assassin and Tom, the amateur, had allowed himself to get into the back of a Range Rover with unknown men. Smith sat in the front passenger seat, he turned to face Tom.

"Smith, this doesn't feel like SOP. What's up?" Tom asked.

"Well, Major Price. That's what we'd like to find out. Not only did someone try to kill Jacques Gagnon last night, we think that Gagnon probably killed or badly wounded a Russian operative."

"Shit," Tom said.

"And, we'd like to know just what you know and what the bloody hell you've been up to in London," continued Smith.

***

The FSB man who had followed Tom from Gagnon's hotel then to the police station and finally to Tom's hotel knew a forced pick up when he saw one. He turned quickly and jogged around the hotel to a service road marked for 'Hotel Deliveries Only'. He took out his phone and called his embassy.

"I think the British just snatched Price," he said.

"Did Price go willingly?" Kamenev asked.

"No, it looked like he was forced but no rough stuff. It looked like an arrest."

"Police car?"

"No, black Range Rover. Security services maybe," the watcher said. "They had enough heavies along in the lobby to stop him running."

***

Tom sat in the middle of the back seat between the two gym-built MI5 men. They obviously weren't covert operatives. Tom could feel his shirt sticking to his back as he sweated. He was in shock; Jacques Gagnon killed someone? He had a knife wound on his chest so he had obviously been in a fight, but what the hell happened? Then, he thought of Nia. If the Russians got to Gagnon they could get to Nia. The SVR, FSB and GRU were, contrary to Hollywood's general impression, skilled and professional practitioners of the dark arts of espionage and intelligence. If they found Gagnon, there was a good chance that they knew of Tom and it didn't take a genius to link Tom to Zalkind/ Kamenev at the BFI which meant a link to Nia.

"Smith," Tom began. "I need to call someone, a civilian. Someone who may be in danger."

"No. Impossible," replied Smith. "There's no call for you whatsoever."

Tom's fear for Nia became all-encompassing, all he could think of was his need to get out of this car and fast.

Tom brought his left hand up to his face as if to scratch his nose, but then lashed his arm out jamming the tip of his elbow into the face of the first heavy, breaking bone and cartilage before any of the men could react. He then turned to the right and attempted to elbow the second man who grabbed Tom's right arm with both hands. Tom quickly countered with his left arm, punching hard and down into the man's groin. The man doubled over and Tom hit him again across his temple putting him out. Smith finally reacted and turned to face the rear seat with a taser in hand. Tom kicked out, hitting Smith's hand just as he discharged the taser. The taser hit the driver who shook involuntarily, made an odd, sustained, high growl like a small dog, and collapsed on to the steering wheel. The big Range Rover lurched to the left as Smith leant over from the passenger seat, grabbed the steering wheel, and fought to regain control. Smith attempted to steer the car and yanked at the handbrake sending the big vehicle into a slide. The SUV swung across the lane of traffic and was hit broadside by a transit van which stopped it.

Inside the Range Rover, Tom was shaken but moved for the door handle. The door opened and he leapt across the unconscious MI5 man for the opening. As the traffic screeched to a halt, Tom exited the vehicle, hurdled a crash barrier and ran down a short grassy bank and disappeared into a shopping street full of people; his right leg aching, his shirt covered in another's blood. Smith, still stuck in the Range Rover, dialled his phone.

"Patel, you won't believe what just happened."

Tom was operating on adrenaline and fear, fear not for himself but for Nia. He walked along the commercial street past the ubiquitous banks, coffee houses and shoe shops and found a cheap high street clothing store. Already the bloody shirt was encouraging disapproving glances and he buttoned up his jacket to hide it. In the store he picked up a new shirt and a cheap overcoat. He explained to the cashier he had a nosebleed problem. The cashier signalled that they couldn't care less. In the shop's toilets, Tom took off his tie and rolled up his bloody shirt. He dumped his shirt and tie in a public waste bin. He put on the new shirt, his jacket and then the new overcoat which he buttoned up to the collar. He exited the store and he moved casually up the street looking for the nearest Tube station. He caught a glance at his reflection as he passed a shop front window. The person who stared back could have been anyone.

The more Tom walked, the more nervous and anxious he became. He felt his limp singled him out, every glance his way became pregnant with suspicion. He wanted to look behind him fully expecting more heavies giving chase. He entered the Tube station and eyed the mass of people on the platform suspiciously, but he could mark no one as Russian or British security services. He was anxious to sit down in the train, take a breather, clear his mind and think. As he took his seat, he eyed his fellow passengers in the train's compartment. Mostly mothers, a few school children and students, and some pensioners, no one appeared to be a threat. He put his air pods in but selected no music and rested his head on the thick window and the only sight he could see now was his reflection and it looked tired. The adrenalin rush of the fight and the escape had dissipated leaving him exhausted and the constant, melodic rocking of the train was soporifically soothing. What the hell was he doing, he thought?

Calm now, Tom concentrated on his next move. The train pulled in and out of stations until it pulled into Marble Arch. The platform was busier here, full with shoppers, tourists and businessmen and women, Tom began to feel uncomfortable again. He stood as the train lurched to a stop at one of Marble Arch's platforms and waited for the pneumatic hiss of the doors to open. They did and he stepped out on to the station platform deep within the bowels of London. He immediately noticed the smell; damp earth, old lubricating grease and electricity. Reflexively he stopped and kneeled to tie a shoelace while scanning the platform. There, about two carriages down the platform, a tall man in a three-piece suit and slicked hair, about thirty, stopped too, pretending to read an advertising poster. How did they pick him up again so quickly, Tom wondered?

There was a hiss behind him as the doors closed and Tom immediately jumped back into the carriage, his shadow did the same. The doors closed further, and Tom stuck his foot in the door, pulled them apart and jumped back on the platform. It had been a basic evasion technique and it failed. The tall shadow stood two carriages away, smiling. Tom ran for the stairs. The long escalators were packed but the wide staircase between the up and down escalators was empty and Tom took the steps two and three at a time, his right leg painful and on the edge of buckling. The bland faces of the people on his left and right stole momentarily glances without suspicion or fear. People were often running up and down desperate to catch a train or to get to some pressing appointment in the city. The stairs opened onto a crowded concourse complete with another series of platforms and another escalator and stairwell. Again, Tom made for the stairs, he wanted to get to the streets. Now, with each leap his leg screamed. He glanced backwards and caught a glimpse of the shadow apparently taking the steps two at a time with ease. The shadow was smiling. Tom wondered whether the tail would risk shooting him and his shoulders involuntarily tensed as if expecting a bullet to rip through his back, but none came. The stairs opened out into the main concourse of the station. People queued to get through the ticket gates while others milled around the ticket machines and small newspaper and confectionary kiosks. Without slowing to a trot, Tom sprinted the last couple of steps and then vaulted over the turnstile. He immediately drew attention from a stern looking ticket collector. Tom heard disapproving shouts behind him as the chase man pushed through the lines and vaulted the gates in pursuit.

With some space to run, Tom turned on his heels and ran for the Oxford Street exit. The street was full of lunchtime shoppers and tourists and Tom quickly limped into the river of bodies. He knew he couldn't go far. His leg ached like hell, and sirens began to blare behind him and from somewhere in front. He turned to see if he was being followed, he was; smiling boy.

The siren in front was getting closer. Tom was glancing over his shoulder when he stepped out on to the street in front of the wailing police car. The police Volvo's brakes squealed but stopped the car inches from Tom. Before the policemen could get out of their car, Tom had limped around to the rear door, opened it, and sat down. The two officers turned to face him with surprise and questions.

"My name's Tom Price and I'm being chased either by the FSB or MI5. And I didn't pay for my last Tube trip."

The two officers turned to each other.

"Fucking hell," said one.

***

Thames House

The deputy director and Patel observed Tom through reinforced one-way glass. Tom was handcuffed to a ring in the centre of a metal table that was bolted to the floor of the soulless room. Tom appeared to be staring at something on the table. The DD glanced at Patel.

"Seriously," the DD said. "What the fuck was all that argy-bargy about?"

Patel shrugged her shoulders. "Smith did say that they didn't show Major Price any ID, that Price was clearly shocked by the news of Gagnon possibly killing one of the Russian agents, but seemed to go crazy when informed he couldn't call a friend in trouble."

"The friend would be Nia Williams no doubt. So, the denial of the option to call her led Major Price to beat up two of my security agents, ruin one of my beautiful Range Rovers, and lead a posse of more of my security operatives on a mad dash across London?" the DD added.

"Yes, ma'am," Patel said. "He managed to do all that and find time for a bit of shopping at Primark."

The DD stared at Patel and then smirked. "Okay. I'll deal with Smith later. Let's bring some professionalism to this cock-up. Time for a chat with Major Price."

Tom could sense he was being watched from behind what he clearly knew was a one-way mirror. So, this was Thames House, he thought, better than some holding cell at the Russian Embassy, or even the interview room at last night's police station, but he was anxious to make sure Nia was safe. A lock was turned, and the door opened. Two women entered. One middle aged, expensive haircut and grey suit and a smaller, younger South Asian woman in blue slacks and cream blouse with dark, intelligent eyes. Both exuded no nonsense demeanours. He was surprised that there were no men present and then felt that Nia would have been disgusted by his apparent chauvinism. Tom had occasionally come across members of the intelligence services and members of the CIA at various times and various postings across the Middle East. He felt he knew what to expect.

He nodded to the two women.

"Major Price," the DD began. "I'm sorry for the cuffs but my security team felt, that after your rather boisterous display this morning, you needed them, but I don't think so, do you?"

Patel moved to the table and unlocked Tom's handcuffs.

"Thank you," he said and reflexively rubbed his wrists.

"I must apologise Major Price as I think my lads may have behaved a little too... operationally. I just wanted you to come in for a chat this morning. We know you didn't... assist Jacques Gagnon in last night's tête-à-tête with the FSB but perhaps you know what the hell this is all about?"

Tom looked into the woman's face opposite him. She was earnest and smart, he thought. Indistinct age, perhaps mid-fifties, more than a mid-career officer and, as she mentioned 'my security team', someone with authority. Instinctively, he felt he could trust her.

"Feodor Zalkind," Tom said looking directly into the DD's face.

The DD glanced sideways towards Patel who shrugged her shoulders as a negative response and began to type into her laptop searching for any records.

"And he is?" the DD asked.

"He's currently a faux cultural attaché at the

271

Russian Embassy going by the name of Kamenev. Gagnon and I ran into him in Afghan but then he was called Zalkind, ostensibly a major in the GRU. Probably SVR or FSB."

The DD nodded. Patel continued to type, Tom wondering whether she was searching or taking notes. She looked as if she was capable of both simultaneously.

"About a decade ago he was running some arms for drugs mission with the Taliban, Haqqani Network, and al-Qaeda among other dirty things. Then I ran into him in London before Christmas while he was masquerading as Kamenev. I contacted Gagnon and let him know too. You probably know about Jacques."

The DD nodded.

"Zalkind was responsible for the death of some of Jacques' men in Afghan," Tom continued. "I know Jacques is Canadian intelligence, so I thought he'd respond through regular channels, informing you guys from his official position, that type of thing, so I was bloody surprised when Gagnon arrived in London. We had dinner last night to talk about how best to approach the situation and when to bring in you guys or MI6."

"And what had you decided about confronting Colonel Kamenev?" the DD asked.

Tom smiled slightly, "Well after a few beers and some big talk about slotting him, we actually decided that we were going to attempt to get eyes on Zalkind, confirm his identity as Kamenev, and then Gagnon would use his intelligence connections to bring you guys in."

Tom stared, at the DD, "Wait a moment, how did you know he's a Colonel?"

"We've been aware of his presence for some time. Were you involved in the fight?"

"No. It happened after I had left. Gagnon called me from his hotel after the fight. Said he'd been jumped in an alley. Had beaten one guy badly and stabbed another in a quick knife fight. He had been stabbed so I went over to see if I could help and to accelerate our involving the security services as this whole thing was clearly getting out of hand. At the hotel, as I got off the lift on Gagnon's floor, I saw a small woman, red hair, dressed as a hotel maid in the door of a room, clearly raise a pistol. You know the rest."

Tom leaned forward and held the DD's gaze. "Look," Tom continued. "I'm worried about my..." what was Nia? "... my friend, err, my girlfriend." He winced when he said it. "Zalkind may have used her to find a link to me and to Gagnon. If so, she could be in some danger."

"Nia Williams is perfectly safe," the DD answered. "We had the local plod out to the filmset this morning. And one of our lads is on set now. No worries, it's secure. We think Zalkind, or Kamenev as he is now called, and, possibly, the injured and or dead SVR or FSB men, have already been spirited away. There was some last-minute activity at London City airport early this morning. The embassy filed a hurried flight plan to Moscow's Vnukovo airport. Private jet flew in and left later this morning. All this was accompanied by what appears to have been an increase in embassy chatter."

"So, you know of Kamenev?" Tom said trying to disguise some of the anger he was beginning to feel.

"Somewhat," the DD said. "We thought he was low level FSB trying to make connections and contacts in the media world. One of those louche Russians who enjoy hanging out with celebrities, keeping an eye on oligarchs, that kind of thing. But over the last few days we picked up an increase in Russian Embassy chatter, followed some FSB imported heavies, and then the link to Gagnon and to you, Major Price, became rather obvious in the early hours of this morning.

"We got CCTV tape of Russian Embassy cars at Gagnon's hotel reversing into the alley, we now assume they were picking up Gagnon's assailants. We purposefully watched the activity in and out of the embassy. Again, an increase in chatter, a quick filing of flight details occurred at London airport and surveillance followed a couple of embassy cars that later headed out to London airport. Two chaps went up the air-steps into the jet. A large bag, which we think probably contained a body, went into the hold."

"So, Gagnon did kill the Russian?" Tom asked, feeling sick.

"It's what we're assuming," the DD noted. "But we're pretty convinced that it was self-defence. We don't intend to pursue the situation any further," she added with a gentle smile.

"And Zalkind's, what, safe in Moscow?" Tom asked.

"I'm afraid so," the DD answered with genuine empathy. "Again, we're assuming that it's too hot for him in London and that he's been recalled to Moscow. I'm sure his reception at Moscow Centre will be anything but pleasant. We'll ask for the suspension of his diplomatic immunity and extradition back to the UK as a person of interest in a violent altercation outside of a London hotel," she sighed. "But we know the Russians will refuse. They don't extradite their own citizens. Let alone an intelligence officer."

Tom grimaced.

"But," the DD continued, "He's now on our radar, and on our allies' radar, too. He won't be able to show his face, whatever face he has now, so his usefulness to the SVR and FSB has been much reduced. Plus, as you may know, Major Price, we have long memories. He ordered the killing of one of our own so we, the Secret Intelligence Service, the Canadians, and the CIA will be very alert to the whereabouts of Zalkind or Kamenev or what the hell he'll call himself. He's a marked man."

"Somehow, I don't feel that's enough."

"No, but it's the reality of the situation," the DD continued. "Worse, perhaps, is that Gagnon, probably will be a marked man. I'm sure he'll now be looking for a new career after his home service deal with him. You too, Major Price, may now be a person of interest to the Russians. I wouldn't plan any trips over there if I were you."

Tom grasped the reality of the situation. "Shit," he said.

"Shit indeed," the DD added.

***

Outside of Ditchling

Daria Kirov made sure there were no cars in front or behind her, nor any pedestrians around when she turned her motorbike into the lane from where the Fiesta had emerged previously. She was nervous as she knew it was a dead end and she could be trapped. She hoped that there would be at least a gate or two which would offer a possibility of egress and escape across farmers' fields if necessary. She slowed the bike and raised her visor while still constantly scanning her rear-view mirrors. She reached the end of the lane and slowed the bike to a crawl. Daria noticed tyre tracks in the mud close to the verge of hedgerows that lined the lane. More telling, she observed, was the pile of fresh cigarette butts. In her mind's eye she saw a Russian waiting in the car smoking, like all FSB or SVR men did, waiting for some signal to pull out of the lane to follow her as she sped past. Her heart raced, she was convinced that her location, and therefore her very safety, had been compromised.

Daria turned the bike around. She pulled a phone from one of her jacket's numerous zipped pockets. She dialled a number and waited for the innocuous automated response that would convince most members of the public that they had misdialled. Daria, however, spoke loudly and quickly. "I need to talk to Patel and quickly," she said. She replaced the phone, gunned the Honda's motor and accelerated out of the lane and onto the adjoining B road.

Thames House

The deputy director sat at her desk digesting the morning's worth of heavy work. Something she couldn't quite put a finger on continued to niggle her. She sat up as if mildly shocked. She went to her door, opened it and called across the hive of cubicles for Patel. The DD liked to preserve a sense of the personal contact rather than summoning one of her team by email, text, or IM. Patel entered quickly.

"Do you have notes from the Price conversation?" asked the DD.

Patel retrieved her laptop, "Yes, ma'am."

"How did Price describe the assassin at Gagnon's hotel?"

Patel scrolled quickly cross her laptop. "As a small red-haired woman," Patel answered.

"I've come across that description before. Can you pull up the reports on the suspicious death of that Russian journalist in Tel Aviv Rabinovich, Viktor

Rabinovich?"

Patel searched through her laptop. She looked up, "Petite, pretty, red-headed woman, possibly Irish."

"And Gagnon also described the hotel shooter as…?"

A click-clack of laptop keys. "Err, pretty, red-headed, and Scottish," Patel responded.

The DD leant forward. "Patel this keeps getting better and better. We have a bloody Russian hit squad operating in London again. Those brazen bastards. Get me all the intel on suspected Russian assassinations of their exiles and a list of their potential targets in the UK. And be quick about it. This is top priority."

"Errr, ma'am, I just got a call from one of our Russian exiles, Daria Kirov, the journalist."

"Go on," the DD said.

"She thinks she was followed. She's been super savvy, ma'am, more so after Skripal. Basically, took herself off the grid and went underground. If she thinks she was followed, she probably was."

The DD thought for a moment. "The redhead in Tel Aviv purported to be a journalist, yeah? Let's get a team over to wherever the hell Ms Kirov is; quietly," the DD ordered. "And, Patel, let's make sure it's an A1 team."

"Yes, ma'am, on it," Patel replied as she moved towards the door.

The DD didn't notice Patel leaving the office as,

reaching for her desk phone, she contacted her assistant asking him to schedule a meeting with the director general.

Chapter Eighteen
Brecon Beacons, Mid Wales, January 14th

The inn was an old coach house on a road that ran through the middle of moorland. The inn owed its placement to the fact that it was at the way point of a coach horses' fatigue between the nearest towns of any size. It was a low, heavy stone building with small windows designed to fight off the violent winds that whipped over the moors. It had survived two hundred and fifty years of vicious winds and harsh winters. It was currently surviving a bunch of pretentious actors and a self-important TV film crew. The landlord was grateful for the business. All his rooms were booked, and he was even earning extra money from the crew parking their caravans, lorries and other equipment on his property. And then there was the money he was making from the food and drink. These TV types liked a drink or two. The poor weather, what did they expect from mid January, had delayed the shoot, so he was making almost as much money as he normally did for the entire high tourist season. He stood behind the small bar drying glasses when the first patron came in, ordered a white wine, and settled into a comfortably worn leather high back on the right-hand side of the roaring fireplace. He continued to dry pint glasses while watching her from the corner of his eye. She sipped her wine while she read a book, feet tucked under her body on the chair.

He wasn't a TV or film buff, but he knew that she was Nia Williams, the Welsh Spitfire. He always liked her as she was Welsh and, he remembered, she used to get her kit off in her younger days. Looked like she still had a decent body, he thought. Ten years and two stone ago, he may have tried to work some charm on her, but he knew, now, that it was not an option. He liked her never-the-less. She was polite and respectful and didn't treat him as if he was the hired help. She kept to herself and was quiet, liked her books and a glass of wine, so unlike the Nia he used to read about in the *News of the World*. She looked up from her book and caught the landlord's eye. She knew he was embarrassed to be caught staring, so she smiled and nodded her head slightly. He smiled back. Yes, he thought, a nice lady.

The landlord had served in the army as a younger man but his postings overseas had only made him long for the cold damp hillsides of home. Since returning to his homeland, he had tended bar and managed pubs across south and mid-Wales for most of his working life. His experiences had made him, he felt, a fine judge of people. He looked over towards Nia and guessed by the way she would check her phone that there was a boyfriend a text away. Mobile reception this high up on the moor was spotty but when Nia received some communication through the ether, the landlord had noticed that she beamed like a lighthouse. Whomever the boyfriend was, he was a lucky fella, the landlord thought. The landlord suspected that Nia's chap was nicer than the guy, the TV film's leading actor he'd been told, who constantly pestered her. Speak of the devil, he thought, as the actor came in.

Goldenboy sidled up to the bar and ordered a bourbon without looking at the landlord. He took his glass without a word of appreciation and sat in the chair to the left of the fireplace across from Nia.

"Another rather beastly night," he said.

Nia looked up from her book.

"Oh, I don't know. There's a beauty in wild Welsh weather," she said authoritatively.

Goldenboy watched her for a moment and then laughed.

"Fuck, Nia," he said. "Really? Already? Oppositional defiance is a disorder you know."

She sighed and closed her book on her lap.

"No, I mean it," she said. "Like this afternoon, the way the clouds formed and darkened over the valleys, how the hills became monotone, and everything became still and silent before the wind and the rain kicked up, was beautiful. It was like being at the birth of a storm. In a crucible of meteorological conditions."

"Oh, that's right," Goldenboy began sceptically. "I heard you went for a walk on the hills. Is this some kind of health kick or are you trying to rediscover your Celtic roots? What do you people call that kind of nostalgia?"

"You people?"

"C'mon Nia, you know, the Welsh, the Celts."

"Hireath," Nia confirmed. "But it's not that. It's just that I like the tranquillity of being in the countryside," Nia responded, slightly curtly.

Goldenboy laughed. "Nia darling, seriously? You hated quiet. You were always the party girl; you got off on the noise and energy from being around people."

Nia frowned, "That was a long time ago. I no longer need the party crowd to energise me."

Goldenboy laughed again but leant forward. He reached out and touched Nia's left knee.

"God, we had some good times, didn't we? And, funny you should mention being energized." He dropped his head, conspiratorially, "I've got some first-class blow in my room. We both could get energised like the old days. We could do some of the other things we did in the old days too. What do you say?" he leant back and beamed, displaying perfect teeth.

Nia smiled. "That's a lovely offer. Thank you. But I haven't had any coke in fifteen or more years, and if it's a shagging you're after then I'd suggest you go back to your room and go fuck yourself."

"Aw, c'mon Nia. Once or twice for old time's sake. We were good, weren't we?"

"No," Nia stated with a raised voice. "We weren't and that was a long time ago. Different people, different places."

"A leopard doesn't change…"

"This one did," Nia said. "Look, for the first time in my bloody life, I'm happy. Really content, really happy." She smiled sweetly but patronisingly, "I'll work with you but I'm not going to shag you. Now piss off and leave me alone."

Goldenboy downed the remainder of his bourbon. "Can't blame a chap for trying, Nia," he said as he got up. He smiled at her again and purposefully looked her up and down as if he was appraising cattle, "You've still got great tits." It was his attempt at a last word.

"And you've still got a small prick," she said.

Goldenboy laughed. "Nice one," he said as he left the bar.

At the bar, drying his pint glasses, the landlord smiled. Well done girl, he thought, well done Cariad.

Nia returned to her book but she had been rattled. Being around Goldenboy had evoked memories of a time in her life that she hadn't actually forgotten but had buried deep, like a time capsule. Now the capsule was opened, she had to revisit events and moments from the past as if they were artifacts. Most were painful, but she had to admit a few were good and happy. Her heart raced. She finished her wine and decided to head back to her room. Like most of the cast, Nia was staying at the inn and she made her way through the bar around the small dining room cum lounge and up steep, narrow stairs to her second-floor room. Her bed was against the room's exterior facing wall, below a small window, which had been mercifully double-glazed. The low ceiling sloped dramatically towards the window and Nia had to duck as she walked around the room. She held up her phone searching for signal bars.

Nia wanted to talk to Tom. She wanted to hear his voice, take reassurance and comfort in it, to tell him about Goldenboy, about her past, to blather on about her work. And to hear him laugh and tell her that her voice sounded like music. She wanted to tell him that the job was a good one for her and there was already some buzz generated about the quality of the piece. She had been her usual consummate professional self and the authenticity she brought to the role had led to the director and screenwriter expanding her scenes and adding dialogue. But the tabloids were already posting headlines about Goldenboy and Nia. She had prepared Tom for such gossip. Tom had told her that he would ignore it, but she worried about how Tom would react if he read such gossip column bullshit.

Nia stood on her bed, head bent but it still touched the ceiling, arm with phone stretched out. She found half a bar, but it vanished back into the ether before she could place the call to Tom.

"Oh Tom," she said to herself. "I wish you were here."

She sat on her bed, grabbed the small pad of paper and pen that rested on the bedside table and began to write a letter.

***

The next morning brought a small break in the weather. There was a gentle mist that had transformed a bright, morning sun into something from a Turner painting. The director liked the light and the almost supernatural feel of the weather and decided to try a location shoot. Nia would be in one long scene. She would appear on the crest of a hill, observing the teacher and his young love interest run across a hassocky sheep meadow into an epic embrace. The longing in her eyes and disappointment across her face would symbolise the cold and passionless old order yearning for what the lovers embraced as the light and energy of modernisation. Nia watched as the crew worked setting up the meadow scene from her mark on the hillside. A drone camera buzzed overhead. The steady-cam operator, who would shoot the close up of Nia's face, kept her company. She was cold, even though she wore long underwear under her full, heavy period costume of long dark woollen dress, white cotton shirt, serge cape, and a heavy woollen shawl. She was still concerned that she'd shiver on camera. Nia asked the steady-cam operator when he would be ready to shoot the scene. He radioed down to the valley floor to the director. Ten to twenty minutes, he reported to Nia. Nia nodded and turned and walked to the top of the hill. She took out her phone, she had broken the director's rule that phones were strictly not allowed on set, for an opportunity like this. She had a bar. She called Tom. The call went through, but he didn't pick up. She left a message. "Tom, I love and miss you," she said to her phone. "I'd love to see you." She hesitated, "Maybe could you pop over?"

Her phone dinged with an incoming text. Her heart began to race with anticipation only to be disappointed to see the text was from Jane, her agent. Nia called her.

"Nia, how's the shoot," Jane began.

"Fine," answered Nia. "Slow and cold but good."

"And Goldenboy?'

"Keeping a respectful distance… now," Nia said. She sensed that Jane was hesitating.

"You know the military advisor I had asked about Tom? Well, he called me this morning. He had heard some top-secret mumbo jumbo about Tom getting into a fight with some Russians in the city."

"Fuck," Nia exclaimed. She was immediately frightened. "Is Tom okay?"

"Don't worry, Nia," Jane said soothingly. "Tom's fine. Probably drink involved. You know boys and their beer. But enough about our boy, now, I think you're going to have to decide about our matron role."

Jane talked about the business, some additional interest in Nia, possibly even some other offers, but Nia didn't really hear any of it. She was relieved when Jane rang off. Nia tried Tom's number again. It rang to voice mail. She texted. "Call me or text me," she wrote. "Love you." She added a heart icon and hit send.

The steady-cam operator waved to her; it was time for her scene. She turned her phone off and returned to work.

London

MI5 had spirited Tom out of Thames House and deposited him at a small plain hotel on the city's outskirts. The plan was for Tom to spend the night at the hotel and then proceed to pick up his Land Rover the next morning and then drive back to North Wales. MI5 had already worked with his former hotel to collect his things, which were waiting for Tom when he entered his new room. The hotel was modern, low slung and basic. It was the kind of hotel that catered almost exclusively to businesspeople needing a night or two between travel and business meetings. There was a queen bed, a small desk and a basic bathroom. Tom was spent. He had had almost no sleep the night before and the morning's chase across London and his interview with MI5 had left him both physically and emotionally exhausted. He worried for his friend, Gagnon, and he ached to be with Nia.

Tom had called his editor and agreed to take the commission. A small advance would wing its way over to his bank account and Tom had received a promise that the publishers would cover the Periwinkle's running costs for the year. The editor was thrilled but had been adamant that Tom's voice be part of the book that the travelogue would have him appearing not just as omniscient narrator but as a character. It was to be a personal memoir in the Rolt vein but with Tom's wit and charm and a little of his personal story undergirding the narrative. It had been a commission that Tom had previously balked at taking. But he felt now that if Nia would occasionally join him on his canal journeys then he could make it work.

After the agent had ended the call, Tom checked messages and texts. None from Nia. He answered a quick text from Rachel as to his ETA and then he texted Nia. He briefly noted he had signed the book contract and that he was looking forward to seeing her again. There was no mention of his most recent adventures. He placed his phone by the bedside table, took off his watch, thought about a shower, but was asleep almost as soon as he closed his eyes.

***

London, January 15th

It was light when Tom woke. He was momentarily confused as to where he was. He had slept late. He quickly showered and felt refreshed. He dressed, packed his bag and checked out. His Land Rover had mysteriously appeared in his hotel's car park, courtesy of MI5. Still no calls or texts from Nia. He called the hospital for an update on Gagnon's condition. Tom was relieved to hear good news. He left a message with Gagnon's ward sister for the Canadian to call him once he was able to do so. He texted Rachel his anticipated time of arrival. He texted Nia that he loved her. He put his phone away, started up his vehicle and began the long drive through the busy commuter traffic.

About an hour outside of the city, both Tom and the Land Rover needed refuelling. Tom was at a Little Chef eating a bacon sandwich and sipping a coffee when his phone dinged with incoming texts. He checked excitedly. It was Nia, "Call me or text me." And then another, "Love you." Tom was both pleased and concerned. He texted back but noticed the text was not delivered. He felt that something was wrong. He opened his phone's GPS app and typed in the address of the inn where Nia was staying.

***

Brecon Beacons

Nia was tired and cold as she entered the inn. The day's shoot had gone well. Nia's scenes were comprised of long takes in close up. The director had asked her to move through a range of love to loss, from yearning to gut wrenching disappointment. She had been asked to display a moment in her character's evolution when she realises that her life would never be the same again, that her hopes and dreams were, essentially, shattered. Nia didn't consider herself a method actor, but she had dug deep into her own history to tap the rich vein of experiences to create authentic emotions. Her tears had been real. As had her exhaustion.

The director had been pleased with Nia's performance and felt that the whole day's shoot had been satisfactory enough to bring the location filming to an end. Most of the cast and crew were looking forward to the traditional end of location wrap party and then moving on back to Cardiff and the warm and dry studios there. Nia wanted nothing more than a warm bath and a text from Tom.

Tom was standing at the inn's bar, chatting good naturedly to the landlord when Nia walked in. Her emotions were already on edge, frayed, after the shoot's requirements. She saw Tom and immediately went up to him at a run and embraced him in a long hard hug. Her eyes were wet.

"Oh, Tom," she began. "I've missed you so much."

Tom held her like a drowning man would a lifebelt, his fear for her safety evaporating. The darkness of his recent experiences, the unease that churned in his gut, dissipated. He felt her quiet sobs. Tom looked at her with concern.

"Hey, hey," he said gently. "Are you okay? I missed you too."

"It's been a bit tougher than I expected," Nia whispered. "The shoot, my character, Goldenboy."

They embraced again. Tom wanted to tell her about London but the flood and melding of their emotions took over.

"I'm so glad you're here," Nia said and she held

Tom's hand and led him up to her room. They showered together and then made love slowly on the soft, squeaky hotel bed. There was now a familiarity with their lovemaking each knowing the other's wants and needs. There was burning, frenzied passion along with a comfort of experience and the confidence that came with love. Nia bit her lip and held Tom tightly as she climaxed. Tom wasn't far behind and they fell together when he came. They spooned through the afterglow.

Tom, again, wanted to tell her about London, Kamenev, and MI5 but didn't feel the time was right. Nia shifted position and laid with her head on Tom's chest. She began to talk excitedly and rapidly about the shoot in her stream of consciousness fashion that Tom had grown to realise signified happiness. Tom listened and smiled. Nia drew a breath and asked Tom about his new book contract. Tom briefly explained the plans for the book, his need to travel along the canals Rolt had travelled some eighty years before. He would update Rolt's observations and expand with his own experiences and anecdotes. Nia was excited to discuss options for her joining him on the Periwinkle for research trips. Her mood elevated by Tom's appearance and the options for elements of a future together, Nia suggested they join the cast and crew for the hastily planned end of location party.

They dressed, Nia in jeans and a black T-shirt emblazoned with a Sun Records logo, Tom in chinos and a blue denim shirt, and they went down to join the shindig. The cast party was in full swing. The inn's restaurant was doubling as an event space. It made for a good party room. Tables had been cleared, lights had been dimmed and filtered, and beer and wine were flowing. The room was full with cast members and crew alongside some invited locals and inn staff mingling around the room and its long bar. Tom quickly checked the room's egress options while assessing the crowd to see if he could make Nia's MI5 shadow. He couldn't. An assistant director from the film crew was belting out a passing rendition of 'Total Eclipse of the Heart' on a small karaoke stage; her voice pure and high and obviously trained. Nia grabbed a small table while Tom went up to the bar.

"Hello Tom," the landlord said with a genuine smile. "'Tis nice to see you and Nia down for the party. I was hoping you two would come down. Nia's much liked by the folks round here. Drinks on the house tonight, courtesy of the production company, what you after?"

Tom ordered the usual; wine for Nia and a cider for himself. 'Total Eclipse' came to its final crescendo.

"Brave that," Tom noted. "English girl singing Welsh girl's big hit."

The landlord nodded as he recorked the wine bottle after pouring a generous serving for Nia. There was an explosion of laughter from the corner of the room where Goldenboy was holding court.

"Prick," the landlord said quietly. He looked at

Tom. "I'll tell you what was brave, the way she put him in his place when he came on to her." He nodded towards where Nia sat.

Tom raised an eyebrow.

"Strong woman that one," the landlord finished and went to serve another party goer.

Tom took the drinks to the small table. He looked over at Goldenboy, his eyes met the actor's and Tom held the stare until the actor looked away with a contrived smirk. Nia followed Tom's stare.

"Nothing to worry about there, darlin'," Nia said with a sweet smile.

"I hear he tried it on," Tom said, matter-of-factly.

"Yeah, but I can handle myself," Nia said and took a long drink from her wine glass. She reached over the small, round iron topped table and grasped Tom's hand.

"Nothing to worry about there, darlin'," repeated Nia. "Nor anywhere else actually. I'm a one Tom woman."

Tom laughed. "I'm very glad to hear it," he said with a full smile.

They both took long drinks simultaneously.

"I'm so glad you came," Nia said. "I was missing you something awful."

Nia smiled shyly with her honesty and vulnerability. It was something she would have buried deeply before Tom. Almost no one who knew Nia thought of her as vulnerable.

The small karaoke stage began to attract some more

interest. One of the film shoot's steady-cam operators had started to belt out an off key and drunken rendition of 'Mac the Knife' in a strong West Midlands accent. Nia went to the bar and the landlord poured another round. The steady-cam operator began 'I've Got you Under my Skin' as Nia deposited the glasses of wine and cider at their table and then went over to the karaoke area to use the system's laptop to search for a song. She returned to the table grabbed her wine, took a long pull and smiled.

"What have you done?" Tom asked.

"A surprise," Nia replied.

Nia waited for the Black Country Sinatra to finish, took another gulp of her wine and went to the karaoke stage. She took the mic out of its stand as her music started.

Already some of the cast and crew began to watch her. Tom barely recognised the opening bars of the song, Bruce Springsteen's 'Sad Eyes', but then remembered Nia had mentioned it as one of her favourites.

Nia had dropped her voice into a lower range and sang beautifully, imbuing the lyrics with personal meaning. She swayed in a simple side to side, two step movement and closed her eyes when she hit the high notes of the song's chorus. Tom's breath caught in his throat.

Nia had captured Tom's gaze. He was smiling as broadly as a circus clown. They were aware only of each other. No one in the room spoke, most eyes were on Nia. A few eyes were cast in Tom's direction. Goldenboy looked at Tom. The actor telegraphed hatred towards Tom.

Goldenboy hated the way Tom looked at Nia, hated his smile, hated the way Nia responded. But, most of all, he hated the surprise wave of envy that gripped him. Nia had never publicly and transparently expressed her feeling for him the way she was doing for Tom. He stared daggers at Tom.

Nia ended her song to rapturous applause, whistles, and shouts for encores. She blushed a little and giggled as she made her way over to Tom's table. Tom stood and they hugged, and Nia kissed him full on the lips, her eyes closed. The crowd applauded again, and wolf-whistled. Tom flushed as they sat down.

"That," he said, "was brilliant."

"The kiss or the song?" Nia replied her dark eyes glowing.

"Both."

Tom leant over the table and kissed Nia again. When they broke the kiss, Goldenboy was standing at the table.

"Nia, babe, why don't you introduce me to your guy?" Goldenboy asked in his plummy accent.

Nia knew his smile was phoney but smiled sweetly back.

"This is Tom."

"Hi Tom, so how long have you known Nia then?"

Tom didn't like the way Goldenboy's questions sounded like orders and he certainly didn't like him referring to Nia as babe.

"Oh, for a few months now," Tom replied unsmiling. He caught Nia's eye to see if he could read her thoughts. He could tell she was nervous as she leaned forward in her chair with her hands together.

"You know she was my wife for a couple of years and girlfriend for a lot longer than that?" Goldenboy's words were beginning to slur a little. Nia looked into his eyes wondering whether he was high or drunk, or both.

"Yes, I'm aware of that," Tom replied. "Quite some time ago though," he added with a fake smile along with a hard stare, eyes like flint. "More like a lifetime ago, I believe, wasn't it?"

Goldenboy smiled broadly, "Yeah, but you never forget your first true love, though do you? Do you Nia?" He moved towards the bar before Nia could respond.

Nia looked at Tom and reached over for his hand.

"Wanker," she said, and Tom nodded in agreement.

Goldenboy returned from the bar with two bottles of red wine. He stopped at the table and put one bottle down.

"Looks like you still like your vino eh Nia?" Nia nodded apprehensively. "Here's a bottle on me. More for Tom than you babe." He turned to face Tom, "She's an animal in the sack after a few wines have been taken, in case you haven't found that out yet."

Tom stood, immediately shifting weight to respond

to any movement from Goldenboy. Tom clenched his fists but kept them down at his sides and took half a step towards the actor. Nia stood and moved quickly to Tom's side. She noticed his eyes had darkened and his jaw had clenched. She put her hand on his arm and felt his body rigid and taught. Tom stared deep into Goldenboy's eyes.

"I think you'd better fuck off now," Tom said slowly and quietly and almost in a growl.

Goldenboy stood for a moment, mouth half open as if to respond. He was fit and strong, still sparred in the gym, but as he looked at Tom, he thought better of a comeback remark or any further physical posturing. He reflexively stepped back slightly and summoned up a broad innocent smile. He nodded slightly and returned to his table. Tom watched him as he sat down, leant over the table and said something to his group who laughed and looked over to Tom and Nia.

Nia's pressure on Tom's arm grew as she tugged him to sit down. She kissed him until the storm in his eyes calmed.

"Thank you," she said.

"Sorry, I wasn't quick enough to stop him insulting you," Tom responded.

"No. Thank you for not beating the shit out of him," Nia smiled and grasped his hand tightly. "I know what you can do, Tom Price."

In Goldenboy's corner the laughter continued. The landlord went by and collected some dirty glasses and empty bottles.

"You were lucky there, boyo," he said in passing.

"Lucky where?" Goldenboy asked.

"Nia's fella," the landlord replied. "Would have taken you apart, mate. He'd have left you a quivering lump of jelly on the floor."

"Yeah?" Goldenboy said aggressively.

"Yeah," the landlord replied softly. "You may play a hard man on screen but that man over there is the real deal. He's put men in the ground." He caught Goldenboy's eye and leant down to pick up a glass and whispered in the actor's ear, "But, I think you knew that, didn't you, boyo?"

***

The hotel room was so dark that Tom struggled to adjust to the darkness. He had woken with Nia spooning him and his leg on fire. He had rolled onto his back to stretch his leg and Nia had snoozily repositioned herself, her head on his chest. He felt her breath on his chest hair. He reached his right hand up to her hair and gently, lovingly began to run his fingers through her thick locks. Tom relaxed deeply enjoying the warmth of the bed and the feel of Nia's naked body stretched along his. He felt uneasy, however. He had meant to tell Nia everything about London, Gagnon, the Russians and MI5 but the opportunity hadn't really emerged and now he felt the moment had passed, that it would feel more contrived, even dishonest, if he was to tell her now. Tom decided he would wait for some time in the future to bring Nia into the picture. Tom expected he would stay awake until morning but, feeling somewhat relieved of a burden, drifted back off to sleep.

Nia woke as the room lightened. She slipped out of bed quietly and went to the bathroom. There, she washed her face and brushed her teeth. She had wanted to ask Tom about what Jane had told her about the fight in London but had got carried away with the emotion of the evening. She smiled at her reflection in the bathroom's mirror with a quick memory of the previous evening. She had been more nervous about working with Goldenboy than she had admitted to Tom, to Jane, to herself. It had been liberating when she realised that she felt nothing for him, that the only emotion he stirred in her was one of regret for ever marrying him. She felt a tiny bit superior as she felt only pity for Goldenboy's continued emotional detachment, his shallowness, his self-absorption. It had been further liberating when Tom had not beaten the shit out of Goldenboy. Nia smiled, it had been enough that Tom had been willing to do so. She knew, after witnessing him in action, what he was capable of. But, more importantly, she felt, that he had been clearly in control. What a paradox he is, Nia thought, such a kind and gentle man but one who is capable of, how did he describe it, massive and controlled violence.

Nia returned to bed with a slight shiver and gently

got back under the covers. She snuggled up to Tom spooning him again from behind. She shut her eyes and considered herself to be entirely content for the first time in, how many years, then realised it was for the first time ever. She had a man whom she loved and who loved her back totally, her career was, incredibly, on the upswing, and she felt emotionally and physically healthy. She was feeling freed from the demons of her past; love had redeemed her. She hugged Tom hard to her body, as if she was trying to meld the two of them as one, he stirred, and Nia relaxed and they both slipped into a warm and comforting early morning slumber.

They spent the day at the inn and took a long, chilly walk in the Black Mountains. Most of the cast and crew packed and left for the BBC Wales Cardiff studios while Nia and Tom were out hiking. After Nia had warmed up in front of the inn's fireplace, Tom drove Nia to her hotel in Cardiff. The hotel, arranged by the film company, was of a trendy, eclectic boutique style. It smelt warm and chintzy with a hint of spice. Nia learnt via text that she would have an early morning call. Tom, tired of hotels, suggested he'd head back up to Rachel's. Before Tom hit the road, they shared dinner at a decent Indian restaurant. Nia had found the unpretentious, somewhat authentic restaurant off the beaten tourist pathways. As they entered, they both inhaled deeply finding the redolent, rich odours of spices and cooking evocative of other times and other places. Nia, to a favourite Indian restaurant in her London neighbourhood, Tom to Afghanistan. After dinner, Tom made sure that Nia was safely ensconced in her hotel room before he headed out.

Tom drove through Cardiff's quiet streets and thought of Nia all the way through to the outskirts of Cwmbran. He had synched his iPhone with the Land Rover's after-market entertainment system and as Cwmbran disappeared in the rear-view mirror he asked, via voice command, the system to call Gagnon.

***

London

Gagnon answered Tom's call on the fourth ring. The tall Canadian was sitting in his hospital room's lounge chair wearing a threadbare hospital dressing gown and a face like thunder. He was still in pain but in no medical danger and was more troubled about the afternoon's meeting he had experienced with representatives from MI5. The meeting had been short and to the point; his personal vendetta against Zalkind/Kamenev was now over, permanently, as was his time in the UK. He was informed that as soon as he received medical clearance to travel, he was going to be quietly escorted to Heathrow and put on a plane for Canada. The rather pompous MI5 officer informed Gagnon that he was to consider himself fortunate that charges weren't going to be held against him. And worse was to come; he was subsequently visited by a pale Canadian intelligence officer from the embassy who, after taking Gagnon's report, informed Gagnon that Ottawa had made a decision to relieve him of duties. Gagnon had expected such news. He was disappointed, yet, he told himself, he was lucky to be alive.

Gagnon told Tom about the meetings with the grey men from the intelligence agencies. Tom asked what Gagnon planned to do once he was back home in Canada. Gagnon had made a few calls to Canadian universities and colleges, some NGOs, and think tanks. An old commanding officer, Gagnon continued, who was now a small private college's president, had been able to secure Gagnon an adjunct teaching gig. Gagnon told Tom that he would now put his PhD to work in higher education. Tom joked that the world of higher education was as cutthroat and political as the dark world of espionage. They laughed together as old friends. They talked through their experiences in London. It inspired them to talk about old times, being young officers, their shared experiences in Afghanistan, their adjustment back to civilian life. As the conversation slowed, Gagnon expressed thanks for Tom's actions that had saved his life. Tom generously brushed it off; simply right place, right time, he told Gagnon.

***

Rachel's Farm

Tom was dead tired when he pulled into the courtyard adjacent to Rachel and Owain's farmhouse. Tom exited his Land Rover and inhaled the farm's scent deeply; sweet hay and fresh cow manure was an oddly pleasant odour. The farm door opened, a crack of warm yellow light spread across the dark flagstones of the courtyard. Jack came bounding out to greet her owner. Tom knelt, allowing Jack to lick his face in her welcoming style. Rachel stood in the door with a small but warm smile. Tom decided to stay the night at the farm and head out to his narrowboat in the morning.

Rachel made a quick round of bacon and egg sandwiches, Owain joined Tom for the late-night snack and Tom told them of his new book contract and his flying visit to Nia on location. He left out the rather juicy detail concerning the trouble with the Russian security services. His phone dinged with a text and he was disappointed that it wasn't Nia but from the young MI5 officer who had been introduced as Patel.

"Gagnon being sent home by week's end," Patel had written.

"Is that wise?" Tom texted in response. He was surprised when Patel replied almost immediately, "Medically cleared. PNG-ed."

Chapter Nineteen
Above Montreal, January 20th

Gagnon was tired, sore and depressed. The flight home had been long and uncomfortable. A six-foot five-inch man, bandaged and wearing a sling, was never going to be comfortably seated in economy. Gagnon closed his eyes and reflected on the past few days as the cabin crew informed the passengers that the big jet had started its descent into Montreal Trudeau.

Gagnon felt the big Air Canada Airbus slide sideways, purposefully dropping altitude. The jet banked over the St Lawrence River on its final approach into the airport below, and Gagnon began to work through a mental checklist of the things he now needed to do. He was so distracted he almost didn't realise the plane had landed and was taxiing to its assigned gate. Gagnon was still in some pain and discomfort as he moved gingerly up the skybridge. Once inside the main body of the terminal, he checked the departures board to double check the time and gate for his connecting flight home to Ottawa. As Gagnon turned away from the board his flight's listing moved from 'on time' to 'delayed'.

Gagnon moved quickly past gates, restaurants,

bars, and the strange assortment of tourist tchotchke and high-end shops that all international airports are populated with. He passed a men's bespoke clothing shop and wondered what he would need to wear at college. He immediately thought tweed with elbow patches and smiled at the cliché. His smile faded when he saw the delayed sign at his gate. His face clouded as he approached the gate agent. The gate's seating area was suspiciously empty, he expected the worse.

Sarah Jones watched the bearded giant approach her customer service station. She thought he looked tired, sore and angry. Oh dear, she thought as he approached but never-the-less gave him a big smile and cocked her head slightly.

"How can I help you, sir?" she asked.

Gagnon was disarmed by the smile and the stunning green eyes. She was tall too, he liked tall women.

"Err, my flight's delayed, just want to know when we can expect to board."

Sarah's fingers moved across her keyboard. "I'm sorry, sir," she began. "It looks as if this flight's going to be cancelled due to mechanical issues. The airplane is still on the ground in Ottawa."

Gagnon scowled. It's an inconvenience, he thought, but at least he didn't now have work pressures on him to get home or get to the office at a set time.

"Are there any options for flights or should I just go ahead and rent a car?"

Sarah checked her computer. She felt sorry for this guy, there was an air of dejection around him.

"Yes," she began. "I can get you on a flight in about four hours."

"Damn, a four-hour wait, and then a one-and-a-half-hour flight, I might as well rent a car."

"I don't mean to be forward," Sarah said with a shy smile, "but can you even drive with that sling?"

Gagnon moved his left arm and pain shot through his chest and across his shoulder. He grimaced. "I'm not sure," he answered.

"Look sir, you look beat. I'll get the ticket for you; we'll comp for the cancelled flight. While I do that, why don't you grab a comfy seat over there," she nodded towards a celebrity chef's diner. "I can give you a food voucher, full disclosure, it won't cover the cost though but it's actually a good place with good service. I occasionally eat there when I have the time."

Gagnon looked over to the diner. It was light, people sat around a bar smiling and laughing. It looked like a happy place and he did feel hungry.

"Okay," he said as he turned back to Sarah. "But, on one condition."

"What's that?" Sarah replied.

"That'll you'll join me," he said. Sarah smiled, she already knew that she liked this tall, seemingly lost guy.

"Well," she began. "My shift's just about over. Give me about fifteen minutes to wrap up here and I'll join you."

"Would you like me to get you a drink?" Gagnon asked.

"Please, a red wine, a Malbec," she replied.

Gagnon was drinking a beer, a Molson, when Sarah entered the diner, saw him, and slipped elegantly into his booth. She had removed her airline company scarf and jacket. Gagnon couldn't help noticing that her blouse and tight pencil skirt outlined a nice, full figure. She smiled at him and reached for the wine glass. She took a big sip.

"Thanks," she said. "It's been a long shift. So, do you come here often?"

"No. But I'm seriously thinking about it," Gagnon laughed and relaxed. More so when Sarah began the conversation which moved surprisingly easily for them both. They talked about travel and the places they had visited. Sarah realised that Gagnon's travels in and out of the Middle East and South Asia must have been related to his having been in the military. She talked about her childhood service-brat life moving from base to base with her Canadian Air Force father. The conversation was light and natural and they both felt they were connecting. They talked of food and wine, of books, and movies. Four hours flew by and another gate agent announced the Ottawa flight.

Gagnon left the diner with Sarah's number in his phone and a date for Saturday night. All of a sudden, the dark clouds that had gathered around him in London appeared to be dissipating. As the Ottawa bound regional jet took off, Gagnon looked out of the plane's window at the lights of Montreal spreading out below him. He smiled. At the gate, Sarah Jones watched the same jet take off. Jacques Gagnon, she thought, he was going to be fun to get to know. She smiled and turned away. It had been a long and interesting day and it was time for her to go home. She was looking forward to Saturday.

***

London

It was a still dawn and the Georgian square appeared almost devoid of life. The SVR watcher, loaned to Kamenev by the Rezident, was observing Nia's house on a laptop screen at a desk jammed with surveillance equipment all crammed into the back of a small nondescript white van. Decals on the van's side announced it was an emergency twenty-four-hour plumber and sewer unclogging specialist. Walkers passing the van would not see anything out of the ordinary and neighbours would be too embarrassed to ask each other which house the van was servicing. The watcher operated under the guise of an itinerant Polish tradesman, and he even had a rudimentary grasp of British plumbing if anyone ever questioned him. He was a highly experienced surveillance expert. He'd positioned the van perfectly so its hidden cameras could focus on the front of Nia's house as well as the comings

309

and goings up and down the street. He also knew how to get comfortable while maintaining the same position for hours at a time, never letting the object of his surveillance leave his sight lines. He had spent many a long hour outdoors in wet undergrowth with mud soaking his clothes and the cold etching into his bones but never leaving sight of his target, so this was a cushy assignment. He was warm, had a padded seat, a Thermos of coffee and sandwiches, and, to cap it all, the woman he was watching was cute.

He liked observing women, less chance of violence and more chance of hitting the voyeurs' jackpot; total unselfconscious, natural nudity. He recalled a recent assignment; posh London hotel, female member of the US House of Representatives. He wasn't sure of her name, but he thought of her as Californian as she was blonde with incredible straight and white teeth and large, fake breasts. He smiled at the memory. Three simple, tiny cameras had provided him with hi-resolution quality images of her walking around the room naked and of her pleasuring herself. Sadly, he thought, rumours of her extramarital affair were not evidenced during surveillance for he would have been thrilled to see some boy-on-girl or girl-on-girl action. As it was, the SVR and FSB did now have some potentially embarrassing pictures and video to present to her at some key moment in her legislative career. Maybe embarrassing enough for her to vote the way the Kremlin would direct. The watcher had also saved some images to his own personal collection which was now quite extensive. It would fuel his fantasies for years.

The SVR agent was snapped out of his reverie by the front door opening and Nia stepping out into the morning cold with a visible shiver. She was dressed for a run and the Russian grinned at her figure in her tight running clothes. Yes, he thought, he would like to get cameras into her bedroom and bathroom. He focused a camera on her as she stretched her calves, then moved into a lunge, and followed up with a quad stretch. He noticed her adjust something with her ear buds and watched as she moved off down the square at a good pace. He radioed her movement and direction to other members of the surveillance team.

Nia liked the quiet, cold mornings when she was able to rouse herself out of bed and go for a run. Although she had become something of a gym rat, she enjoyed the freedom and simplicity of a road run. She felt she got a better workout than the gym's treadmill could offer, in half the time of a gym trip, and she enjoyed being out and about in her neighbourhood. She had enjoyed her towpath runs with Tom and she felt close to him as she ran, even when apart. More so this morning as she had downloaded another playlist, he had sent her. The Verve's 'Bittersweet Symphony' played quietly through her ear buds, she wanted to be aware of the noises that emanated from the roads, houses and parks along her running route.

The opening chords of Bonnie Tyler's 'I Need a

Hero' began as Nia ran through a neighbouring Georgian square's central beautifully kept park. She guffawed out loud, getting Tom's habit to include a Welsh singer in every playlist. Still, Nia thought, the song had a good driving beat and she increased her pace. She ran through deserted streets, the city still slumbering, through another square and across another park accompanied now by XTC's 'Making Plans for Nigel'. She noticed another female runner across the park. Nia didn't recognise her but couldn't miss the young, petite woman's flaming red hair and her blistering pace as she closed the distance between them. Nia noticed that the redhead's face was set almost in a grimace. Nia raised her head to give the usual runners' nod as the young woman passed. It was not necessarily unusual for a runner not to acknowledge the greeting, but the redhead appeared to diverge from her direct path, drop her shoulder, and her elbow caught Nia a glancing blow as they passed. Nia's right bicep immediately ached.

"Hey," Nia shouted. She stopped and turned but the redhead was already sprinting away across the park, through its gate and was gone.

"What the fuck was that?" Nia thought, as she rubbed her bicep. She shook her arm and then began to run again. "Bitch," she said out loud.

Nia continued her run turning onto pavements that bordered major streets, now filling with early commuter traffic. She ran down a few more streets before beginning to circle back closer to home. She ended the run with Elton John singing 'I'm Still Standing', enjoying another of Tom's jokes. Once home and in the shower, she noticed the bruise on her bicep.

Outside of Nia's home, the Russian listened in to the surveillance team's radio conversation, his English comprehension was excellent. He heard a woman's voice, accented, implying that the actress was an easy mark and that they could take her out at any time. The surveillance man recognised the deep voice that entered the conversation: Kamenev. The watcher heard Kamenev order the hit for the next time the actress took a solo early morning run. In his embassy office, Kamenev ended the call. He picked up the hard copy of the newspaper with Nia's photo from the BFI *Vampire Moon* event. Lovely looking woman, he thought with a sigh, collateral damage in the ongoing dirty war. He had approved her removal via a Georgi Markov type hit. The redhead would run past the actress bump into her as she had today but, the next time, she would inject her with enough insulin to cause a massive heart attack. A sloppy pathologist would simply pass her death off as a coronary brought on by exercise, but a good pathologist would find the needle mark, the insulin, and it would be filed under a mysterious, pointless homicide. Any parallels between her death and the 1978 assassination of Bulgarian dissident, Markov, poisoned with ricin via a stab of a sharpened umbrella, were too few to draw any conclusions as to the murders. And, Kamenev

313

reflected, the post Brexit Brits were so anxious to keep up trade treaty negotiations with Russia they probably wouldn't even pursue any investigation that led to Moscow. The Russian smiled and took a sip of his hot tea.

***

Ditchling, January 22nd
The MI5 team was good, very professional and experienced. They had quietly infiltrated the village, unobserved. They established furtive observation posts across the village at strategic points. Anyone entering or leaving the village by road would be viewed and identified. Three members of the team had snuck unobserved by neighbours into Daria Kirov's cottage under cover of darkness. From their observation positions, they continually monitored the quiet street in the front of the cottage and the meadow behind.

Daria had agreed to the deputy director's plan of, essentially, using herself as bait. Daria had called her agent and suggested a meet with the Irish daily that had expressed an interest in publishing the Russian's work. The DD hoped that such a ploy would lure out the red-headed assassin and her Russian support team. Like clockwork, Daria's agent called her and suggested a meet with the Irish journalist at a rather popular pub in Brighton. Daria said that, as she was about to move to a new house, she was fine with meeting the journalist at her Ditchling cottage if the Irish newspaper sent some information on their journalist. MI5 had thought it safer for Daria and the local civilian populations if the Russian could be contained in an area where there wouldn't be any chance of collateral damage. Within minutes of her agent's call, Daria received an email with a short biography, links to some online pieces, and a photo of the journalist. She was petite, pretty, with long red hair.

At Thames House, the DD was alerted to the email.

"Right, Patel," she said. "Looks like we're a go. Alert the onsite team."

Patel nodded and took notes on her tablet.

"Also trace the incoming information from the newspaper, they obviously have a bad actor in their midst aiding and abetting our little ginger assassin."

"Yes, ma'am."

It was dusk when the first MI5 agent at one of the Ditchling observation posts radioed an alert about a suspicious vehicle. Its make, colour and number plate didn't match any of the local cars and didn't match any of the visiting vehicles that had recently been through the village and the subsequent vetting. Several pairs of MI5 eyes were on the vehicle, a grey Ford Focus, as it drove past Daria's cottage. It didn't slow suspiciously but the MI5 watchers noticed that both the driver and passenger observed the little house intently as they drove by. Photographs of car and occupants were taken by hi-resolution optics and sent to Thames House for analysis.

"We've got movement behind the cottage," a voice came over the radio. Through binoculars the MI5 agent on observation duty at the rear of Daria's house had spotted a couple of figures taking up tactical positions in the meadow behind Daria's house. The security service had planned for such an eventuality and moved an outlying team into position behind the two men they now considered active Russian agents.

"Two cars stopping, adjacent street," another voice came over the secure communication system, surprisingly calmly. "Look like Audi Q5s, black."

The DD listened into the conversations and observed movements in Ditchling through real-time hi-def video from an operations centre in the bowels of Thames House. Patel sat next to her.

"Two people leaving the first car," the radio voice continued. "Visual confirmation: petite, redhead. Repeat: petite redhead. Accompanied by unidentified male carrying large camera bag, probably a gun bag."

Patel's fingers flew across her keyboard pulling up a still photo of the Russian with the bag and cross-referencing it against faces in MI5's extensive database.

"Got an ID, ma'am," she said excitedly. "One of the Holyhead Russians."

"This is all coming together, isn't it?" the DD asked rhetorically. "Shit. Alert the team. Weapons hot."

The DD passed on that information to the agent in charge.

As the redhead and her faux cameraman approached Daria's cottage, MI5 vehicles slowly and quietly moved into place blocking all the entry and exit roads into the little village. Effectively locking down Ditchling.

The Russian agent with the camera bag dropped back allowing the redhead to get a house length in front of him. He slowed and knelt and opened the bag and he appeared to be rummaging around in it. In the body of the bag, the agent chambered a round in the small Skorpian machine pistol and moved the safety catch to off. He nodded to the redhead. The assassin approached Daria's front door and knocked loudly. She moved her hand into a deep coat pocket and flipped the safety catch of her Walther PPK/S to off.

"I'm in the kitchen," Daria shouted from inside the house. "Can you come round the back?"

The redhead tentatively tried the door handle, locked, and then stepped back from the door. She thought for a moment, assessing her options. Then, she gestured with her head for the camara bag agent to follow her and moved to the side of the house. She made her way slowly around to the back of the cottage. There, she noticed Daria's motorbike, and smiled. So, the Russian bitch was indeed in, she thought. She tried the back door, again locked. She knocked.

"Just a moment," Daria shouted from inside and she was instantly pulled upstairs by the MI5 agents.

The redhead stood outside the door for a moment

and then stepped back. In one fluid movement, she pulled her gun out of her coat and kicked at the door. The door lock splintered, and she moved quickly and smoothly into the kitchen, pistol at the ready. Her adrenalin flowed and she was on heightened alert to any movement but what she saw as she entered the kitchen was unexpected. She hesitated a moment before she raised her gun towards one of the two figures that greeted her in black combat fatigues. Her eyes widened, mouth opened, and her breath paused, she dove to her right, firing and hitting one of the dark figures low in the chest. She hit the kitchen floor hard and attempted to roll while bringing her gun up to sight on the other figure in black fatigues. A red pinprick of a laser sight jostled on her rolling body until it momentarily settled on her forehead. The bullet that followed killed her before she could pull her own trigger a second time.

The MI5 shooter went over to the red-headed assassin's body and kicked the Walther out of the prostrate woman's reach. It was just procedure; the shooter knew his round had killed her instantly. Once satisfied that the red-headed assassin would kill no more, the MI5 agent radioed that the assassin was down and dead. He then went to his colleague who was sitting up a little uncomfortably rubbing a spot below his left ribs.

"Shit," he said. "She was bloody fast. I've never been shot before."

"Good thing she went for a torso shot," the standing

shooter replied with a smile. "Your vest saved you." He put out an arm to help his slightly embarrassed colleague up.

On the street in front of the cottage, the Russian with the camera bag reacted to the sound of suppressed gun shots. He appeared to hesitate for a moment before he pulled the Skorpion sub-machine gun out of the bag and made a move towards the cottage. Before his first foot fall, he was brought down by a single head shot from the MI5 sniper from the upper floor of a cottage on the other side of the street.

The two Russian agents observing the events from the field behind the cottage knew the mission had gone pear shaped. They retreated under cover of the field to their car only to be apprehended by the waiting MI5 snatch team. The Russians, outflanked and outgunned, surrendered meekly.

Kamenev, in one of the Audis that accompanied the redhead, knew from his team's radio chatter and hearing the gunfire that the simple assassination mission had gone seriously wrong. He radioed the drivers of both Q5s to get out of the village as quickly as possible. The first FSB driver was a good one. He immediately put his big Q5 in reverse and accelerated, executing a textbook J turn. He slammed the car into first gear and headed out of town. Kamenev's Audi followed close behind. A police BMW and an MI5 Range Rover formed a roadblock on the Audis' egress road. Kamenev radioed the first driver to ram the roadblock. The driver gunned the motor as he approached the security services' vehicles. He accelerated, aiming his SUV for the front noses of the blockading vehicles. The Audi crumpled into the Range Rover before cartwheeling over the Rover's bonnet and landing on its roof. The police BMW had been pushed perpendicularly into the curb and Kamenev's driver swerved up on to the right-side pavement clipping the police car and forcing enough room between the BMW and a cottage's hedge to speed past. The Russian driver floored it. Kamenev lay across the rear seat fearing British bullets entering the back of the Audi. None came and the driver accelerated out of the village and on to a larger B road. Traffic speed cameras flashed as the car sped past.

On the video screen at Thames House, the DD stood as she watched in real time as the Q5 made its escape.

"I want eyes on that car," she ordered. "Get a chopper in the air. I want chase vehicles and roadblocks. I want that bastard."

Kamenev's driver followed an emergency contingency plan. Before MI5 eyes had caught them, the Audi had been swapped for a small, silver Ford Focus. Kamenev lay across the Focus' rear seat while the driver headed for London. Kamenev quickly radioed one of his most trusted men still at the embassy to make arrangements. His secure mobile began to light up with messages from the embassy as well as from Moscow. He ignored them all. He was going rogue. He could imagine that communiqués were already being prepared disavowing any recognition of Kamenev's mission. He knew that Ditchling's failure well and truly meant not just the ignominious end to this career but probably arrest, deportation and execution. As his car sped north towards London on the M25, Kamenev imagined that Moscow's plans for his own fatal accident would already be on the President's desk awaiting approval. His disappointment, frustration and anger were distilled into only one thought: revenge upon Tom Price.

Chapter Twenty
Shropshire Union Canal, February 3rd

Tom woke to the sound of a tractor mowing on the other side of the towpath's hedgerow. He checked his watch; it was seven a.m. Jack looked up expectantly from the foot of the bed. Tom had moored outside of the little Cheshire village of Wrenbury after a long trip the day before. He had tied up against the towpath on a lovely treelined spot where he and Jack had enjoyed a glorious sunset from the Periwinkle's bow. Tom was back on very familiar territory.

Tom and Jack went through the regular morning. routine on the canal boat before Tom headed into Wrenbury to shop and resupply the Periwinkle with some essentials. He put Jack on her lead and popped in his air pods. He found one of the playlists Nia had created and hit play. Norah Jones' *Come Away With Me* started and Tom smiled. Although they had talked the night before, Tom was excited by the prospect of seeing and holding her again. His step into the village was light.

Back from the short shopping trip, Tom took the Periwinkle down the canal under Wrenbury's electrically powered swing bridge and then on his way to the village of Marbury just a short two-hour journey to the west. The canal meandered lazily through postcard-like Cheshire countryside. Tom had traversed this stretch of the canal numerous times over the last five years. He had enjoyed almost every trip through all kinds of weather but, on what was a beautiful late winter day, Tom was feeling a level of contentment that he had never really experienced. He steered the narrowboat reflexively, his thoughts very much on Nia.

Nia was on the 10.10 a.m. from London Euston. She would be in Crewe before noon and had already arranged a taxi from the station to her lunch date with Tom at the White Swan in the tiny Cheshire village of Marbury. She, too, was excited. She tried to read but found herself reading and re-reading the same page repeatedly. Her thoughts were very much on Tom. She was looking forward to a few days with him, Jack and the Periwinkle. Nia had become enamoured with her time on the canals and had specifically asked Tom for a trip back towards Llangollen to again experience the majesty of the countryside combined with the canal builders' art.

Nia stretched out in the first-class seat and watched the countryside pass by at express speed. It wasn't fast enough as she was anxious to be with the man she loved. She returned to her book, *Hadfield's Illustrated History of British Canals*. It was rather dry and she was distracted. She was tired too, her latest role, the 1960s' lesbian matron, had just wrapped. She had spent one night in her home before heading out for the rendezvous with Tom. She hadn't noticed that the small white plumbing van had returned to her Georgian square or that it had followed her taxi to Euston station that morning. Nia had no idea that two carriages behind her a Russian SVR agent was reading the morning's *Daily Mail* while occasionally updating his boss with texts.

***

Outskirts, London

The hotel was north-west of London on the outside of the capital city's greenbelt. The hotel's heyday, if it ever had one, had long since passed. It was threadbare, barely surviving on travellers with very limited budgets, the accidental passers-by needing a late-night check in with no other options available, or prostitutes booking in for a four-hour 'nap'. Its selling points for Kamenev were that it took cash, indeed it was preferred, waived ID, and had no cameras. In a corner room on the first-floor, Kamenev sat on a single bed reading texts on his phone. He tapped out a short response and then put the phone back into his jacket pocket.

"Go gas up the car," he ordered his driver. "It looks as if we are heading to a place called Crewe."

The driver got off the room's second single bed with a grunt. He was glad for an opportunity to get out of the shithole hotel they been cooped up in for the past few days. He grabbed his small hand grip, his go bag, that contained cash, three separate identities with passports and other identification, and a Skorpion. He left the room and headed out of an unalarmed emergency exit to the small car park and the silver Focus. Kamenev, too, was pleased that things were once again moving.

Kamenev knew that as a rogue agent his time was short. The driver and the surveillance man had begun to question the total communications blackout with the embassy, the Rezident and Moscow. It wouldn't be long before one of his team breached the radio silence and the British security services or, worse, the FSB or SVR tracked them down. He didn't enjoy feeling like prey. His field craft was good enough to evade the forces aligned against him for some time but he much preferred being the hunter. He was focused on his own hunt and that hunt was now accelerating. The actress was now being followed and she would lead him to Tom Price. Then, at least, he would settle the account that began long ago and far away in Afghanistan. He grabbed his own go bag. He pulled out his heavy Makarov semi-automatic pistol and chambered a round.

***

Crewe

Nia's prearranged taxi was waiting for her as soon as she exited Crewe station. She took a quick look at her watch to calculate the time it would take before she would see Tom again. She didn't notice the man who had followed her out of the station nor the cab that tailed hers. She didn't see the following taxi stop when hers pulled into the White Swan's car park in Marbury. She failed to notice the man who got out of the taxi and shadowed her, at a distance, as she entered the pub.

Tom had arrived at the pub before Nia. He had chosen a table in the corner of the lounge, hard against a floor to ceiling bookshelf, that allowed him to tactically observe the pub's main entrance. An exit was directly behind him. He saw Nia enter the pub and look around. She was elegant as usual. Her hair was tied back but looked as if it had been prepared by a stylist. She wore her new Barbour coat over a red wool jumper, a white tailored shirt and cropped jeans with brown Dr Martens. She was toting a smart leather weekend bag. Tom stood up as soon as Nia made eye contact with him. He felt her broad smile warm deep inside. They moved together and hugged as if they had been apart for months. Nia kissed Tom hard and he reciprocated. As they broke their kiss Tom noticed the entry of a pub patron who stared at them before he made his way to the bar. Tom ushered Nia to the corner table. Nia kissed him again as she sat down and removed her hat and coat. They quickly fell into conversation. As Nia talked quickly and excitedly about her recent acting role Tom caught the eye of the same pub patron in the bar back mirror. Instinctively, Tom assigned the patron's facial features to memory, but he became quickly engaged in listening to Nia and her rapid fire, almost stream of consciousness conversation.

After lunch, Tom and Nia held hands as they walked through the high hedgerowed country lanes and down to the canal. They had enjoyed the excellent food served at the White Swan but were both looking forward to getting back on the Periwinkle. Nia was also looking forward to seeing Jack again. Out of their sightlines behind them, Kamenev's SVR man watched them through a small pair of binoculars. He moved stealthily through a farm field and lay down, hidden by the hedge that separated the field from the canal. Through his binoculars he watched Tom and Nia make their way down from a humpbacked road bridge and down onto the canal's towpath. There was only one narrowboat moored on the bank and the Russian watched as Tom and Nia entered it. The Russian noted the boat's name, the direction it was pointing, and texted Kamenev.

***

Periwinkle

Jack greeted Nia with her usual welcoming licking routine before the terrier rolled on her back in anticipation of a tummy rub. Once Jack was satisfied, she allowed Nia to unpack her bag in the narrowboat's cabin. Tom had once again made space for her things in the cabin's small cupboard and closet. Tom was on the stern deck going through the routine of engine starting while Nia was in the cabin folding her things. Tom had planned on letting the engine tick over for about twenty minutes before they headed off westward up the canal.

Tom came down the stern cabin's steps whistling. The tune he was butchering stalled when he noticed that the cabin's curtains were drawn, he recognised the sweet scent of Nia's Floris No 89, and then he saw Nia was under the covers of the bed. He smiled.

"Well, hello," Tom said in a posh louche accent.

Nia laughed and she pulled back the duvet. She was wearing a pink silk camisole set.

"C'mere," she said with theatrical lasciviousness and patted the bed next to her.

"As you command," Tom replied and began to slip out of his clothes.

They fell together hungrily. After, they lay spooned together as Nia ran a hand through Tom's hair.

"That was lovely," Nia said. "Do you know what would make it perfect?"

Tom turned on his side so they were face to face.

"Errr," he responded. "A cup of tea?"

Nia smiled, "Tom, you're a genius."

"What's with you and all the sex and tea?" Tom joked.

"It's Welsh thing," Nia replied laughingly.

Tom got out of bed.

"You are a gentleman genius," added Nia. "And with such a fine arse too."

She slapped Tom's bottom.

"Oh, I haven't had this much affection since basic training," Tom said as he put on some boxer shorts and Nia laughed.

"I love you, Tom Price," Nia said as Tom disappeared down the small corridor to the galley. Jack ran into the cabin after being sexiled in the lounge and jumped up on the bed. She licked Nia's hands before settling down, after her usual circular nesting motion, at the foot of the bed. Nia lay back enjoying the warmth of the bed, the weight of the dog on her feet, and the diffused light that emanated through the curtains. She sighed with happiness.

The afternoon's trip down the quiet canal was uneventful. Tom steered the Periwinkle and Nia joined him at the stern taking in the countryside and the tranquillity. She was a little nervous as the narrowboat approached the first of three locks. Nia's confidence returned almost as soon as she had opened the first lock gates. Tom pulled the Periwinkle in and Nia closed the rear lock gates before she moved to the front gates and opened the sluices to fill the lock. They worked well together through the next two locks and Nia was a little disappointed that the lock flight at Grindley Brook would require the assistance of a lock keeper.

Tom pulled the Periwinkle up to a water station after the final lock. Nia walked up from the lock after a quick chat and a word of thanks with the hirsute, friendly volunteer lock keeper. A shiny red and gold narrowboat moved into position to go down the lock flight. Nia took the tiller as Tom pushed the Periwinkle away from the water station and then stepped on board. The late afternoon sky moved from shades of reds to oranges to yellows.

Nia took a turn at the tiller and increased the revs. Tom noted, again, that there wasn't any speeding on the canal as well as no running around the locks, another thing Nia continued to do. Nia slowed down and steered the Periwinkle into the canal banks to let Tom off to open the swing bridges that marked this stretch of canal. Nia was always quick to wave and shout out a greeting to the few boaters that passed by. She received friendly 'hullos' or 'how do' in return and the occasional double take of recognition.

Tom enjoyed watching Nia at the tiller. She had quickly become a competent helmsman and was now confidant enough to control the boat around sharp bends, into locks, and even steering the middle course between narrowboats on her port and starboard sides. Tom finished making two steaming mugs of tea and brought them back to the stern.

"Ummm, lovely," Nia said taking one of the mugs. She was squinting in the lowering sun but had zipped up her coat over one of Tom's fleece jackets against a wind that was progressively getting colder.

"It will be a chilly night once the sun drops," Tom stated. "Do you want dinner in a village or on the boat?"

"Let's stay on the boat," Nia replied.

They both looked at each other and smiled.

"Like a real couple," she added and immediately regretted the turn of phrase. Her smile faded.

"What's wrong?" Tom asked.

"I'm sorry, I didn't mean to be presumptuous," she said.

"Nia, don't you see us as a couple?"

She thought for a moment, "Yes, of course I do, I love you so much, Tom. It's just that it sounded strange to announce it publicly."

"Publicly? There's only the two of us. And Jack."

Nia laughed nervously and moved to hug Tom. She felt vulnerable but wanted to make sure that Tom was okay with where the conversation was going.

"I do love us being a couple, doing couple's things," she said. Then she added, reticently, "I haven't felt as if I needed to be a part of a couple for a long time now... but now, with you, I do."

Tom lifted Nia's chin gently and kissed her.

"To us, being a couple. Let's toast to that," Tom said and raised his mug of tea and Nia reciprocated with a throaty guffaw as they clinked mugs.

Tom had actually thought of himself and Nia as a couple since the drink they shared in the theatre bar after her performance in *Blithe Spirit*.

Nia drove the Periwinkle through the wetlands of Prees which she thought felt like a nature reserve and then on past the meres outside of the aptly named Ellesmere. Tom suggested they push on past the village with its busy wharf and eventually moor up at a more

331

bucolic stretch of canal. The canal took a rightward turn passing the junction for the Montgomery canal. Tom and Nia pushed on through the two locks at New Marston until Nia chose a mooring spot on a quiet, heavily wooded stretch of the canal.

The Periwinkle's engine clicked through its cooling and contraction stages as Tom locked the stern doors and he, Nia and Jack went for a run down the towpath. Hidden in the undergrowth at the side of a small canal bridge to the rear, the Russian agent observed them through his binoculars. He was thankful that his run across fields, down county lanes, and on the occasional towpath, shadowing the Periwinkle, had finally ended. He watched the narrowboat and its occupants until the evening dark made further observation impossible and the Periwinkle's curtains were drawn. He slipped back through the hedgerow and stretched his cold and aching limbs; he was exhausted from the physically demanding day. He walked quickly across the field to a breeze block farm equipment shed. He forced the lock with ease. He lay out some hay and pulled a coat from his day pack, a can of Coke and a power bar. He made a makeshift bed and settled in for a long, cold night.

***

The Next Day, Seven a.m.
The small narrowboat yard was situated at the end of a twisting, turning, oft overgrown country lane. Hard

against the canal side, it was ideally positioned for canal traffic. A light burned in the yard's office as the manager made an early start to his working day. The yard's secluded nature made it the ideal spot for Kamenev and his driver to approach. The SVR watcher who had followed Nia was waiting for them as they pulled into the ancient boat yard's small car park. The surveillance man was dirty and sore from his night in the machine shed. He slipped into the Focus' rear seat and quickly apprised Kamenev and the driver as to Tom Price's location.

The boat yard manager, surprised by business so early in the morning, greeted the Russians suspiciously. Kamenev quickly assuaged the manager's concern with his cut-glass public-school boy accent and a wad of cash. The manager was quick to rent Kamenev a narrowboat. Kamenev had told the manager that he and his friends had planned an early trip to Llangollen and back, two days and one evening. Kamenev overpaid for the rental, much to the yard manager's delight.

The three Russians entered the forty-five-foot-long narrowboat along with the yard manager who quickly ran through the boat's operations. The manager cut his usual orientation short as Kamenev had convinced him that he was a veteran of numerous narrowboat trips. The Russian driver retrieved the two go bags from the Focus as Kamenev bought some basic supplies of food and beverages and caps emblazoned with the boat yard's name from the small office. Kamenev was keen to make a start and another exchange of cash, as a tip, quelled the boat yard manager's concern about Kamenev's desire to start his canal trip before the eight a.m. approved start time.

The watcher, rather dirty from his time tromping across fields, muddy towpaths, and hiding under hedgerows and machine sheds, cleaned himself up in the boat's small bathroom. The driver, taking up his customary role, this time at the tiller, waited for Kamenev to reboard the canal boat and then he pulled the tiller to the left and increased the engine revs, and the narrowboat moved slowly off from its mooring and into the canal's main channel. It was heading west. The watcher joined the driver at the stern.

He handed the driver a cigarette, lit it, and then yawned widely and loudly.

"Fuck, I hardly slept at all last night. This country is always frigging cold."

The driver nodded not really listening and not caring.

"Crazy this, isn't it?" the surveillance man continued. "Now we're chasing some Brits in a boat that can go what… four miles per hour? High speed chase, *da*?"

The driver didn't see the humour in the situation.

"It's our job. The boss knows what he's doing."

"I don't know," the watcher replied in a whisper. He shivered, "I don't feel right about this. Something's not right and I'll be happy when this shit is all over."

He flicked his half-smoked cigarette into the canal and went into the body of the boat where Colonel Kamenev was cleaning his Makarov.

***

Tom and Nia woke early. The morning was bright but chilly and they had lain in bed chatting and giggling and listening to the cooing of wood pigeons from the copse that bordered the towpath. Once up, Tom had taken Jack for her morning walk while Nia made breakfast. Later, Nia made coffee as she washed the dirty breakfast bowls and plates. Tom checked the engine's fluids and then fired it up. Tom went back into the boat as Nia sat on the stern gunwale, drinking her mug of coffee. Jack lay down at Nia's feet. Ducks quacked demandingly on the canal.

A goose waddled down the towpath towards the Periwinkle's stern. Nia and Jack watched the goose's slow progress intently, Nia raised her coffee mug in a silent greeting, Jack wagged her tail. The goose slipped into the canal with hardly a splash. The ducks quacked their displeasure at the goose's arrival. Nia smiled, she was enjoying the little dramas of canal waterfowl, the warmth of the coffee, and the company of the terrier. The Periwinkle's redoubtable engine hummed contentedly beneath her feet. At eight-thirty a.m., Tom cast off the lines, pushed the Periwinkle away from the canal side, and joined Nia at the tiller.

The Periwinkle made good headway as the canal wound its way around the border town of Chirk and through its first tunnel. Nia noted how the more natural, river-like appearance of the canal changed to something that had been obviously cut through the landscape by the picks, shovels and dynamite of man. She wondered about the canal builders' hard lives, of how much blood had been spilt to build the canal, bridges, tunnels and aqueducts. She thought of the builders' wives and families. Tom was aware of the history of the canal, particularly, this stretch, which he considered his home stretch, but enjoyed Nia's enthusiasm for the story. He watched her face as she recounted canal builders' tales, he watched her eyes shine, how her lips parted over her teeth. He loved that she now shared this passion.

They passed over the border between England and Wales at the dramatic Chirk aqueduct. Nia increased revs to fight the increase in the canal's current as the Periwinkle traversed the aqueduct and then through another tunnel. A little later, Tom suggested they moor up for lunch below the little Welsh village of Froncysyllte before they travelled across the most dramatic aqueduct on the British canal system. Nia pulled the boat into the right-hand bank of the canal hard against some mooring points. Tom stepped off the Periwinkle and made the boat fast.

The afternoon warmed and Tom and Nia enjoyed a post-lunch cup of tea on the stern. The low winter sun had inspired their use of sunglasses. Tom made some notes in his log while Nia skimmed a script. They were pleasantly interrupted by an ancient towpath walker who greeted them with a robust 'hello' along with a wave from his walking stick. Tom and Nia both smiled and nodded to the walker.

"Where are you two from?" the walker asked.

"Here," Tom said. "And London," he added, with a nod in Nia's direction.

"Funny I haven't noticed you before," the walker continued. "I usually walk the towpath most days. At my age, I've got to keep moving or I'll seize up. I'm eighty-six you know."

"Well done you," Nia said. "I hope to be as active as you when I'm eighty-six."

"Yes, it's about two, two and a half miles, my walk. And I see all kinds of things."

Nia was intrigued, "Oh, like what." She smiled slyly to Tom.

"Well, some wonderful wildlife; hawks, badgers, an occasional fox," the old man looked off into the woods that bordered the towpath. "And, erm, some people need to close their curtains when they're on the boats more. I've seen people in their toilets, and in the bedrooms. In all kinds of undress. Not that I'm looking mind!" He shook his head with some kind of memory. "It's not right. Kiddies walk and cycle on these paths you know. And the number of people who can't handle the boats. I've seen all sorts; people who can't steer or control the boats, I've seen crashes into the canal sides

337

and into other boats. All sorts of malarkey."

"Have you indeed," Tom said.

"Why just about ten minutes ago a boat tried to pass under the swing bridge back there," the old man signalled where with a directional shake of his walking-stick. "A boat tried to rush through the swing bridge even though it had been opened by someone from a boat that was patiently waiting on the other side. Both boats then tried to get under the bridge at the same time and scraped each other with a terrific noise. Cheeky buggers too, they were, the people on the boat at fault. All loud and shouty. Foreigners, they were."

Nia and Tom glanced at each other anticipating a pro-Brexit turn to the conversation.

"Russians, I think."

Tom froze.

"I served in West Berlin when I was in the army," the walker continued. "Used to meet some Russkis at the checkpoints there. Recognised the lingo."

"Which way was their boat travelling?" Tom asked with barely concealed concern in his voice. Nia stared at him.

"Oh, this way," the walker said. "Towards the aqueduct." He turned and looked back down the canal, "Yes, that's them now. Silly buggers."

Tom quickly moved to the open stern doors and grabbed a small pair of binoculars that were hanging in a storage compartment there. He focused on the boat. It was a battered old purple rental, and it was moving faster than was acceptable on the canal. Its wake was visible, and it rocked moored boats as it passed, clanging them into the canal's sides. Tom didn't recognise the two men on the tiller but for a fleeting moment he saw a third head pop up to stare over the boat's long cabin. Even through the binoculars he recognised Zalkind/Kamenev.

"Nia," he commanded. "Cast us off." He turned to the walker, "Sir, you better get the hell out of here. Make your way back down the towpath. Try to act naturally, keep your head down. Call the police when you've passed the purple boat."

There was something in Tom's voice that the old walker didn't question. He nodded grimly and immediately started to walk back from the way he came. Nia untied the bow rope and made her way back to the stern rope. Tom cut it with a knife and held his arm out to her as she stepped up on to the stern deck. Behind them, the purple boat appeared to slew sideways across the canal.

"They're blocking the canal," Nia said with alarm creeping into her voice. "Who are they?"

"Russians," Tom replied. "I think they're after me."

"Holy fuck!" Nia stated, eyes wide.

Tom increased the revs and the Periwinkle moved into the centre of the narrowing canal. He quickly tied the tiller so that the boat maintained a straight course. He moved quickly into the Periwinkle's long cabin. Fuck, fuck, fuck, he thought. He knew that whatever was about to happen would change the trajectory of his and Nia's lives forever and probably not for the better.

Kamenev watched the Periwinkle leave her moorings and move out into the narrow canal.

"I'm going on foot," he shouted to his two agents. "Stay here."

He jumped off the purple narrowboat and began to run down the towpath towards the Periwinkle. He darted into the woods on the side of the towpath and used the trees for cover. He stopped when he felt he was in shooting distance of the Periwinkle. Kamenev was a good shot and he was confident of bringing anyone down who stepped out on to the stern deck.

Inside the Periwinkle's cabin, Tom knelt in front of the little Morso stove and opened an almost invisible hatch in the oak planked floor. He retrieved a small fire safe and unlocked its combination in a fluid movement. Nia moved closer and peeped over his shoulder. She saw passports, some legal looking papers, cash and, troublingly, a heavy semi-automatic pistol with an extra ammunition clip.

Tom picked up the pistol, a Browning Hi-power. Expertly, automatically, he cleared the breach, released the magazine that nestled in the pistol's handle, checked it, slid the magazine back, chambered a round, and clicked the safety catch to off. He turned to Nia. She stared into his eyes and noticed that his eyes had almost turned flint black. Tom's pupils had dilated almost across his entire irises, his jaw was set, and he clenched his teeth. It was as if his face had become one of chiselled granite. His look of grim determination momentarily scared her.

"Stay here," he commanded. "Call the police. Tell them they'll need an armed response unit and they should contact the security services." He attempted a smile, "I'll be back."

Nia nodded but reached out her hand and touched him on the shoulder. "Tom," she said. "Don't kill anyone, I couldn't stand it if you did."

Tom paused momentarily. "I can't promise that Nia. These are different people. Not London street thugs. They're a Russian hit squad. I think it's, literally, us or them." He pushed past her and moved swiftly through the narrowboat. He turned momentarily to look back at Nia. "I'm sorry," he said then moved quickly up the stern steps and was gone.

Kamenev observed the Periwinkle from the thick undergrowth at the canal's side. He watched as Tom jumped off the stern and ran towards the Russian narrowboat down the towpath. Kamenev brought the Makarov up took quick aim at the running Tom, but then lowered the ugly pistol. He let Tom run past. The Russian grinned with a new tactic. He'd go after the woman.

Tom ran holding the Browning down by his side. The Russian's boat had been poorly moored. Tom jumped up and on to the bow on the run. He kicked open the cabin's front doors. They gave easily, wood splintered and glass smashed. The SVR agent, the driver, was in the cabin and registered surprise but was well trained enough to swing the Skorpian machine pistol into a firing position. He was a breath too slow as Tom fired twice. Both bullets caught the Russian around the heart, and he was thrown back onto one of the cabin's bench seats. Tom was down on the cabin floor and fired five times through the thin plywood bulkhead that separated the lounge and kitchen from the bathroom and bedroom at the boat's rear. Tom had fired knowing his nine-millimetre bullets would move through the thin cabin wall into the bathroom and on into the rear cabin with ease. He heard a grunt and the sound of a man folding in on himself. Tom changed his magazine and chambered a fresh round. He worked his way quickly through the narrow passageway and saw the crumpled Russian, the watcher, Tom recognised him from the White Swan, in the bathroom doorway. Tom squatted and checked the Russian's pulse. Ropey, but he'd survive if he received medical attention. Tom picked up the man's Makarov pistol and went up the stern steps. Kamenev wasn't there, he wasn't on the boat at all. Tom threw the Makarov into the dark canal.

"Fuck," he thought. He jumped down to the towpath and sprinted back towards the Periwinkle. "Fuck, fuck, fuck." He knew that Kamenev had outflanked him.

The Periwinkle was moving at walking pace and had entered the narrow channel of the aqueduct. There wasn't anyone at the tiller and the boat gently bounced into the canal's sides but kept its slow forward momentum. Kamenev stepped out from the undergrowth and made his way to the Periwinkle. He kept his gun hand close by his side. As Kamenev approached the Periwinkle, Jack bounded off the narrowboat's stern and, sensing the Russian's evil intent, leapt up at him. She grabbed his left arm between her powerful jaws and bit down hard. The Russian shouted in pain and brought the butt of the heavy Makarov down on her skull. Jack bit deeper before Kamenev brought the butt down again. The terrier fell on to the towpath. The Russian thought about shooting the dog but instead kicked her with a curse. He made his way up on the stern and into the cabin. Nia emerged from the front cabin, she saw Kamenev and her face went white with fear. Kamenev took a quick step towards her and kicked her viciously in her stomach. Nia collapsed in shock and pain. She felt immediately sick as the pain burned and radiated through her body. Kamenev knelt down with one knee on her back and grabbed her by her thick hair pulling her head back painfully. Nia gasped for breath with a fresh trauma that was devastatingly familiar.

***

Cottage Hospital, West Coast of Scotland, Eighteen Years Previously

The pain was unbearable. Nia felt her insides stretch to a breaking point. She gasped for breath as an elderly nurse placed an oxygen mask over her nose and mouth. The strong plastic smell of the mask made her want to throw up. Then her insides were on fire. She felt her blood and life fluids coursing out of her body; warm, wet and sticky already pooling underneath her and across her thighs.

"Please, stop it," Nia screamed.

It didn't help. They all knew what was happening, she and the nurses, and the old doctor. The doctor shook his head sullenly.

"There's no foetal heartbeat," he said.

Nia's physical pain was heightened by the emotional pain. The sense of loss was already overwhelming her.

"Please no," she wept to herself. She could taste the oxygen and then something metallic. She was drifting off into chemical fuzziness. Pitocin coursed through an IV into her veins. She was being induced but wasn't ready to let go. She tried to grab her large tummy bump, but stronger hands held her back. The pain burned again. Nia heard the doctor tell the elderly, grey haired nurse that Nia was going to need some blood. Some disembodied voice told Nia to push while the doctor assisted with forceps. Nia was lost in a miasma of pain where she didn't know where she ended and where it

344

began.

At some point the fog cleared and Nia was aware of her stillborn baby being placed on her chest. Nia looked at the baby and then turned away. Her visions of motherhood, of nursing and nurturing, of loving and being loved had been terribly wrenched from her. She sobbed for the lost baby, the lost husband, and for all the loss that had been distilled to this point. She cried with the pain. She cried with the knowledge her life would never be the same again. She cried with an understanding that her grief would be constant. A nurse took the baby away while another gave Nia yet another drug through her IV and then the darkness moved in like a shadow to fill all her empty spaces.

***

Pontcysyllte Aqueduct, The Present
The Periwinkle was moving slowly through the narrow iron trough of the aqueduct. Tom approached his boat at a run and saw Jack lying prone on the towpath. He could see the shallow fall and rise of her chest. He stopped running only when he saw Nia move onto the stern deck. Behind her, Kamenev emerged from the cabin holding the heavy Makarov at Nia's back. Tom continued to walk towards the boat just yards in front of him. He could see the fear in Nia's eyes.

"My dear Major Price," Kamenev said in his impeccable Oxbridge English. "I am so pleased you could join our little coterie. Please do absent yourself from the nasty weapon you're holding."

Tom placed his pistol down on the towpath. He continued to walk very slowly at the side of the boat. Tom's eyes, unblinking, drilled into Kamenev's skull. The SVR man continued.

"We have come across each other twice now, Major Price. There won't be a third time."

He raised the Makarov towards the general area of Tom's chest and smiled. He then slowly swung the gun to point to Nia.

"Would it be more painful for you to catch a couple of bullets or for you to lose your actress whore?" the Russian smiled evilly.

Tom dived backwards towards the Browning. Kamenev was fast and fired twice. Startled crows took to the air from the trees on the valley floor below the aqueduct. The first shot had splintered harmlessly off the towpath but the second went through Tom's left shoulder blade. Still, the prone Tom continued to inch forward, his right arm reaching for his gun. Kamenev smiled as he took careful aim. Nia was paralyzed with fear as she watched Tom belly crawl along the towpath with the expanding bloom of blood on his back.

"Major Price has cost me everything," Kamenev said to Nia. He looked over his left shoulder at her with a smile that sickened her. "I'd be too generous to give him a quick death. This man caused this." Kamenev waved the heavy pistol in front of his face. "He deserves a painful end."

Kamenev fired at Tom catching him high in the left arm. Tom stopped moving. He lay on the towpath and Nia didn't know whether he was alive or dead. A police siren sounded somewhere in the middle distance. Kamenev turned to face Nia.

"Ah well, my dear, unfortunately events conspire to prematurely bring my bit of fun to an end." He smiled, "Him first, you second okay?"

Kamenev swung around to face Tom, now some distance back down the towpath, just as the drifting Periwinkle banged heavily into the canal's iron side. The boat appeared to shudder and the Russian wobbled off balance and lowered his gun. Nia's paralysis of fear finally broke. Instinctually she screamed and punched out at Kamenev catching him heavily in the throat. He gagged and reached for his neck with both hands. In a move practiced hundreds of times in her cardio-boxing class, Nia shifted her weight and kicked him in the groin. Kamenev doubled over, stumbled, stepped backwards on to the stern deck's low gunwale and tripped off the boat, off the aqueduct and into thin air.

The valley floor lay calm and quiet one hundred and twenty feet below. The annoyed crows settled back onto their perches even as sirens grew louder and closer.

***

The aqueduct's towpath was full of people. Tom, still on his stomach, drifted in and out of consciousness.

347

Police were everywhere. He knew he was being worked on by a pair of paramedics. He was aware of Nia kneeling next to him holding his right hand. The old towpath walker was at Nia's side.

"Nia," Tom said weakly. "Thank God you're okay."

Nia smiled wanly and squeezed his hand. "Oh Tom," she said through tears.

"You going to be okay?" asked the walker.

"I think so," Tom grunted in reply. He felt Nia squeeze his hand.

Tom heard the unmistakable sound of rotor blades and was aware of an air ambulance landing somewhere nearby as the paramedics continued to work on him.

"What's that for?" Tom asked one of the paramedics.

"That's for you mate."

"Really? I hate those fucking things," Tom said.

Chapter Twenty-one
Hospital Room, Wrexham

Tom was coming out of the anaesthetic from his surgery. His vision was cloudy and his thinking fuzzy. He began to focus; Nia was sitting next to his bed. He smiled at her. She had been crying and she looked pallid, tired and drawn.

"Nia," he said. "Thank God you're here. You look beautiful."

"Tom," she said simply. She smiled.

Tom began to focus and noticed a doctor at the foot of the bed and behind her a high-ranking police officer and a middle-aged woman with a severe hairstyle and a well-cut business suit. The deputy director from Thames House. Tom thought he had smelled MI5 even before his eyes opened. The doctor, a young south Asian Muslim woman wearing a hijab, turned and told the visitors that they could now talk to Tom. The police officer asked Nia to leave the room and he nodded towards the doctor who left as well.

The DD sat in the chair that Nia had just vacated.

"How's my dog?" Tom asked quickly.

"Err…" the DD turned to the police officer.

"At a local vet. Concussion and requiring some stiches I understand," said the police officer. "But a full recovery expected," he added.

Tom smiled and relaxed with the news.

"Now then," the DD began. "Tell me what the hell just went on."

Outside Tom's room, Nia sat in the waiting lounge with the doctor who again confirmed that Tom should now make a full and complete recovery from the bullet wounds. Tom had lost a considerable amount of blood, his left lung had collapsed, his scapula had been broken, and there was a fair amount of tissue damage to back, chest, and arm. It would be just a matter of rest and time, the doctor told Nia reassuringly. Nia was relieved but a fear continued to gnaw at her.

For nearly twenty years Nia had shut herself down emotionally, never allowing herself to feel content, denying herself deep and meaningful personal connection. The loss of her almost full-term baby had left her with a void that she had refused to fill in an act of self-flagellation, an act of displaced penance. Once, she had retreated into work, into her empty house, into herself. There, she had avoided hurt and pain but had sacrificed what it meant to feel, what it meant to be whole. Then Tom had blundered and stammered into her life and had brought her joy. He brought a love that she had never experienced. But then, she considered, he'd brought deceit, pain and he had brought death. He had lied to her. She didn't know how to deal with the maelstrom of conflicted emotions that were spinning in her head. She only knew how to retreat from them. Nia knew how to walk away, it was what she always did.

Nia went into the small bathroom that was adjacent to the lounge. She washed her face and ran her fingers through her hair. She looked at herself in the bathroom's mirror. She was pale and her dark eyes were red rimmed. She took deep breaths, determined to get into character. It began to feel natural, muscle memory took over, the moments before stepping on stage or in front of a camera she was able to disassociate her thinking and her body from her real self. She watched her face in the mirror change subtly, but enough. Her eyes appeared to darken, as if the light that had so recently burnt there for Tom was extinguished. He lied to her. She shook her hair so it fell in an unfamiliar style, she let curls fall over her face. She straightened her body almost unnaturally and held the position, she smoothed her sweater over her hips. She stepped out of the toilet in character.

Nia waited in the lounge for the MI5 women to leave Tom's room. She sat, straight backed with her hands folded in her lap. The DD, her assistant and the high-ranking police officer emerged and walked quickly past Nia. The DD slowed momentarily, turned and told Nia that MI5 would contact her soon for an interview back in London at Thames House. Nia nodded but then looked down at her hand and missed the DD's return nod and slight smile. The police constable on station outside of Tom's room nodded to Nia as she entered the hospital room. She smiled weakly and took the seat on the left side of Tom's bed. It was still warm.

351

Tom's left arm, chest and shoulder were heavily bandaged, and tubes and wires appeared to link him to a number of beeping and flashing machines. He brightened visibly when Nia came in. He was glad to have some alone time with her, to catch up. To move on together.

"Aw fuck, Nia," he began. "I had no idea all this would happen. I'm so sorry that you had to go through all that. I'm so, so sorry. I should have told you about that bastard Zalkind/Kamenev and about what happened in London. But I thought it was all over and done with. I never expected any of this kind of thing to happen."

Nia turned to him and with as much steely determination she could muster. Tom watched her face and felt his stomach hollow.

"Yes, Tom," Nia said through clenched teeth. "You bloody well should have told me. You've lied to me. Something you said you would never do. It was the only thing I asked of you Tom, not to lie to me."

A horrible fear gripped him.

Nia knew she was playing a part and she wanted to transform herself into a character to temporarily divorce herself from the very real emotions, the crushing emptiness that was beginning to envelope her. Nia needed to imagine that those icy tendrils of pain and loss and heartbreak that were already enfolding her were not actually hers.

"Tom, I don't feel that I know you. What you did

to the muggers in London and to the Russians on the canal, it's like you are some kind of terminator." Nia paused and stared down at her hands resting on her lap knowing she needed to avoid looking into Tom's eyes. "Look, I think things have moved so quickly for us. Maybe too fast," her voice was flat, devoid of warmth and intonation.

"No wait, Nia," Tom reached over with his right hand for her hand but Nia didn't take it. Pain shot through the left side of his body. "Please don't do this. You don't have to do this."

"I think we need to take a break. We got too serious before I could feel that I really know you. And, after all this, I don't really know who you are. You never told me about your parents' death, you lied to me about the Russians you ran into in London. You kept a gun on your boat Tom. You killed a man and shot another one. You're some kind of hunter killer. I saw that side of you, Tom, a different side of you, and I can't get my head around that. It scared me. You scared me, damn it. I know you're hurting but you have hurt me, Tom."

Tom saw the pain on her face and stopped himself pointing out that she, too, had killed someone.

"I never, ever meant to hurt you. That was the last thing I ever, ever wanted to do, Nia," Tom said his voice cracking. "I was trying to protect you. I love you."

"I thought I loved you," Nia lied. "But now I'm not sure and I need to take some time. I need some time for myself."

"Nia, you can't mean any of this. We have something, you and I, and, and... I know you love me. Don't do this."

"Tom, you're a nice guy. I told you some time ago that I'm not a nice person that I'm selfish, that I have no time for other people. That I burn through people, Tom. I'm sorry but that's the way it is. That's the way I am." Her eyes welled but she struggled to maintain control as she got up to go.

"You don't have to do this," Tom pleaded.

Nia felt she had to leave, or she'd break down and take it all back. Her voice wavered, she wanted to take it back but then she summed up some steely determination from the depth of her actor's training.

"Look, give me some time to get my head around all this and I'll get back in touch," she said. "We'll talk more then."

Tom stared at Nia, but she lowered her head and avoided his eyes. "You once told me that no one can hurt you like the people you love," Tom said, the pain obvious in his faltering voice.

Nia turned at the door.

"I love you Nia. I always will," Tom said and then she was gone.

Nia walked quickly down the hospital corridor with tears rolling down her face. What have I done? she thought, and the thought reverberated in her head.

Tom laid back on the hard hospital bed. He was shocked and confused. What the bloody hell had just happened?

Before Nia, Tom had been emotionally spent, full to the brim with pain and sadness and sorrow with no space left for anything else. Then Nia had wafted elegantly into his life and had taken the broken pieces of him and rebuilt him as strong and resilient as a dry-stone wall. She had shown him that his capacity for emotional connectivity was infinite. Or at least it was until Nia walked out of his hospital room and out of his life. He felt utterly incapacitated.

***

London, February 28th

Nia had returned from the hospital to her London home and retreated to her bed and then her study. She couldn't bear to look at the painting of the Periwinkle and removed it from her study's wall. She ignored calls and texts from her friends, even from Jane. Nia cried frequently. She regretted what she said in the hospital and how she had said it. She called the hospital for updates on Tom's recovery. She drafted a desperate apologetic text to Tom but deleted it.

Nia attempted to console herself in the knowledge that even though she had overreacted, as all her relationships crashed into bitter ends, that it was better to end this one sooner rather than the inevitable later. She would convince herself that she was right, that she was okay, and then she'd be overwhelmed. Nia felt herself spiralling into a depression but didn't have the strength nor the will to stop and pull herself out.

The MI5 deputy director was true to her word and requested Nia's presence for a debrief at Thames House. Nia was significantly intimidated to receive a summons to the shadowy security service's headquarters, although she wouldn't have admitted her apprehension to anyone but Tom. Tom. Even his name, his face in her mind's eye, made the pain a blunt and bitter reality. She questioned herself again about her actions; why had she impetuously walked away? He had lied to her, she thought, but she had lied, by omission, to him. Her thinking got stuck in a mobius ring of recriminations and second guessing. Tom had made her happy, yes, but she didn't deserve happiness. He was a nice person and she wasn't. She hadn't answered Tom's phone calls and responded to his texts with a curt "Not ready to talk yet."

At Thames House, Nia sat in a spartan private waiting room deep in the building's bowels. She was wearing a stylish navy suit, and a pearl silk blouse, the kind of outfit someone would wear for a middle management job interview at a corporate headquarters. A visitor's badge on a lanyard hung around her neck. She wasn't sure why she had dressed as she had but wanted to project a sense of her own authority. It wasn't working. She had already been intimidated by the establishment types that had stepped into the affray on the aqueduct and who had then controlled the aftermath. She knew they moved people, including Tom and herself, around as if they had infinite power and authority. She had already signed a copy of the Official Secrets Act at the Wrexham hospital, but an officious receptionist reminded her that she wouldn't be able to discuss the events with anyone, ever.

An establishment type, and a young south Asian woman entered the room. Nia recognised the establishment woman who sat at the plain table across from Nia as the woman who was clearly in charge in North Wales. The south Asian woman, who didn't introduce herself, took a seat against the wall and appeared to make notes in a file.

"Ms Williams," the rather posh voice said. "I'm Deputy Director Davies. We met briefly at the hospital in Wrexham but I'm sure that was probably a blur for you. I'm hoping that you're feeling better about things now."

Nia looked at the DD and saw a hint of genuine concern in the older woman's eyes.

"I'd like to thank you for coming in today," the DD continued. "I know this isn't easy but it won't take long, just a few clarifying questions to ask."

Nia nodded.

"Obviously, everything we discuss is covered by the Official Secrets Act and you may have realised that we issued a 'D Notice' denying the press the option of reporting on the events. As far as the public is concerned, some Russian tourists had perished in a terrible barge mishap. Such things are rare on our canals, but they do happen."

"Narrowboat, not barge," Nia corrected reflexively.

"Quite," the DD responded.

Nia simply stared at the DD. The DD waited for Nia to say something else then proceeded to go through what seemed to Nia a perfunctory set of questions around dates and times, trip details, whats and wheres. Nia answered seemingly satisfactorily. The DD smiled and nodded to the south Asian woman who closed the file, both collected themselves as if to leave.

"How's Major Price doing?" the DD asked.

Nia's stomach churned. She knew that her expression couldn't disguise her pain, which was palpable.

"I don't know. I haven't been in contact with him,' Nia answered. She noticed the DD's expression show a little surprise.

"He wasn't the man I thought he was. He lied to me. He brought violence and death into my life," she added defiantly.

"Oh, I don't know about that," the DD said with a sly smile and looking Nia straight in the eye. "Actually, Ms Williams, when you think about it, it could be said that it was the other way around. Wasn't Zalkind/Kamenev made aware of Major Price at one of your events? We believe it was a press photo of the two of you, Major Price and you together at the BFI that led to Kamenev operationalising his vendetta. And then, it was you who Kamenev followed to the Llangollen canal. Quite frankly, he used you to get to Major Price."

Nia felt shaken.

"So," the DD continued, smiling falsely again. "In some way, it was you who brought pain and death back into Major Price's life. And God knows that poor man has had enough of that."

Nia looked down, her eyes welled, and tears began to fall onto her shoes and the floor.

"What have I done?" Nia asked herself. She looked into the DD's eyes searching for an answer, for something that would make the regret and hurt go away, something to give her hope.

"Additionally," the DD continued. "The Russian agent we arrested in Kamenev's narrowboat, the one Major Price wounded, was rather forthcoming during our... interrogation. His information has been vital for our national security. So, you see, Ms Williams, although this whole bloody mess has been one monumental cock-up, we actually have some positive results. You and Major Price actually helped us save the life of an innocent young woman, an incredibly brave Russian journalist, and we appear to have broken up, would you believe it, an international assassination ring."

Nia moaned audibly. She looked over to the south Asian woman, who immediately looked down to her tablet and typed in some notes, and then to the DD. Nia thought the DD smiled matronly back at her.

"Ms Williams, perhaps, you should talk to Major

Price," the DD said softly. "You have both shared a terrible experience. It would be helpful, for you both, to talk through it. Instead of pushing you apart, it should bring you together. So, maybe, you should give him a chance Ms Williams, I know he's a good man."

The DD nodded to Patel and they left the small room with Nia still seated inside sobbing gently to herself. The DD asked an assistant seated outside of the room to get Nia a coffee but to first give her a few minutes to cry it out and compose herself.

The DD turned with Patel and they moved up the corridor and on to a lift.

"You didn't mention that this all started out as Gagnon and Price's muddleheaded revenge scheme," Patel said after the lift doors closed.

"Well yes, but I chose not to. Why complicate things when there's really no need for her to know more than she already does. She really was pivotal in all this you see. If Ms Williams hadn't gone to the BFI event, Price and Kamenev wouldn't have come into contact, Jacques Gagnon wouldn't have gone all Rambo in the streets of London, and three Russians wouldn't be in the morgue, and I wouldn't have a ton of difficult paperwork on my desk to deal with. But that journalist, Kirov, may have been disappeared or found dead under some mysterious circumstances. As far as Ms Williams and Major Price are concerned, their part in this clusterfuck is all over. It's best that they move on, together I think."

Patel faced the DD with questioning eyes, "And that last piece of advice to Ms Williams?"

"Ahh, that was just part of the service," the DD answered. "The things we do for love."

"Really, ma'am?" Patel couldn't keep the incredulity out of her voice.

The DD faced Patel, "You ever been in love Patel, real love?"

"I-I don't know," Patel stammered a little embarrassed.

"Then you haven't," the DD said. "I have friends who have been married twenty years or more who don't have half the connection I saw Price and Williams have. I hope she stops being silly about it."

The lift stopped and the DD nodded a goodbye to Patel as she got out of the elevator. The DD crossed the busy floor, cubicles buzzing with activity, and closed the door to her office quietly. She stood for a moment in front of her office window that overlooked the hive of activity across the analysts and communications officers' section. They were always busy and getting busier. The DD felt the fatigue of her responsibility. The domestic threat web continued to expand almost exponentially; jihadists sneaking home after the fall of the Caliphate, the SVR, FSB and the GRU treating London as if it were a St Petersburg Saturday night, the Real IRA sharpening swords, all along with the usual suspects of home-grown threats.

The DD flipped a wall switch that turned her office

glass opaque then sat in silence for a moment. She booted up her computer and Tom's file appeared on one of her monitors while Nia's appeared on another. The DD liked these two people. In a different time, a different life, she thought, she could have imagined meeting them at a dinner party. She so very much wanted them to be happy, to be happy together. But, she thought, I have a man of action, bruised and battered, but someone who can still operate to the highest level of professionalism and someone adept at assuming the roles and personas of others. Together, they'd be a great team, a great MI5 asset. The DD clicked her mouse and saved the files to a desktop folder she had labelled 'future prospects'. She sighed. "Done... done for now Ms Williams," she whispered to herself. The DD moved her mouse and brought up a minute-by-minute review of how her team was doing in a Europa League match. She smiled; they were winning.

***

Llangollen Canal, Two Days Later

Engine compartment checked, Tom gingerly lowered the cover, difficult with only one good arm. He pressed the start button and the engine coughed into life. Tom went back into the cabin to let the engine warm up. The shoulder ached as he took his arm out of the sling. The physical pain that shot through his body was a welcome relief from the deep, emotional pain that gnawed away at his core.

He removed the sling and threw it on the little cabinet that stood at the foot of the bed. The sling landed next to two small framed pictures. There was a framed photo of Nia, laughing in the snow, on the morning after their first night together. Next to it was the photo of him as a young platoon leader in Afghanistan surrounded by twenty-five servicemen and women. All were smiling. His air pods lay on the cabinet unused; there was no playlist to assuage this pain. The oft-read letter Nia had written from the inn in Brecon, which professed undying love, lay under the air pods.

"Okay Jack," Tom shouted. "Morning piddle."

***

The black Porsche Carrera snaked through the narrow country lanes as smoothly as if it was a slot car racer. The driver changed gears effortlessly and well. The engine responded to the subtle press on the accelerator, the large disc brakes slowing the car down when the driver's phone beeped with a speed camera alert. The Porsche pulled into the scenic overlook and stopped abruptly, skidding ever so slightly on some loose grit. The valley spread out below like a quilt. Frost glittered. To the right, across the valley and up on the hill, a castle's sandstone walls reflected the morning sun back across the valley. The silence could almost be felt. The Porsche's driver stepped out and observed the canal below through small binoculars. The watcher was patient and, eventually, patience was rewarded as a narrowboat emerged from the woods that shielded the canal down to the watcher's right. The watcher changed the binocular's optics and zoomed in onto the narrowboat. There, on the bow, a happy dog wagged its tail, barking at something in the water or on the unseen towpath. The watcher then moved the gaze down the boat's polished green paintwork to the man at the tiller. It was Tom. The watcher smiled involuntarily.

"Gotcha!" she said as she lowered the binoculars. Nia let out a sigh. "Oh, thank God," she said out loud as her heart pounded in her chest. She raised her binoculars again and watched Tom. Nia thought he looked older and fatigued and her stomach hollowed. He was pale, had dark circles under his eyes, and wore a scruffy beard and she noticed that he occasionally grimaced as he pushed or pulled the tiller. She observed him until the Periwinkle moved behind a canal-side copse of trees and she could see the boat and Tom no more.

Nia was relieved she had found him. Earlier that morning, she had stopped at Periwinkle's home marina and the staff were reticent in sharing any information with her until one of the grounds' crew recognised her. He thought Tom was heading for a slow trip to Ellesmere and an overnight at the wharf there. Nia had followed the road that ran roughly parallel to the canal's meandering path, stopping at overlooks and the occasional bridge to see if she could find the Periwinkle.

Now that she knew where the boat was and where it was heading, she returned to the Porsche and settled back into the deep, leather bucket seat. She pushed the start button and the three-litre, flat-six inter-cooled engine fired into throaty life. The car's media centre blinked on. She used the on-screen commands to move to playlists and found the playlist she had labelled 'Boat Songs'. Elvis Costello's 'Shipbuilding' began to play. Ironic she thought. Nia gunned the motor and whipped the car around the overlook's lay-by. The Porsche's nineteen-inch wheels sent arcs of gravel flying, and then the car headed back out on to the main road.

On the canal, Tom positioned the Periwinkle to go under another bridge. Although scores of bridges traversed the canal, he never tired of them. They were obvious and gentle reminders of the history of the changing nature of canal life and landforms. Tom slowed the elegant narrowboat, the engine so quiet that the boat appeared to almost glide along the canal, slightly faster than the ducks and geese who occasionally swam alongside. The brick bridge approached and Tom felt the connection with the bargees of another era who would have gone through the same routine umpteen times a day. He gently leant on the tiller and looked to the towpath to his left. On such a quiet day he could imagine a boy guiding the boat horse along the towpath and hear the hooves click and clap as the horse walked on the brick pathway under the bridge. He wondered whether his Victorian narrowboat kin ever took the time to stop and behold each tree and field that was presented for viewing.

The Periwinkle nosed under the brick bridge. The bridge had remained relatively unchanged since the day it was completed one hundred and fifty years before apart from where the generations of ropes that once connected horses to canal boats had worn smooth and deep grooves into the masonry. Once these bridges connected neighbours' farms, provided paths to church on Sunday, or eased the shipment of goods to the nearest village for market day. Tom felt a sense of melancholy knowing most of the bridges, were now bridges to nowhere. As the Periwinkle emerged from under the bridge, Tom noticed that no footpaths remained leading up to or down from either side of the bridge, that it was no longer walked or ridden over. Yet, it still stood, a testament to its simple design and quality craftsmanship. He thought about pulling to the canal side, mooring up temporarily, and taking Jack for a walk up and over the bridge but it would be a pointless and futile gesture. He thought of Nia and whether more attempts to call and text her would be as futile.

Tom pushed the engine control forward increasing the revs and the Periwinkle responded by moving a bit faster. Tom checked the stern of the boat to make sure he wasn't causing too much of a wake. He rounded a long and gentle bend as the Cheshire countryside gently sloped upwards to his left. An hour later, he approached the entrance of the wharf. Tom pushed the tiller to the left and steered the Periwinkle into the right-hand side of the canal. He then swung the tiller far right to bring the forty-eight-foot narrowboat around to make the sharp left turn. He normally liked the meandering nature of the canal as it cut its way gently following the imperceptible contours of the Cheshire and Shropshire countryside. His heart ached at the memory of the last time he had travelled on this part of the canal with Nia in the boat, with Nia in his life.

Tom was nauseated at the emptiness he felt knowing that, without Nia, his life would never be as vital, as bright, and as fun as he once, prematurely, thought it was going to be. He would be like the brick bridges he frequently passed; sturdy, resilient, fit-for-purpose, but forgotten, lost and unloved. "Fuck, fuck, fuck," he said to himself trying to snap himself out of his unhealthy reverie. Tom squared his shoulders, he would just have to get on with it. He knew he would love Nia always and he knew that the pain he felt at her leaving would now follow him forever. He would be as emotionally broken as his right leg was physically. Yet he wasn't sorry that he had met her, for the last few months burned with a light and an energy and a fervour that he would savour always. It was better to have loved and lost than never to have loved at all. Yeah, he told himself, not really a comfort at the moment.

Jack's barking from the bow brought Tom back to the present. He stretched to see over the boat's length as to what had caught Jack's attention. There, up ahead, on the wrought iron bridge that spanned the canal was a solitary figure. The Periwinkle nosed into the marina's channel and Tom brought the revs down and the boat slowed to walking pace. He looked at the figure as the bridge inexorably approached. Jack ran through the boat's cabin and joined Tom on the stern deck. Tom could see that the figure was female and leaning with her arms on the bridge's balustrade. His pulse quickened. He was sure it was Nia, but he swallowed that thought in fear of disappointment. The woman wore a green, waxed coat, tight jeans, red bobble hat and a blue and white scarf. A small overnight bag lay at her feet. She removed her hat and her thick hair whipped in the wind just as the boat nosed under the bridge. She waved down at Jack and Tom. It was Nia. Jack barked in recognition; Tom sat on the deck fence staring up at Nia. She stared down, cupped her hands around her mouth. "I love you," she shouted as the Periwinkle's stern went under the bridge.

Tom steered the narrowboat towards the canal's side. He put the engine into reverse to quickly stop the boat's forward momentum. He stepped off and quickly tied the boat to a mooring ring only by the centre line. Nia had walked off the bridge and down to the towpath. She dropped her overnight grip and ran towards Tom and into his arms. She was cold and she was crying.

"I love you," she said again. "I'm a fucking idiot. I'm so sorry. I was scared and I panicked." She buried her face into Tom's chest. He could feel her tears. Tom smiled with a sense of relief for life with Nia had been a rollercoaster ride and now he knew that the ride would continue.

"I want us to be together." Nia sobbed. "I was in shock, Tom, I was so fucking scared."

She held on to him afraid to look into his face.

"I didn't mean what I said in the hospital, I didn't even believe it. I regretted it as soon as I left your room. And you were so hurt and lying on that bed all bandaged, I was such a bitch to you. A really stupid bitch."

Tom gently moved her chin up and they locked eyes.

"Without you, I'm broken," Nia said. "I love you Tom. I know that I'm not easy to be with, I understand that, but I want to us to be together. I want to be with you more than anything."

"That's what I want too. That's actually what I've always wanted since sitting next to you on the plane." Tom said.

Nia hugged him again, beaming. She broke the embrace to retrieve her bag.

"Look," she said holding up the bag. "I'm packing lightly."

"Probably just full of knickers."

Nia laughed and held Tom's right hand as they turned to walk to the Periwinkle.

"How long are you planning on staying?" Tom asked, a little worried by the small size of the bag.

Nia appeared to think for a moment, "If you'll have me, forever. I have a much larger suitcase in the car."

ACKNOWLEDGEMENTS

No creative work is developed in a vacuum. I owe a debt of gratitude to my good friends, Jean Drasgow, Dena Lawrence, and Keith Marshall, who generously shared their time and ideas. As always, Beth's support and encouragement and patience were instrumental in my finally completing a novel.